EARTH HOWL (BOOK 4)

BOOK 4 IN THE EARTH SONG SERIES

NICK COOK

ABOUT THE AUTHOR

Somewhere back in the mists of time, Nick was born in the great sprawling metropolis of London. He grew up in a family where art was always a huge influence. Tapping into this, Nick finished college with a fine art degree tucked into his back pocket. Faced with the prospect of actually trying to make a living from his talents, he plunged into the emerging video game industry back in the eighties. It was the start of a long career and he produced graphics for many of the top-selling games on the early home computers, including *Aliens* and *Enduro Racer*. Those pioneering games may look crude now, but back then they were considered to be cutting edge. As the industry exploded into the one we know today, Nick's career went supernova. He worked on titles such as *X-Com*, and set up two studios, which produced

Warzone 2100 and the *Conflict: Desert Storm* series. He has around forty published titles to his name.

As great as the video game industry is, a little voice kept nagging inside Nick's head, and at the end of 2006 he was finally ready to pursue his other passion as a full-time career: writing. Many years later, he completed his first trilogy, *Cloud Riders*. And the rest, as they say, is history.

Nick has many interests, from space exploration and astronomy to travelling the world. He has flown light aircraft and microlights, an experience he used as research for *Cloud Riders*. He's always loved to cook, but then you'd expect it with his surname. His writing in many ways reflects his own curiosity about the world around him. He loves to let his imagination run riot to pose the question: *What if?*

For everyone struggling during the COVID 19 pandemic. We will get through this.

CHAPTER ONE

I woke up to see a golden hint of light creeping through the bedroom window. My consciousness began to surface and I was filled with a deep sense of peace as the warmth of Jack's body soaked into me. There wasn't a hint of tension in any muscle of my body – quite something considering the gymnastics of last night's antics.

I breathed in Jack's comforting scent, trying to extend this magical moment as his naked body contoured round mine.

He kissed the top of my head. 'Are you awake, Lauren?'

'Busted...' I raised my head, turning it to gaze into Jack's ocean-blue eyes. The swirl of sparks rippled through my abdomen.

A wide smile filled his face as I pulled away a fraction to look at him.

'Mmm, now that's the way I'd like to get woken up every morning,' I said. 'You're so much better than an alarm clock.'

'I have an idea that would make that wish come true.'

'OK, I'm listening,' I said, narrowing my gaze on him.

'What do you say to us sharing a room together? We practically live in each other's spaces anyway.'

I raised my eyebrows. 'Six months of wild dating and you're already thinking about us moving in together?'

'Well, if you don't think it's a good idea...'

I started to walk my fingers up his chest. 'Oh, I think it's a fabulous idea.'

'Thank god for that!'

He rolled me on top of him and started to attack my shoulders with kisses. And when his mouth sought out mine, those sparks grew to a forest fire.

With every other guy I'd slept with, I'd often felt self-consciousness in the cold light of a new day. But not so with Jack. This just seemed so right – so easy and meant to be.

His hands grabbed my bum, things beginning to get really interesting, when a loud knock came from the door.

'I thought you'd both like to know that Jodie has managed to persuade Mike to join us for breakfast,' Alice's voice floated in from the corridor.

I exchanged a wide-eyed look with Jack. 'Mike's finally left the infirmary?'

'Yes,' the president of the Sky Dreamer Corp. replied. 'Not only that, but he says he's ready to get back to work today in the lab too – although I told him there was absolutely no rush.'

'I guess he couldn't keep away from the big day with Lucy,' Jack said.

Alice laughed. 'Basically, yes.'

I felt a little twist of apprehension at the reminder of that event. 'It will be great to have Mike back on the team,' I said.

'Absolutely,' Jack agreed.

'It will also be good for Jodie. She's been running herself ragged. Anyway, when... ahem... you've finished up here, doing whatever it is that you're doing, you'll find coffee already brewing downstairs.'

Jack grinned at me as I buried my face in his shoulder. We'd obviously been louder than either of us had realised.

'We'll be down in a few secs,' I replied, doing my best to ignore Jack who was very unhelpfully kissing my neck again.

We heard the creak of boards on the landing as Alice manoeuvred her wheelchair towards the lift.

I reluctantly slid myself off Jack. He made a soft groaning sound deep in the back of his throat.

'Later, I promise,' I said as I stood grinning over my shoulder at him.

'Oh, I am so holding you to that.' He gave me a smile like a cat who'd very much had the cream and wanted to come back for more.

I began to hunt for my clothes. Along with Jack's they were scattered in all four corners of my room. I gave up trying to find my knickers – maybe they'd combusted during the explosive sex we'd had after getting back to my room yesterday.

I grabbed a towel and turned to see Jack's eyes lingering on my naked body. I returned the gaze. God, he was seriously gorgeous. After previous dancing around each other, at last it seemed this Viking god was all mine.

'What state do you think we'll find Mike in?' Jack asked, obviously not aware of the direction of my thoughts.

'Hopefully not as down as usual. The number of times I've visited that guy in the infirmary and I've found him staring at the ceiling.'

'I know – the fight has really gone out of him since losing his leg,' Jack said.

'Let's just hope that going back to work is the start of him rediscovering his mojo.'

Jack nodded. 'This is something I saw way too much of on the battlefield – young soldiers whose spirit was crushed by a life-altering injury like Mike's. And I can't help wondering if deep down part of him blames me for what happened.'

My gaze sharpened on Jack. 'How many times are we going to have this conversation, Jack? Mary said the medical team would have given up way earlier than they did if it wasn't for you. You kept pushing them on to try to save his leg. No one could have done any more. The important thing is that you saved Mike's life – that's what really matters.'

Even though Jack nodded, I could still see the swirl of pain behind his eyes. Mike would never be just another patient to him. This was far too personal. Even it was rationally wrong to do so, Jack would always blame himself for Mike's medical outcome.

If I was honest, it wasn't just Jack who was beating himself up over what had happened to our friend. After all, I'd been the one in charge – I'd led us out on that crazy mission in the first place. The icing on this guilt-trip cake was that Lucy had also been shot down by a TR-3B Astra on the same mission and hadn't rebooted since...

I sighed and gave Jack a hug as much for my own sake as his. I reluctantly let go of him and headed off to the bathroom to grab a much-needed shower and to try to make myself look at least halfway respectable.

When Jack and I eventually headed downstairs, we found Alice, Jodie and Ruby sitting across the dining table from Mike. Our own little bubble of happiness dissolved away as I took in our friend's appearance.

In stark contrast to everyone else, Mike looked pale. It seemed as if the short trip from the infirmary had already taken a lot out of him. Just like Alice, Mike was also sitting in a wheelchair. But unlike our illustrious leader, there was an awful flatness in his jeans from his right knee down that everybody was doing their best to ignore.

This was what the human cost of trying to save the world looked like.

Mike had lost his lower leg after being wounded during a firefight with Alvarez and his soldiers amidst an operation to retrieve a downed Tic Tac UFO and its alien pilot. That mission had morphed into an attempt to retrieve another micro mind from Area 51 – part of the scattered consciousness of the alien AI that we called Lucy. The clock was well and truly ticking down to an alien invasion, so we badly needed to find these micro minds hidden around the world. According to Lucy, the secret to defending our world from this alien race who were coming to harvest our planet like an all-you-can-eat buffet was hidden within those micro minds.

No pressure or anything.

Mike looked up from the scrambled eggs he'd been picking at and managed a faint *honestly, I'm doing OK* smile. 'Hey guys, good to see you.'

'You too, Mike. I thought you were in danger of becoming a fixture in that hospital,' I replied.

I tried to use humour wherever I could with Mike. After all, what could you say to someone who had lost their leg that didn't sound trite in the awful, life-changing circumstances?

'No danger of that with Jodie on my case,' Mike said, reaching across and squeezing his Swedish girlfriend's hand.

Jodie looked to Mike. 'Hey, being your chief motivational coach is a tough job, but someone's got to do it.'

She managed a faint smile for him, but she looked just as washed out as Mike did. For a woman who'd been previously full of boundless energy, these days she was more like a husk in comparison.

It seemed Jodie was as worried as the rest of us and couldn't hide it as well. Mike was making good progress physically, but it was his mental state that we were all concerned about.

Alice nodded towards us and then the coffee pot. 'You're both going to want to load up on caffeine. You have a very full day ahead, what with the training session followed by Lucy's reboot attempt.'

I felt the colour draining from my face at the last bit. This was going to be the final roll of the dice in our attempts to get Lucy up and running again. I was filled with a sense of foreboding at what we were going to do today – a sense that had been growing inside me for months.

Alice broke off part of her croissant and looked at Jodie. 'So you're going to get to try out the new WASP drones today, Ruby?'

'I am and they are going to kick ass, especially in my hands, hey, Lauren?'

I rolled my eyes at her. 'If you say so.'

She took a large bite of her minute steak sandwich topped with caramelised onions and grinned at Jack and me. 'I so do.'

Mike gave Jodie a quizzical look. 'WASP drone?'

'It's the acronym for Weapon Aerial Suppression Programme,' Jodie replied.

'Please don't tell me you've been working on yet another project – not with everything else you've already got on your plate?'

Jodie gave him a shrug. 'Pretty much, but that's what Alice pays me the big bucks for.'

Alice raised her hands. 'Just keep me out of it. I've been the first one to tell you to slow down, but you've just ignored me, Jodie.'

Mike's gaze immediately narrowed on his girlfriend. 'How many times have I asked you if I could help, even if it was just looking at data on a laptop? Every single time you've just fobbed me off saying you had it all covered.'

Jodie's neck broke out in pink blotches. 'I didn't want anything to distract you from your recovery, Mike. That's all.'

His face hardened and he stared down at the tabletop. 'I see...'

I had the distinct impression that we were just glimpsing the peak of a very big iceberg of a conversation that these two had been having for some time. It seemed that Mike's long convalescence wasn't just down to him and was partly due to his girlfriend being overprotective.

Mike looked up to meet Jodie's gaze again. 'We've talked this over a thousand times. You need my help more than ever now. So please stop shutting me out of what you're up to. I'm more than ready to take on an active role again. That's why I'm here at Eden.'

Jodie chewed her lip. 'Only if you think you're really ready.'

'Honestly, I need to do this for my own sanity if nothing else.'

Jodie nodded. 'Of course.'

Mike seemed satisfied and turned towards Jack and I. 'Guys, there's something I need to tell you.'

I took a mental breath. 'What is it?' I replied, hoping he wasn't going to use the opportunity to lay into us for his injury.

'To be honest, I think my days in the field are probably over. Let's face it, I've been more of a liability on missions than a help.'

I let out that mental breath and relaxed a fraction. This conversation I could cope with – even if I wasn't generally happy with the idea.

'No, you were never anything like that,' Jack replied before I could.

I quickly nodded. 'Mike, you've always been an integral part of our team and you always will be. Having said that, I will respect your decision. But if you ever change your mind, please just know the door will always be open to you getting involved in future missions.'

'What, even limping along on my peg leg, holding you all up?' Mike asked with a thin-lipped smile.

Alice shot him a sharp look. 'As you know full well, it won't be anything like a *peg leg*. It's a state-of-the-art active joint prosthetic leg that you've been measured for. It's been 3D printed and is ready to be fitted.'

Mike started to fiddle with his ear. 'Sorry – I realise everyone has worked really hard on it and I wish I could be more enthusiastic, but you know I feel uncomfortable about it...'

Alice slowly nodded and sighed. 'Yes, unfortunately I do. I really hope that will change.'

I poured myself a coffee as I pondered the conversation. If anyone in this room understood the journey that lay ahead for Mike it was Alice. And she was exactly the right woman to push him when he needed it. She'd lost the use of her legs after the stunt aircraft she'd been flying had crashed. I also knew that she would go out of her way to guide Mike through the challenges he would face, both physical and mental. It sounded as if using a prosthetic leg was the first mental roadblock that Mike was going to have to overcome.

Mike sat back in his wheelchair and his eyes sought out mine. 'So today is the big day with Lucy,' he said brightly, in a very obvious attempt to change the subject.

If he was looking for something to take the spotlight off himself, he'd hit upon the perfect subject – one about which I was worried sick to the core of my being.

Alice's gaze flicked towards me. She knew exactly how I felt and had already heard my arguments a dozen times about why we shouldn't attempt this.

I sat down at the kitchen table and nursed my coffee cup. 'You all know I'm still very nervous about attempting this. It's got risk written all over it. We have no way of knowing how it will play out.'

Alice sat back in her wheelchair. 'Look, I understand your concern, Lauren. However, as you yourself have said on many occasions, we've tried absolutely everything else.'

'I know, but that doesn't stop attempting to merge Lucy with Red being a huge risk.'

'What's Red?' Mike asked.

'That's the highly original nickname I gave the Area 51 micro mind – because of the colour it glows,' Ruby explained with a shrug as she finished off her steak sandwich.

'Maybe *demon* would be a more appropriate name, especially after your encounter with it at Area 51, Lauren,' Jack said.

I sipped my coffee, letting the caffeine sharpen my thoughts. 'Any AI entity that can conjure up a hell version of Machu Picchu obviously has a certain amount of issues to work through.'

'But isn't that because it imprinted itself on Cristina Garcia in the same way that Lucy imprinted herself on to you?' Alice asked.

'With one major difference,' Jack replied. 'Cristina had basically been brainwashed by the Overseers into believing that we killed her husband and child. That could account for a lot.'

'We also don't know what experiments the Overseers ran on Red that could have made it behave in that way,' I said.

'That could definitely be a factor,' Jodie said.

Alice leant forward in her wheelchair. 'The bottom line is, we're all painfully aware that if we can't bring Lucy back it will have serious consequences for us trying to defend this planet from the Kimprak invasion.'

Everyone was silent for a moment. The implications of that were truly off the scale.

Mike gazed around at all of us. 'OK, I can't believe I'm the one actually having to say this, but let's keep positive, people.'

Jodie nodded. 'You're right, Mike. I wouldn't be supporting this attempt if I hadn't run countless simulations and come up with an eighty to ninety per cent probability that merging the micro minds will work out all right.'

Mike scratched his neck. 'And even if it doesn't, there's always the option of recovering another micro mind – one that hasn't been imprinted by a woman mad out of her mind with grief – and trying again. Then, before we know it, Lucy will be back to her old self, causing the usual trouble.'

'Oh joy,' Jodie said with a small smile.

One thing was for certain: by the end of today we would have leapt well and truly into unknown territory.

At that moment a knock came from the porch door. We looked round to see Tom, our chief of intelligence, and Niki, our head of security, standing in the doorway.

'Are you all ready for the training exercise?' Tom asked. 'We have Ariel locked and loaded with the prototype WASP swarm.'

'Hell yes,' Ruby replied. 'I'm itching to serve you guys your asses on a platter. What do you say to a small wager?'

'The confidence that comes before a fall, hey, Lauren,' Jack said.

'Absolutely,' I replied with a broad smile that I so wasn't feeling on the inside.

CHAPTER TWO

As JACK and I crept through the undergrowth towards the target, the jungle soundtrack of birds and insects was almost deafening. In the stifling humidity, sweat was already running down my back and soaking through my camouflaged combat uniform. The trees started to thin ahead and we both stopped as the three-hundred-metre-wide clearing came into view.

I pulled my safety googles up on to my Kevlar helmet and peered through my compact Zeiss Terra ED 10x42 binoculars. There it was: the silver flight crate and a trailing parachute, in the middle of the clearing after its airdrop. It looked so tempting, sitting there waiting for us with not a hostile to be seen anywhere. Which of course was exactly the point.

'How are we doing, Lauren?' Jack said as he checked the magazine for his Glock 19. He'd increasingly started to favour the weapon on the firing ranges.

'Objective is in sight. Apart from that I'm feeling hot, sticky and already in desperate need of a shower.'

'I really didn't need that mental image to distract me right now,' Jack replied, casting me a smile.

I grinned back at him. 'My bad.'

I heard a click in my earbud.

'OK, if everyone is in position, report in,' Niki's voice came over our platoon's channel. He was the one in charge of us and all the other squads in this training exercise that promised to get very interesting.

As it was Jack and I, technically we weren't a squad as that needed a minimum of six people. However, that aside Niki had roped us into the exercise, which we'd been more than happy to help out with. Also, although I wouldn't admit it even to Jack, it brought out the competitive streak in me and I wanted to prove to our head of security how good we were, even when it was only two of us.

I swung my binoculars right and looked into the thick under-growth. I was only able to spot Niki's team in their combat uniforms because I had my binoculars pointing straight at them. Twenty-five of his best security guards had been split into squads and were already in position, ready to begin the recovery mission.

The five other squads called in before I took our turn.

I pressed my fingertip against my earbud to activate its inbuilt mic and keep the channel open. 'Foxtrot squad ready for your orders.'

'All teams get ready to begin the phased assault on my command,' Niki replied.

I turned to Jack. 'I really don't understand why they haven't already attacked us. Ruby knows we're out here.'

'She's probably waiting for us to make the first move before showing her hand,' Jack replied. 'One thing's for sure: the next few minutes are going to get real interesting fast.'

'That's definitely a given.' I unholstered my Mossad .22 LRS pistol that had become almost an extension of me during combat and took a centring breath. My hardened battle-calm dropped over me, sharpening every instinct – the soldier version of myself that I could now turn on whenever I needed it. Though part of me still couldn't believe how I'd been transformed by the experiences of the last few years, and if I was honest, I wasn't always entirely comfortable with.

'Bravo squad, fire smoke rounds into the target area,' Niki's voice said through the earbud.

'Affirmative,' a woman replied over the comm channel.

Several *thunking* sounds came from the trees around us. A split second later, dark canisters arced out from the edges of the jungle and thudded down near to the silver crate. Each cylinder began to billow thick grey smoke that quickly covered the clearing with a thick pall of fog.

'Bravo. Charlie and Delta squads, go now,' Niki said.

I caught a brief glimpse as the flurry of security officers burst out of several points around the clearing. Within seconds they were lost in the smoke as they raced towards the flight crate.

'Alpha and Foxtrot squads, go, go, go!' Niki said over the comm link. Immediately his squads were up on their feet and sprinting forward.

Jack nodded towards me. 'We're up.'

'Let's go and show the others how this should be done,' I said as I thumbed the safety off my LRS

We dashed forward, keeping our heads low and our weapons drawn. The weight of the Kevlar body armour kicked in and slowed me a fraction. But it was necessary and Niki had insisted on it as a safety precaution.

We burst out of the jungle as the previous squads had done and plunged into the bank of billowing smoke. The world became a landscape of grey smudges and indistinct figures running ahead and around us. Thank god this was only an exercise, as adrenaline was already pumping through my system. I didn't want to show even a hint of fear beneath my icy calm exterior.

Of course, Ruby, our resident sniper and tactical officer, was always going to be waiting for us to make our move.

We'd barely even glanced towards our objective when a faint whining sound sped unseen over our heads, the source hidden by the fog. That single sound was then multiplied a dozen times, seemingly coming from every direction at once. Ruby had launched her WASPs, our new swarm combat drones and I knew she wouldn't pull any punches.

'Everyone get ready. Incoming hostiles,' Niki said through our earbuds.

Crackles of live gunfire erupted all around us, followed by a lot of swearing over the combat channel. Although this was a training exercise and an opportunity to shake out the combat performance of the WASPs, that didn't mean a live round couldn't do a lot of damage to flesh and bone.

But this was Niki all over - totally old school. A background in the special forces had made him a fan of live-fire exercises and he maintained it focused people's minds like nothing else.

'Echo squad, give us covering fire into the air now,' Niki said, his voice cool and calm.

The bark of heavy machine-gun fire opened up from the jungle behind us, tracer rounds blazing through the smoke above our heads in glowing trails.

The swearing fell away, but the roar of fire increased around us. Then came the short hissing sound of incoming projectiles, every one of which ended in a cry from a security team member.

'Damn it. Ruby's just picking us off. We need to start improvising,' Jack said.

'No, we follow Niki's orders. The first squad to reach that flight container grabs it and makes a dash back to the jungle.'

He gave me a sideways glance as we ran. 'Look at you actually following orders for once. But even if we reach it, there's no way Ruby's going to let us waltz out of here.'

'I know, but this is Niki's party and we're going to follow his lead,' I replied. 'You're the one always lecturing me about the chain of command.'

'Yeah, I do, don't I?' Jack said, pulling a face.

Three sharp whistling sounds came from close by and to our right, three of Niki's squad, crumpled to the ground, groaning and clutching their stomachs. Just as worrying was the machine gun fire quickly growing quieter as distant cries came from behind, in the jungle beyond the clearing.

'Great – sounds like Echo squad is being taken out too,' Jack said, his voice tense.

'And with that goes our covering fire as we try to retrieve the crate,' I replied.

But there was no time to talk. It was our turn.

Adrenaline tanged my tongue as I spotted a blur of movement almost directly above us. Immediately, all my experience in the field kicked in. I dropped to my knee, sighting the fast-moving object along my LRS's barrel, and pulled the trigger. Sparks erupted from the stubby-winged grey WASP. It spun away, crashing unseen in the smoke to the ground with a dull thud.

'Nice shooting,' Jack said as the silver flight crate loomed in the fog ahead of us.

'I'd certainly love to see Ruby's face right now.'

But as we raced towards our target, I was painfully aware that there wasn't any sign of the other squads.

'Oh, this isn't good,' Jack said as the realisation set in.

Niki appeared out of the mist before I'd even a chance to mentally process how the odds had badly swung against us. He had a Benelli M3 tactical shotgun in one hand and an Agie Plate in the other – one of the antigravity lifting devices we'd reverse-engineered from the Overseers. Without pausing, Niki slapped the Agie on to the large silver crate.

'Attention all squads, we have secured the target and are

making our way back,' Niki said, his finger pressed firmly to his earbud.

No response came over the comm channel. Perhaps even more disturbingly, the sound of gunfire had fallen silent too, leaving just soft groans coming from around us in the smoke.

'Oh crap, I think that means we're on our own,' Jack said.

An itch of fear started to grow inside me. Despite being a training exercise, this was beginning to feel uncomfortably real.

Nike reloaded his Benelli. 'You two, get that crate out of here and I'll give you covering fire.'

Jack and I grabbed the handles and hoisted it between us. Even though I knew what the Agie plate was capable of, it was still a surprise to my muscles as we easily lifted what should have weighed a good hundred kilos, but was actually more like ten.

We could run almost at full speed towards the edge of the jungle as it began to appear through the thinning smoke. It was a hundred metres away...then ninety...eighty...

My senses went electric as three more WASPs, each about half a metre wide, swooped down from the sky straight towards us.

Niki pumped his shotgun, drawing in on our position, firing twice in quick succession. Two of the craft exploded as the Benelli's twelve-gauge anti-personnel rounds shredded them.

But the WASP in the middle was still closing fast, randomly spiralling, which made it a tougher target. Whilst still at a full speed, Jack tried a one-handed shot, but his Glock's bullet went wide of its target. I could imagine the glee on Ruby's face as she watched our frantic efforts to defend ourselves whilst she closed in for the kill.

In that frozen second, I felt vulnerable – that no end of training could save us from every eventuality in combat. And just like that, my cool detachment shattered, no matter that this was a training exercise. Fear buried its claws into me.

A puff of pale gas erupted from the stubby barrel mounted on the belly of the WASP. We dived sideways, but Niki was too slow. A red patch exploded on Niki's stomach from the paintball round and he toppled like a felled tree.

The small craft streaked over our heads, its small wings rotating and the whine of its motors growing louder as it scrabbled for maximum lift.

Any sense of calmness in me was totally blown now, my fear replaced by anger.

'Not so fast, you bitch!' I hissed. I aimed my LRS and squeezed the trigger.

A hole appeared in the craft's fuselage as it tried to speed away, then its nose dipped and it ploughed into the ground, shedding its wings as it tumbled end over end.

A spark of hope lit up in me.

'We can still do this, Jack!' I shouted.

He nodded, the muscles cabling in his neck as we lengthened our strides to a full-blown sprint. Thirty metres towards the relative safety of the jungle...twenty...

There was another whining sound directly ahead of us. Three more drones shot out from the jungle and sped towards us, skimming low over the grass like hawks coming in for the kill.

As one, Jack and I dropped the crate and raised our weapons. Too slow. Too little. Too late.

A projectile blurred into Jack's shoulder and spun him round. It felt as if someone had struck my combat helmet with a sledgehammer as I sprawled to the ground.

I lay on my back, panting for breath. Red liquid began to drip on to my goggles from the impact. It might have been a paintball round, but part of my psyche still interpreted it as being genuinely shot.

'Jesus, that hurts,' Jack said, nursing his shoulder.

The fear that had become anger that had become hope was

overwhelmed by the sense of frustration rolling up through me. We'd lost and losing was something I didn't do. This time it had been a paintball round, but next time it could be a real bullet.

A deafening whoop came through my earbud as the three drones peeled away, performing barrel rolls in the sky. The smoke thinned to a haze just in time for me to see the other drones buzz out of the forest, rising in formation.

'Thirty-six kills to five lost WASPs. Damn, I'm good!' Ruby's voice gloated in our ears.

A circular shape rippled above us as *Ariel* materialised like a ghost out of thin air, her chameleon cloak now deactivated. Three small iris hatches opened in the belly of Sky Dreamer Corp's very own UFO and Ruby's remaining WASP drones disappeared up into them.

'I think that's a definite win for team Ruby and her WASP swarm and a lose for team Niki,' Tom, our chief intelligence officer, said over the comm link.

'Yah, yah, yah,' Niki said as he appeared in my sights, standing over me.

He handed me a cloth and I sat up, I began to clean the red paint from my goggles. Jack got slowly back to his feet, still clutching his shoulder.

'Jesus, those supersized paintball pellets hurt like hell,' he said.

'And leave a pretty good memento too,' Niki replied, pulling up his shirt to reveal an expanding purple bruise on his stomach.

Soldiers had begun staggering out of the jungle to join the members of the platoon, who were recovering. Every single one of us had been tagged with a splodge of red paint somewhere on the body.

I unstrapped my helmet. 'Bloody hell, talk about a massacre.'

'Maybe, but as a demonstration of the effectiveness of a

WASP drone swarm, I think it was very impressive,' Tom said over the channel.

'So you've been watching this exercise the whole time?' I asked.

'I've got something of a ringside seat. I'm up here on-board Ariel as a spectator, watching Ruby put the WASPs through their paces.'

I peered upwards towards the craft hanging in almost perfect silence over us, still surreal despite all the flights we'd had inside it.

I did my best to summon up what was left of my dignity. I wanted to sound magnanimous. 'That certainly was an impressive bit of shooting, Ruby. But then I expect nothing less from you.'

'As tempted as I am to take all the credit, I have to say those little WASPs were a dream to control and did most of the heavy lifting. Their thermal vision made it a breeze to spot you all through the smoke – even beneath that thick canopy.'

'On that high note, now you've proved that a WASP swarm is so effective in a troop suppression scenario, are you ready for the next challenge, Ruby?' Tom asked.

'What challenge?' Ruby replied. 'Right now, I'm ready to collect on my bets at the Rock Garden over a beer or three.'

'Really, this isn't so much of a challenge for you – all you'll need to do is press a few buttons in the CIC seat,' Tom said. 'But it will be a serious test of the skills of your pilot.'

'I assumed you were flying, Tom?' I said over the link.

'No, this flight is in the far more capable hands of Commander Troy Armstrong. Troy, are you ready to help test Ariel against Eden's new defence grid?'

'Of course, I'd be more than happy to put this silver girl through her paces,' a man replied with a Texan twang.

Something about the guy's name pulled at a memory, but I was damned if I could place it.

'Excellent, because you will help train Delphi's new flight and combat control systems for *Ariel*. Her basic flight AI routines are already good, but they need some honing for combat.'

'Then I'll do my best to be a good teacher,' Troy said with more than a hint of amusement.

I turned to Jack. 'Who's this new test pilot guy? I thought I knew everyone on the rota, but Troy is a new name on me.'

Jack shrugged. 'No idea, but something tells me this is going to be quite a show if Tom is happy for this guy to train the AI combat systems. Alice told me only the best of the best are allowed to do that.'

I pulled my helmet off and rubbed my seriously aching head. I was definitely going to need to take some pills to ward off the threatening migraine when we headed back down to Eden, our hidden base a good three hundred metres beneath our feet.

'Time to get the second part of this exercise underway,' Tom said. 'Delphi, initiate the test run of Eden's defence grid.'

'Initiating defence grid,' the base's AI, Delphi, replied.

Across the jungle, large metallic cylinders rose above the trees on their hydraulic jacks. As they cleared the canopy, each cylinder split apart to reveal a large central barrel surrounded by circular magnets. These were linked together by copper rods that were starting to steam in the humid air of the jungle – already running hot and ready for action.

This was the new railgun defence system, another of Jodie's many ongoing projects. Although this particular tech was based on the weapon system from the Astra TR-3B that Tom and I had stolen from right under the noses of the Overseers back at Area 51. On our return to Eden, Jodie and the R&D team had reverse-engineered the whole craft. One of the fruits of that research was about to be tested for the first time.

Above us, *Ariel* rotated on her axis until she was pointing almost directly upwards. With not so much as a sigh, the ship zipped away. Troy engaged *Ariel*'s active chameleon camo system, adding to the eerie nature of the craft. With a slight ripple, she disappeared as the panels transformed to the same colour and texture of the sky around her.

'Begin exercise,' Tom said over the link.

'Locating target,' Delphi replied.

Columns of shimmering hot air lanced out from large parabolic reflectors mounted on the top of each railgun. Their beams began to sweep the sky like spotlights – it was something straight out of a Second World War movie.

'That's the first time I've seen the microwave sensor net operational,' Jack said.

'Yeah, me too,' I replied.

This was another product of the TR-3B's reverse-engineering. The Overseers had previously had the edge over us because their microwave sensors had been able to detect *Ariel* even when cloaked. Jodie's answer had been to develop her new ES – electronic shield – a countermeasure that was now fitted on *Ariel* and would hopefully tip the balance in our favour in future encounters with them. That was the theory but this would be the actual test.

With a series of cannon-like booms, huge red spheres shot out from the railguns and sped up into the sky.

I turned to Niki. 'Bloody hell – those look like massive paintball rounds being fired.'

'That's because they are – ones travelling at subsonic speed,' Niki replied over the comm channel. 'After all, we don't want to endanger *Ariel* with live rounds.'

'Not to mention her friggin' crew,' Ruby butted in, her tone already strained.

Jack traded a grin with me. I hated to admit it, but I was

slightly reassured to hear that the usually ice-cool Ruby was rattled by this training exercise too.

In fact, her day was about to get much worse.

'Target located,' Delphi calmly announced.

Shot after shot was soon blazing upwards as the shimmering beams of microwave energy directed them like a laser sight. Troy was flying the rivets off *Ariel*, based on the way the beams danced through the air, trying to lock on to the ship. Every so often I caught the faintest blur as the active camo failed to keep up with the craft's high-speed manoeuvres. Troy jinked *Ariel* through the sky at every angle imaginable. I'd seen plenty of great flying displays, but nothing quite at this level.

However even a skilled pilot as Troy began to run out of sky and the beams started to converge on a single spot in the sky.

It was then that silver confetti started to fall from that area, flickering in the sunlight as it descended towards earth.

My concern immediately ratcheted up. 'Has something critical been hit on *Ariel*?'

'Relax,' Jack said. 'That's the new chaff decoy system that Jodie designed to fool any radar. I'm not sure how good it is against microwave detectors though.'

Sure enough, the shimmering beams ignored it and continued to track *Ariel* as Troy threw everything in the pilots' book into his manoeuvres, clearly determined to shake the lock that the railguns now had on the craft.

'Ruby, don't you think it's about time you engaged your ES against the microwave detector net to make Troy's life a bit easier?' Tom said over the link.

'Damn it, yes! Powering up the ES now.'

'And that right there is why we have training exercises,' Niki said, giving us both an amused *she had it coming* look.

The boom of the railgun rounds fell silent as the beams of energy began to sweep the sky again.

'Target lost – ending attack simulation,' Delphi announced over our earbuds.

With the hiss of hydraulics across the jungle, the railguns started retracting into their hidden silos.

'Kiss our asses!' Ruby shouted over the link. 'That was a batshit-crazy level of flying, Troy. I look forward to toasting your skill down in the Rock Garden.'

'Why thank you, kind lady. I'll hold you to that,' he replied.

'All in good time, people,' Tom said. 'First of all we need to get *Ariel* back to her hangar. And I want a full technical report about how all the new systems have checked out on my desk ASAP.'

A loud sigh came over the link. 'You really know how to rain on a soldier's parade, you know that, buddy?' Ruby said.

'All part of the service,' Tom replied.

Ariel slid silently away through the sky towards the hidden entrance of the landing bay silo next to Alice's laboratory.

I shook my head at Jack and Niki. 'There's definitely a strong streak of evil lurking under Tom's pleasant exterior.'

Niki chuckled as he headed back towards the jungle.

Jack gazed at me. 'I don't know about you, but all this talk of beer has got me thirsty. I need a drink or three to take away the pain of that damned paintball round.'

'Later, but first, pills, lots of pills, followed by a hot bath.'

Jack gave me an overly innocent look. 'Now your plan sounds way better than mine.'

I smiled, holstering my LRS. 'You do know you have a one-track mind?'

'So shoot me already.' His smile sharpened into a grin. 'I can't help that you are crazy gorgeous even in combat armour.'

There was a cough in my ear. 'Lauren and Jack, you might want to mute your private conversations,' Tom said.

Before I'd even had a chance to even blush, Niki gave us an amused look over his shoulder.

'Anyway, I hate to be a killjoy,' Tom continued, 'but Jodie has just radioed in. They are ready to begin the experiment with Lucy and they need us down in the lab ASAP.'

And just like that, any sense of lightness was swept away and foreboding took hold of me again.

'On our way,' I said, gazing at Jack.

He raised his eyebrows at me as we turned and headed back towards one of the concealed entrances in the jungle along with a number of battered and bruised security guards shuffling along ahead of us.

CHAPTER THREE

HEADING FOR ALICE'S LAB, Jack and I walked along a large gantry set over a large underground factory. Below us several huge industrial 3D printers were creating dozens of XA103s, the unimaginative official designation for *Ariel*, testament to Alice's philosophy of rapid prototyping and development.

Partly constructed curved hulls stretched away towards the end of the cavern. Yellow and blue painted robots with various tool attachments fitted to their multiple arms, worked alongside people wearing either blue coveralls or white lab coats.

Our new mechanised workforce units were called Mircats, a mashup of the acronym for 'mobile industrial robot' and the caterpillar tracks that they manoeuvred on. The robots had been built to augment our human efforts to speed up production as much as possible, running round the clock.

The Mircats were one of the many recent developments to come out of the Forge – a nickname that had been given to Jodie's very own department, which Alice had promoted her to run. The Forge was Eden's equivalent to the Skunk Works, the official pseudonym for Lockheed Martin's Advanced Development

Program, which was behind no end of top secret US military projects. Under Jodie's guidance, the Forge had already more than proved itself as a worthy competitor.

An almost completed X103 was being towed by one of the Mircats whilst floating under its own power, heading towards a far cavern where dozens of completed craft had already parked. Alice had nicknamed this area the paint shop – where the active camouflage polymer display panels were glued on to the titanium hulls of the craft.

'Looks as if Alice is building an armada down there,' Jack said.

'Unfortunately there's nowhere near enough craft for that yet – according to Jodie,' I replied. 'She was telling me they are having increasing difficulty sourcing enough materials, especially the titanium. Although hopefully that's a moot point since it's our plan B in case we can't Lucy get back online.'

Jack shot me a thin-lipped look. 'Let's pray it won't come to that, especially as Mike and Jodie seem pretty confident that this reboot attempt of Lucy is going to work.'

I winced inwardly. No one, even Jack, seemed as concerned as me that this reboot could be risky.

'I just hope that optimism is well-founded,' I said as we reached the end of the gantry and entered a lift.

A few moments later we emerged into the launch bay with its memorial wall to all that had fallen at the hands of the Overseers. As intended with its design, every time I walked past it, I was reminded of just how ruthless that organisation had been with people's lives over the years.

I often found myself visiting it when I was alone to gaze at the names and lose myself in my thoughts. I sometimes even found myself reflecting on the number of Overseer lives that I had taken. No doubt they all had families who were mourning them too.

In some ways the memorial wall had become my version of a church – or maybe even a confessional where I could face my sins, if only to myself.

On one of the landing pads stood *Ariel*, a craft that had now very much proved herself in combat. Beside her was a similar saucer-shaped ship, but twice her size at more than fifty metres across. Apparently it weighed in at five hundred tons thanks to its thick armour plating, heavier even than some of the biggest passenger jets. This was the new XA104 and a heavy transport variant of *Ariel*. It had quickly been christened the *Pangolin* in honour of the *Armadillo* that it would eventually replace in regular active service.

Half the guts of the new ship were exposed as technicians and Mircats worked on it, giving us a clear view through the exposed airframe of a large cockpit deck. Like *Ariel*, the flight deck was designed to be kept gyroscopically level whilst the hull rotated round it.

Jack whistled as we headed past the *Pangolin*. 'Wow, that's some serious progress the Forge team are making. That prototype was little more than a blueprint the last time I was down here.'

'Alice is keen that we have it as soon as possible. She was telling me that it can carry up to thirty people and has full crew quarters along with a significant amount of cargo space for long, sustained missions. And with its heavy armour it will definitely be useful on missions where we need serious backup.'

'Well, it's certainly impressive. If I was a TR-3B pilot I'd think twice before attacking it,' Jack replied.

I nodded as we entered Alice's lab. The tension across my shoulders immediately increased and my gaze travelled straight to the transparent room that we'd nicknamed "the Cage". This was the holographic area designed to work with the synaesthesia-based communication system of the Angelus. The reason for my growing tension lay inside it.

Lucy's darkened and shattered micro mind was sitting in the middle of the chamber, hooked up to a bank of monitoring equipment. Even if Lucy didn't have a pulse, for me the resemblance to an intensive care unit was uncomfortably real.

Outside the Cage sat Red, the micro mind we'd stolen from right under the noses of the Overseers at Area 51. It glowed its usual dim and slightly threatening ruby colour, in stark contrast to the two small, shining blue Agie plates that had been attached to it. They made manoeuvring the two-ton tetrahedron-shaped crystal relatively easy. Currently the large crystal was being held firmly in the hydraulic mandibles of one of the new three-metre-tall Mircats. In fairness, it could have easily lifted the micro mind even without the Agie plates.

Beyond the Cage, Jodie was sitting at a workstation with Mike, Alice and Tom, all of them gazing up at the large screen. On it was a live feed of Lucy along with dozens of scrolling data windows that monitored activity, or the lack of it, in her crystal matrix.

Yes, to take the ICU analogy further, Lucy was in a coma.

My gaze flicked to the countdown timer above the main screen – the reason that Alice had decided we had to risk taking this chance to reboot Lucy.

It displayed three years, five months and eighteen days – the length of time until the Kimprak would arrive in our solar system to destroy it. Very much like the memorial wall outside, the timer focused everyone's minds on what was at stake here.

Alice had been talking to Tom, Mike and Jodie, but pivoted her wheelchair towards us as we approached. 'Good, we've been waiting for you. We're all set from our side. Lauren, are you ready to begin? Did you bring what you need?'

'Absolutely.' I slipped the Empyrean Key out of the small rucksack on my shoulder.

Jack raked his hand through his blond hair. 'So what's the plan exactly, guys?'

'We're going to order the Mircat to place Red into the Cage with Lucy,' Jodie replied. 'We're hoping that once the micro minds are within close proximity of each other the self-repair icon will appear over Lauren's Empyrean Key and then she'll be able to activate it.'

I nodded. 'OK, but are we ready to lock down the lab if anything goes wrong?'

Tom gave me a straight look. Out of everyone, he'd taken my concerns the most seriously and he'd already told me he'd put an insurance policy in place.

Sure enough, he gestured towards a number of black boxes mounted to the walls of the Cage. 'I've had some C4 charges attached in case everything goes tits up. Hit the emergency button on the wall and you'll have thirty seconds to get out of the Cage before blast panels slam into place round it to contain the detonation. This is obviously a last resort option – it'll leave very little of any of the micro minds inside apart from crystal dust.'

'Jesus, you think it might go that badly wrong to take such a crazy Armageddon step?' Jack asked.

'No, but we need to be prepared for every eventuality,' Alice said, meeting my gaze.

Maybe people had been listening to me after all. And ironically, despite the massive implications, I felt the tension in my shoulders release a fraction. Without Lucy in the driving seat when merging these micro minds together, we were about to jump into the unknown. So it was good to know that a fallback plan, even such an extreme one, was in place. It started to hit me that I might be the verge of losing an AI that I'd come to think of as a friend for ever.

'OK, everyone, we're going for it,' Jodie said. 'Get ready to pray to whatever deity or greater power that you believe in.'

Jack leant in towards me. 'I'm sure it's going to be all right, Lauren.'

Yes, he could so read me. 'I hope so, for all our sakes,' I replied.

I stepped in through the glass door of the Cage and closed it behind me. There was a slight hiss of air as the pressure equalised.

Up close to Lucy, the damage she'd sustained was shocking. Numerous fissures ran through her six-pointed star crystal structure. There was even a huge gouge mark from a strike by a railgun round from one of the pursuing TR-3Bs. All this damage was significantly worse than the single bullet hole I'd managed to put through her back at Skara Brae. Lucy had been able to self-repair from that. But could she really cope with damage this big?

Mike's voice came through the speaker in the ceiling. 'OK, Lauren, I'm turning on the carrier frequency to activate your synaesthesia.'

'Understood.' I raised the Empyrean Key in my hand so that the camera overhead had a clear view of it. 'Ready whenever you are.'

'Activating now,' Mike replied.

A crystal clear tone rang out from the speaker in the ceiling. Not so much as a glimmer of light appeared over the stone orb clutched in my hand, even though my synaesthesia ability should have converted the sound into a visual pattern.

A sinking feeling filled my stomach. I knew exactly what that meant.

'We're not seeing anything on the monitors, Lauren. How about you?'

'No, not a thing, just like before,' I replied, trying to make my tone sound less flat than I felt. The next step was growing inevitably closer.

I reached out and ran my hand over the cold surfaces of the

micro mind crystals. 'Lucy, if you're in there, please just give me a sign before we try anything with Red?'

I held my breath but once again, not so much as a flicker passed through her surface.

That was it, the last chance saloon.

My gaze strayed to one of the C4 charges outside the room before I turned to face the others watching me through the glass. 'It looks as if we really have no choice but to proceed.'

'OK, I'm going to commence bringing Red into the Cage now,' Jodie said through the speaker mounted in the ceiling.

Outside the room, one of the Mircat's free mandibles reached forward and opened the door as delicately as a human hand, impressive for something strong enough to rip it off entirely. I stepped to one side and the robot trundled into the Cage, holding Red's tetrahedron shaped crystal in its outstretched arms. As it manoeuvred the micro mind into position over Lucy, I held my breath and gazed down at the Empyrean Key.

Please god, let this work... I thought to myself.

This time a single icon shimmered into existence – an orb with concentric lines round it. The self-repair icon.

I felt my heart lift. At least this was a good sign.

'See, I told you it was going to be fine,' Jack said over the intercom.

He could see exactly what I could thanks to the Cage's system, which interpreted what I was witnessing with my synaesthesia and relayed it to the large monitor in the lab.

I braced myself as the sense of foreboding grew stronger. I selected the icon and flicked the Empyrean Key forward with my wrist.

Red started to emit a low buzzing sound like the hum of an electrical transformer. Then the ruby light began to intensify beneath his crystal surface. With a slight crackle of frying electronics and wisps of smoke, the Agie rings mounted either side of Red went dark and dropped to the ground.

'Releasing Red from the Mircat's grip now,' Jodie said over the intercom.

As the robot's mandibles opened, the glowing crystal floated free under its own power and my mouth grew dry.

We'd already passed the point of no return.

Static washed over my skin as the air began to smell strongly of ozone – the aroma you get at the seaside.

Red's humming grew louder as he floated up to the top of the Cage, now fully under his own antigravity power. With a snarl of wind, whirling crackles of energy began to dance between Red and Lucy's broken remains.

'Lauren, get yourself out of there now!' Mike shouted as he starred at the readouts in front of him. 'We're getting rapidly building energy levels.'

He didn't have to tell me twice. I could almost taste the threat to my life in there. I dived for the door just as a whiplash of red plasma earthed itself on to the Mircat and sent sparks flying. I rushed outside and slammed the door shut behind me, taking several deep breaths.

'Are you OK?' Jack asked, heading over to me.

'My anxiety levels are through the roof, but otherwise I'm fine. The real questions is: what about Lucy?'

We headed back to the others and I noticed Tom's hand placed strategically close to the C4 detonation button under its protective panel. Good – at least somebody was prepared if this situation deteriorated rapidly.

Everyone had grown noticeably quiet, suggesting I wasn't the only fearful one, as we watched the red tetrahedron crystal rotate directly over Lucy until one of its tips pointed down towards her.

'The energy readings are off the charts in there,' Mike said, shaking his head at the read-outs.

The glass started to bend violently inwards as the roaring winds intensified.

'Just say the word and I'll blow those charges,' Tom said.

Jodie held up a palm. 'No, I think we're good. The energy levels seem to levelling out and that glass is strong enough to resist a hurricane.'

'Resist as in not break?' Jack asked.

'I guess we're about to find that out for certain,' I replied.

But then Jack's eyes widened as he looked past me. 'Holy crap, will you look at that light show now?'

I turned back towards the big screen. It showed the camera view from inside the glass room, with geometric patterns cascading all over Red as he descended towards Lucy. Lightning was lancing out from his tip. As it hit Lucy, little pulses of red energy rippled through her, surrounded by swirls of blue light that had suddenly burst into existence.

'Well, that's looking highly promising,' Alice said.

A sound that reminded me of haunting whale song began as the red micro mind slid into Lucy. A burst of intense starlight blazed through the lab and we had to turn away to shield our eyes.

What was happening was no longer being contained within the Cage. The whole lab shook as equipment racks toppled over.

Tom rested his hand over the C4 detonator button. 'Just give me the order,' he shouted over the roar.

But I was increasingly starting to feel all right about was happening. This was very close to what we'd seen before when the micro minds had merged back in Peru.

'No, this is all good – we just need to hang in there,' I called out.

Alice's gaze met mine and she nodded. 'Stand down, Tom.'

He slowly withdrew his fingers. 'I just hope that's the right call.'

Before I could reply, the whale song was replaced by a rising tone so impossibly loud we all had to clamp our hands over our ears. I heard something creaking loudly above us and spotted a light rig in the roof of the cavern swinging wildly. With the crack of its suspension cables breaking free, it came plummeting down, straight towards Jack.

I hurled myself towards Jack, knocking him to the ground a microsecond before the light rig smashed down on to the spot where he'd just been standing.

Jack shot me a grateful look, but before either of us could say anything a roar of sound came from the Cage so intense it felt as if every fibre of my being was being torn apart. A moment later, every single light in the lab flickered off, plunging us into darkness as the thunderstorm inside the Cage died away to nothing.

My ears still ringing, I let go of Jack and rolled on to my back to see small whispers of smoke rising from the now nine-pointed crystal star floating within the Cage.

I noticed the faint cascade of red light rippling through the combined micro minds as the blue swirls round them began to fade. What did that mean?

'Has it worked, Lauren?' Alice asked, wheeling her chair across the debris-covered floor towards the Cage for a closer look.

'Only one way to find out,' I replied.

As I got back to my feet, I couldn't help but notice that Tom had once again positioned his hand as close as possible to the kill switch.

When I stepped through the door of the Cage the smell of cordite flooded my nostrils. Any doubt of the amount of energy that had just been unleashed in here was swept away by the puddle of molten metal still bubbling on the floor. I carefully stepped round all that remained of the Mircat.

'Alice, can you give me a carrier tone? Let's see what we're dealing with here,' I said.

Alice cupped her hand to her ear and mouthed, '*I can't hear you*,' to me.

I headed back to the door and opened it.

'Sorry, the electrical storm seems to have fried the speaker system,' Mike said.

I nodded. 'Then we'll do this the old-fashioned way.'

I re-entered the Cage, taking out my tuning fork and striking it against the Empyrean Key.

Elation surged inside me as a pulsating red circle with four red arrows pointing in towards it appeared hovering over the stone ball – the self-repair function was now up and running.

I almost sagged into myself as I stepped back outside.

'Well?' Alice asked.

I turned to face the expectant gazes of the others. 'It worked. The repair of Lucy's matrix is underway.'

And just like that everyone was whooping and applauding. There were quite a few hugs too, particularly between Jack and me. Even Mike's drawn expression seemed to lighten a fraction as Jodie wrapped her arms round him.

'I have to admit I was a little bit worried for a moment,' Alice said as she wheeled her chair up to me.

'You and me both,' I said. 'Maybe next time we need two micro minds to merge, it should happen in a wide open area above ground – definitely not in a contained space like a cavern, hey?'

Alice smiled. 'That might be a very good idea.'

'So how long is this repair going to take?' Jack asked.

'Honestly, I have no idea,' I replied. 'The damage to Lucy is certainly more extensive compared to what happened to her back in Orkney. We could be talking a week, maybe longer.'

'Well, the sooner Lucy is back to her old sassy self, the happier I'll be,' Alice said. 'Have you any idea why the combined micro mind is red rather than blue like Lucy's original crystal?'

I shrugged. 'I've been wondering that myself.'

'Then we'll have to wait for the answer to that particular riddle when Lucy can tell us,' Tom said as he joined us.

'What happens in the meantime?' Jack asked.

'We keep an eye on the completed TREENO network,' Jodie said from across the room. 'We're overdue another micro mind waking up.'

I nodded. For the first time in months, I felt as if I could start looking forward again. 'Good. I don't know about you, Jack, but I'm itching to get back into the field.'

Jack's mouth twitched. 'A glutton for punishment, hey?'

'Something like that,' I replied with a grin.

But then I caught the pained look on Mike's face. We were talking about heading out on a future mission without him.

I shook my head. 'Sorry, me and my big mouth, Mike.'

'No, don't worry about it,' he replied. 'As I said, my place is here with Jodie doing the real heavy lifting to help make the tech magic a thing. I don't mind you two and Ruby going off gallivanting round the planet.'

'We'll make sure we bring you back a present from the duty-free shop,' Jack quipped.

Mike snorted. 'Yeah, yeah.' He raised his palm and Jack high-fived it.

The calmness in his expression seemed to be sticking around this time. Whatever he was dealing with on the inside, maybe there was already a glimpse of light at the end of the tunnel.

I leant into Jack as he wrapped an arm round me, the tension I felt draining away for the first time in months now it looked as if Lucy really was going to be all right.

Yes, there was definitely going to be some celebrating tonight and god knew we all deserved it.

CHAPTER FOUR

Two weeks can feel like an eternity when you are waiting for something to happen, stirring up memories of childhood as time dragged on towards Christmas Day. But unlike the definite reward of unwrapping those presents you'd been eyeing up under the tree, with the current situation it felt as if there was no end in sight. Despite everything looking promising initially, Lucy still hadn't booted up.

I sat in the lab rubbing my thumb over the Empyrean Key, threatening to wear a groove in it, as I watched the fused micro minds through the glass walls of the Cage. A slow-motion dance of light was still rippling through the combined crystal tetrahedrons. Apart from the visible fissure damage slowly disappearing as the days had passed, the only other notable change in the last fortnight was that the light display emanating from them had subtly shifted. Now, small motes of blue surrounded by swirling pools of red hypnotised me as I watched them.

Mike was peering at the scrolling readouts with Jodie as he sat in his wheelchair. He hooked his hands round the back of his neck and sighed.

'Problem?' I asked.

'I just wish we could understand what the hell is going on inside those micro minds. This is the longest time so far for Lucy's self-repair routine to complete.'

'At least on the plus side all those fractures in her crystal structure have been repaired,' Jodie said.

'So why hasn't she burst back into life by now?' I asked.

'No idea, but we do know something is happening in there,' Jodie said. 'According to the readouts, there's been a lot of electrical activity within the micro minds. And of course, there was that one memorable incident a week ago when anything metal within a metre of the Cage was magnetised and stuck to its glass walls, although thankfully that didn't last long.'

'Yeah, especially as my wheelchair was one of those objects – with me in it,' Mike said, shaking his head and raising a smile. 'Talk about my magnetic attraction.'

We all groaned.

'Anyway, our best guess is that Lucy is integrating Red's micro mind into her own matrix and that's just taking time. Then once she's finished spring cleaning his code, she'll hit the restart button and boot herself up.'

I placed the Empyrean Key down on a bench and started to pace up and down. 'But if this red light routine is a manifestation of this process, why haven't we seen it before? After all, this isn't Lucy's first rodeo when it comes to repairing herself.'

Mike shrugged. 'Lucy is a lot more damaged this time around, so I'm guessing it's everything to do with that.'

The hum of motors came from the corner of the lab.

We all turned to see a large round block descending from a hole in the ceiling down a transparent tube. This was actually Alice's office, the entire room built on a lift mechanism that could transport it from the upper production floor level down to her private lab and inner sanctum, where all the really interesting work in Eden happened.

'Looks as if Alice is about to put in an appearance,' Jodie said.

'I haven't seen her for days,' I said.

'That's because she's been heavily involved in adapting plans for the Mars settlement project,' Mike explained.

'In what way?'

'Not sure – she's been vague about it whenever I've bought the subject up.'

The room came to a gentle stop with a soft sigh of hydraulics and the door opened to reveal Alice and a guy with cropped grey hair and penetrating eyes who looked to be in his mid-forties. He walked towards us with a confident stride alongside Alice in her wheelchair.

Even before he opened his mouth, I could tell he had history in the military by the way he held himself.

'Jodie, can you power up the live link to Ymir 3? I've just relayed it from my office to workstation three in here,' Alice said. 'It's reached its destination and is already sending back some very interesting data.'

Jodie stared at her. 'Hang on – Ymir 3 isn't due to reach the target asteroid for another year yet.'

A smile flickered across Alice's face. 'Let's just say that a little side project we've been testing during the mission has worked out better than anyone could have hoped for.'

'That has to be the understatement of the year based on what I've already seen,' the man said with a hint of a Texan twang.

I suddenly realised where I'd heard that voice before – this was the exceptional pilot who'd demonstrated his considerable skill during the railgun defence test.

'Troy?' I asked.

'Guilty as charged,' he replied, reaching out a hand and

taking mine in a firm handshake. 'Commander Troy Armstrong at your disposal.'

I peered at him. 'I know I've seen your face somewhere but I can't quite place it.'

Alice smiled and shook her head. 'You should know, Lauren – you've watched this man at work enough times.'

I gave her a blank look. 'Sorry, still none the wiser.'

'Then I'll put you out of your misery,' Troy replied. 'You've probably only ever seen me in a pressure suit and on a screen.'

Part of me became instantly star-struck – the man standing before me was a real-life astronaut. 'Of course, you're the guy leading the Mars simulation programme. Former test pilot in the military and several missions up in the International Space Station.'

His grin became as wide as his home state of Texas. 'Yep, that's me, ma'am.'

'Apologies – I really should have been able to put your face to the name sooner,' I said.

'Tricky when it's hidden behind a golden faceplate,' Troy smiled. 'I'm guessing you must be the one and only Lauren Stelleck?'

'You've heard of me?'

'I doubt there's a single person in Eden who hasn't heard of the incredible achievements of you and your team.' He turned to Mike. 'And you must be Mike Palmer, the hot shot physicist I've been told so much about?'

'That's me,' Mike replied, holding out a hand to shake Troy's.

'I'm a big fan of your work,' the commander said.

Mike dragged his hand through his hair. 'Seriously?

'Seriously and I've been reading up about your reports into this E8 higher dimension. I'd love to pick your brains about it over a drink sometime.'

'Anytime,' Mike replied.

'Now, where's Jack Harper? I'm keen to chat to him; I'm a bit of an amateur archaeologist myself.'

'He's monitoring the TREENO network from my house in the cavern next door,' Alice replied.

I nodded. 'Yes, Jack loves using the virtual dome projection system in there whilst sprawled out on a lounger. He says it's like having the ultimate ultra-wide monitor.'

'It guess it beats sitting at a workstation,' Troy replied.

The commander's gaze flicked to the Cage and the glowing crystal micro minds inside it. 'And that's the alien AI, Lucy?'

'The very same, although at the moment she's still offline,' Jodie said as she stood up and shook Troy's hand too. 'Good to see you, Troy.'

'You too, old friend.'

'So why aren't you out and about digging up rock samples or planting potatoes in your biodome, Troy?' Jodie asked.

'That's because we decided to terminate the Mars simulation programme a week ago,' Alice said.

I turned and stared at her. 'But why? I thought it was running really well.'

'It was, but we needed to urgently reassign Troy and his team to a new project after we received a particular feed from Ymir 3. Everything will become clear when you watch it,' Alice said.

Intrigued, Mike spun his wheelchair round and flicked a few buttons.

On the main screen the view of scrolling sine graphs was replaced by a grainy black and white image of a large egg-shaped asteroid floating in the void of space.

The air caught in my chest as I took in the stark ethereal beauty of the monochrome object pulling hard at my astronomer's heart strings.

'Which asteroid are we looking at exactly?' I asked.

'That's 16 Psyche, an M-type asteroid that's one-sixteenth the diameter of Earth's Moon,' Alice replied.

'M-type as in a metal asteroid?' I asked.

Troy nodded. 'Correct. Jodie, could you pull analysis from the core sampler that the Ymir 3 just recovered? It'll explain why everyone is so enthusiastic about this particular beast of a rock.'

Jodie nodded and tapped a few more keys. A long list of data appeared down the right-hand side of the image.

My eyes widened as I began to process what I was reading. 'Large amounts of iron, nickel and even titanium, but also significant amounts of platinum, gold, iridium, palladium, osmium, ruthenium and faint traces of rhodium,' I quoted the text scrolling past.

'We basically hit the jackpot,' Alice said. 'Needless to say, an asteroid of that size would give us near limitless resources.'

I looked between Troy and Alice as a cog turned over. 'Hang on, are you saying what I think you are?'

Troy gave me a slow smile. 'That depends on what you're thinking, Lauren Stelleck.'

'I'm thinking that you're going to attempt to mine that asteroid and use the materials from it to support a sustained increased production rate of the X103s and X104s.'

'No flies on you,' Troy said. 'Anything else you can deduce?'

My eyes tightened on him. 'The fact that you've been pulled out of the Mars simulation programme suggests that you and your team are going to be actively involved somehow?'

'Good work so far, but for the grand prize: how so exactly, Lauren?'

I gazed over Troy's shoulder, gathering my thoughts. My eyes landed on the half-constructed *Pangolin* visible through the door to the hangar.

I turned back to stare at him and Alice. 'Hang on, we're not talking about a crewed mission to the M-type asteroid on-board that X104?'

Troy nodded with a grin. 'You've nailed it, ma'am.'

Jodie's jaw literally dropped open. 'Seriously, you're talking about sending the *Pangolin* out into space before we've even finished building the prototype?'

'Absolutely,' Alice replied. She gestured towards the big countdown timer. 'You know as well as I do what those numbers represent for humanity. That's changed all our priorities around here. There certainly won't be much of Mars left if the Kimprak get here first and we aren't in a position to challenge them. Think of this as plan B, C and D all rolled into one. Troy will lead what will effectively be a proof-of-concept mission out to the asteroid belt to target 16 Psyche and run a test mining station there.'

'Hang on,' Mike said. 'Aren't you talking at least a couple of years to get a crewed mission to reach something as far out as the asteroid belt?'

'Not if you have a propulsion system that can get you close to the speed of light,' Troy replied.

Now it was my jaw that dropped. 'You have a new drive system?'

'We most certainly do,' Alice replied. 'We're looking at equipping the *Pangolin* ships with a helical drive system.'

By now both Jodie and I were gawping at her like two goldfish.

'You're talking about the Dave Burns theoretical drive, which uses a helical drive to generate net thrust?' Mike asked, his eyes even wider than ours.

'The very same,' Troy said. 'Although it's not so theoretical now.'

Alice nodded. 'We had one of the science research teams rapidly prototype it and a smaller version is fitted to Ymir 3. We launched that probe five months ago and initiated the helical drive once it was clear of the atmosphere. It took a while to accelerate up to forty per cent the speed of light, but once it did, it travelled the three AU distance to 16 Psyche in a relative blink of an eye – although it's been spending most of its time decelerating now.'

'AU?' Mike asked.

'Astronomical unit – the distance from the earth to the sun,' I said, my mind now well and truly blown as I processed what I just heard. A near speed-of-light drive was the stuff of my sci-fi dreams.

Jodie slowly shook her head. 'I can't believe you kept such an incredible breakthrough from me, Alice.'

'I am sorry about that, but I think if I started talking to you about theoretical particle accelerator drives along with everything that's been riding on just your shoulders recently, your head might have been in danger of exploding.'

'Alice has a point there,' Mike said, squeezing Jodie's hand.

She nodded. 'But if this new drive really does work, it makes all sorts of things possible.'

'Including a test crewed mission to 16 Psyche by the sounds of it,' I said.

'Exactly,' Troy replied. 'Also, thanks to the gravity reduction aspect of our REV drive, there is less mass in the craft for the helical drive to initially accelerate, so we can use a relatively compact design for the new engine. With that fitted, we believe we can get a *Pangolin* out to 16 Psyche in around three months, allowing for acceleration and deceleration times.'

'Hang on,' I said. 'What about all the solar radiation you and the crew will be exposed to?'

'That's where the larger design of the *Pangolin* comes in,' Alice said. 'We can build in layered shielding that will include water tanks constructed just beneath the hull to help absorb any radiation. In addition to that, we'll also be using the latest hydrogen-rich polymers and rare earth-doped high-density rubber that's proved far more effective than aluminium for shielding during prolonged space missions. And as a final precaution, we'll also include a small, thick-lead-walled room built into the flight deck for shelter – just in case a really big solar storm hits during the voyage.'

'Good god, you really have thought of everything,' I said. 'And you actually believe this could work?'

'I have to admit it's going to be a gamble, but if it pans out, just think about the near limitless potential,' Troy replied.

Alice nodded. 'We could even build a factory on the surface of Psyche 16 to produce *Pangolins* right there.'

I laughed. 'If anyone else had said anything half that mad-sounding, I would have laughed in their faces. But if I've learnt anything from you, Alice, it's not to underestimate anything that you put your mind to.'

'Lauren has so got your number, Alice,' Troy said.

'Oh, she has indeed,' Alice agreed, smiling.

Before I could respond, the door at the opposite end of the lab burst open and Jack came barrelling through it.

'Where's the fire, mate?' Mike asked as Jack practically skidded to a stop in front of us.

'No fire, but an alert has come in from the TREENO network. A CubeSat just detected a major neutrino burst at one of the main candidate sites for a waking micro mind.'

My pulse amped. 'Where exactly?'

'Atlantis,' Jack replied, his face alight.

'You have got to be kidding me?' Mike said, stating exactly what we were all thinking.

'Do I look as if I'm joking?' Jack replied. 'But come and see for yourselves. Tom is already on the way down, along with Ruby, to help us put together a mission profile. This is it, people – the next micro mind we've been waiting for. And this time there is every chance we will get a major jump on the Overseers and beat them to it by quite some margin.'

'OK, anything to do with Atlantis, I've got to see,' Troy said.

Everyone followed Jack towards the cavern.

But despite the incredible news, I hung back a moment, sparing a last glance at Lucy.

You would so love this, I thought to myself.

Then I tore my gaze away from her and headed after the others.

CHAPTER FIVE

In Alice's personal cavern, a simulated version of autumn was currently running. The leaves of the maple trees round the lake had turned to deep reds and golds, and there was a slight chill in the air, heightening the sensation of it being a real change in season. A perfect reconstruction of Alice's family home had been erected in the cavern and recently she'd lit a log burner in the house that we all took turns to feed with wood. Of course, in the closed confines of the cavern, a smoke scrubber had been fitted to the chimney to remove any toxins.

At first I'd thought Alice was crazy to simulate the seasons like this. After all, why not have summer all year long? But the longer I'd spent down here the more I had appreciated the rhythm of the passing year. Just like for Alice, it so reminded me of home – and that was an especially big deal when Eden was situated in the temperate climate of a jungle where seasonal variations weren't a thing.

Wrapped up in jumpers and fleeces we'd grabbed from the house, we all now sat in recliners gazing up at the virtual fluffy white clouds gently sliding across the deep blue sky, a hint of frost on the lawn around us that still hadn't thawed.

Jack had begun to brief us on the location of the energy burst that had been picked up by the TREENO network and had opened up a number of computer windows over the cloudscape above. I gazed at a graph showing the level of the neutrino spike that had been detected by one of the CubeSats less than twenty minutes ago.

'So, you're being serious when you say that you detected this burst at a candidate site for Atlantis?' Tom asked. He and Ruby, who was still soaked in sweat from being halfway through a gym workout, had just joined us.

'I haven't been more serious about anything in my life,' Jack replied.

'But I thought it just a legend?' Troy said.

'It is, but like most legends, it's based on an element of truth. And in the case of Atlantis, there's always been a lot of indirect evidence that it was a very real and significant city.'

'One that's meant to have slipped beneath the ocean,' I pointed out. 'Isn't that going to make this technically demanding to get to?'

Jodie chewed her lip. 'Actually, with the REV drive, in many ways water is just a thicker version of air, so it should be possible to adapt the gravity bubble round the craft and make it possible to move underwater and protect the hull at depth. But we're still going to need to engineer a solution for the multimode vectoring propulsion system to adapt it—'

Jack held up his hands to stop Jodie's flow of problem-solving. 'Slow down there, Jodie. I didn't say the site is actually underwater, did I?'

'But if it's Atlantis, that's where it's supposed to be,' I said.

'Yes, that may have been the case for a short while, but one of the strongest current candidates for that ancient city is actually above sea level. More precisely, in the province of Western Sahara in Mauritania. And that's exactly where we've just detected the signal burst.'

Jack clicked a remote in his hand and a large pop-up window overlaid the others. It was at least thirty metres across and showed an 8K satellite view of North Africa above our heads.

'OK, time for a crash course history lesson,' Jack said. 'The legend of Atlantis first surfaced from Solon, a Greek who recorded the story about it from his visit to Egypt around 500 BC. Six generations later, his account was then picked up by Plato, who included descriptions of Atlantis in his dialogues, Critias and Timaeus. In them Plato stated that the King of Atlantis was none other than Atlas, the son of the god Poseidon.'

Jack's gaze swept over us, his eyes shining with enthusiasm as he hit his stride. 'The first real clue that the site the neutrino pulse came from is something to do with Atlantis is that there were a group of people known as Mauri who came from Mauritania. And guess what – it just so happens that their first king was called Atlas of Mauritania. So, what do you get if you join up the dots?'

I took a sip of the hot chocolate that Jack had shared out from his flask when we'd arrived. 'That Atlas of Mauritania and King Atlas of Atlantis are the same person?'

Jack nodded. 'So that narrows down the location of Atlantis to the modern republic of Mauritania. But to zero in even further we have to look at the work of another Greek known as the father of history, Herodotus. He died years before Plato published his account of Atlantis. The thing that helps our investigation is that Herodotus was famous for his incredible maps of the known world around 450bc. And he happened to create a map which included the position of Atlantis. Guess where that was?'

'Also in Mauritania?' Mike asked.

'On the nose, buddy.' Jack clicked a button on the remote and an old-fashioned, hand-drawn map appeared below the satellite image. 'This is Herodotus's map with the position of Atlantis.' He took a laser pointer and played over an area of sea between Africa and Europe. 'This area is now known as the Strait of Gibraltar, but back in Herodotus's time it was called the Pillars of Hercules.' Jack moved the pointer's green dot down to a line of mountains on the map. 'And these are the Atlas Mountains. Guess who they were named after?'

'This dude King Atlas?' Ruby asked.

'Right again.' Jack moved the pointer south again and started to rotate it round a name of the map: 'Atlantes'. 'We can see the position clearly labelled. And this is where it gets very interesting – it bears a striking similarity to something called the Richat Structure in the Sahara Desert, also known more popularly as the Eye of Africa. And here it is...'

Jack clicked on the remote and a satellite image was superimposed over the map. The view began to zoom in on an area of desert that corresponded to the location of Atlantes on the ancient map. It kept zooming in on a region of the Sahara until we could see a structure of a series of huge concentric rings to the west of a mountain range.

'You're telling us that's the real-life site of Atlantis?' Alice asked.

'The similarities to Plato's description of a ringed structure are striking,' Jack replied. 'The Richat Structure even has the same number of rings that Plato described and matches its dimensions at fourteen and a half miles across.'

'But what about the myths of Atlantis disappearing beneath the waves?' I asked. 'I don't see how that happened in the middle of the Sahara.'

'You have a point there,' Jack replied. 'The Richat Structure is currently thirteen hundred feet above sea level. However, the area has suffered numerous major earthquakes which have raised and lowered whole plain round the Richat site, no doubt fuelling the legend of the original city disappearing into the ocean. Locals claim to have even seen fish skeletons in the moat structures. Supporting that is the tale of non-fossilised whale bones found in the surrounding area, meaning being underwater would be well within the time frame of Atlantis. Even today there are wells at the site producing salt water. And if that's not enough evidence for you, Plato described a freshwater spring – one that still exists in the middle of the Richat Structure today.'

'And the location of the neutrino burst came from exactly here?' Tom asked.

A wide smile filled Jack's face and he clicked a button on his remote again. The view zoomed in on the centre of the concentric circles, a faint rectangular line appearing in the middle.

'That looks like some sort of structure, maybe even a temple. More importantly for us, the position of the neutrino burst...' Jacked tapped the remote and a red pulsing dot appeared overlaid on the exact centre of the rectangular building.

'Bloody hell, you mean the Angelus actually visited Atlantis and left a micro mind buried there?' Mike asked.

'They may of course have buried the micro mind long before the establishment of the city. It isn't much to stretch the imagination to how Atlantis could have later grown up over it. Maybe it was even viewed as some sort of mystical site by the locals, very much like Skara Brae.'

'Once again, Jack, your insight into something like this is extraordinary,' Alice said. 'So now with all the evidence pointing towards this being the next micro mind awakening, how do we need to proceed?'

'To leave for the site as soon as possible,' Jack replied.

'I'll second that,' I said. 'And it could be the perfect outing for *Ariel*, particularly now she's equipped with an ES field and should be totally invisible to that damned detector of theirs.'

'I have to say I agree, but you should go fully equipped for any eventuality, especially as we haven't currently got Lucy for backup,' Tom said.

Ruby shrugged. 'Even if the Overseers do turn up, I more than fancy our chances now, especially as we have my new WASP swarm. They should be more than able to hold their own.'

'Yes, but we will need to sort you out a pilot for this mission, especially as Delphi's automated AI flight systems still need refining,' Alice said.

Tom scowled at her. 'I hope that doesn't mean you're going to put yourself forward again? Not after what happened last time during *Ariel's* test mission – nearly killing yourself and Lauren.'

'I wouldn't dare. I know I'd never hear the end of it. I suggest we look through the test pilot rota to see who's available.'

Troy sat up straighter in his seat. 'No need to do that, Alice. If Lauren agrees, I'd love to be the pilot for this mission. I could certainly do with some serious stick time with an X103 craft whilst we wait for the *Pangolin* to be completed. I may have done plenty of simulations, but that's no substitute for flying the real thing on an actual mission.'

Alive narrowed her eyes on him and then slowly nodded. 'In terms of further advanced training of Delphi's AI flight algorithms, I can think of no better pilot to do this than you. What do you think, Tom?'

'I agree, but this is Lauren's call as she's the mission leader,' he replied.

Troy gave me an expectant look. 'Well, what do you say, Lauren?'

I turned the thought over in my head. With all respect to the guy, I didn't know him. Troy was a colonel and technically outranked me. Would that mean he would want to try to run the show?

I gave him a level look. 'I don't want to be rude, especially as

I've witnessed your amazing flying skills for myself, but we have a fairly unique way of going about missions.'

'You're telling me,' Ruby said, rolling her eyes. 'But this guy is the real deal, Lauren. I'd be more than happy for him to be our chauffeur.'

Troy laughed. 'Same old, Ruby, hey?'

She grinned at him. 'Pretty much.'

His gaze tightened on me as he held up his hands. 'If you don't want me along, I completely respect that decision, Lauren. You need to choose the people on your mission – not have ones that are foisted upon you.'

Jack gave me a sideways look. 'It sounds like a good idea to me.'

I couldn't help but notice how Mike was looking away and I realised the real reason behind my reluctance. It was almost as if Troy was taking his place, even if this was a one-off.

Alice remained quiet, but I knew she could read me. And maybe she got it as someone with great responsibility. Bringing someone new onboard wasn't a casual decision, especially as somewhere along the journey we'd become a closely knit team. And she wasn't alone. Tom was also giving me the sort of calculating look that suggested he could guess what was going through my head at the moment. Then he spoke, which left me in no doubt.

'I think Troy would be a major asset to your mission and we do need to train Delphi's combat systems with the best pilots. He also had considerable combat experience flying missions before joining NASA as a test pilot. Plus Troy was awarded the Navy Cross for single-handedly shooting down an entire squadron of MiGs that were bombing a civilian refugee convoy, despite his own F18 having half a tailplane missing. And he has more space walks under his belt than any living man or woman. Of course, Troy's far too modest to tell you any of that himself.'

Ruby nodded with a look of obvious approval. 'This guy is a real-life American hero, Lauren, in every sense.'

Troy just shrugged. 'As far as I'm concerned that's just the past. It's how I contribute now to humanity that matters.'

And right there I caught sight of the real man and the history behind some of the lines that spidered out from his eyes. Any lingering reservations of mine were swept away.

'In that case...' I met Troy's gaze, 'I'd love you to join us. Sorry for the hesitation, but I just needed to think it through.'

'No problem, I did kinda spring the idea on you. A good leader always thinks through their options before committing.'

I smiled at his understanding.

He sat forward. 'And thank you for this opportunity, Lauren. It will be great to spread my pilot wings again after being stuck in that Mars simulation for so damned long.'

I nodded. 'That I so understand.' But then I noticed Mike picking at his knuckles. He caught me looking. And just like that I was drowning in deep water with no idea of how to navigate this discussion with him. Instinct told me that despite what he'd said previously, he really wanted to come with us.

But then he gave me a small wistful smile and gestured towards his chair as if he had read my thoughts. 'Don't stress it, Lauren. I'll be cheering your mission on from the side-lines whilst I get on with the real work back here with Jodie.'

She reached out and squeezed his hand. 'I could certainly do with your help, especially if Lucy decides to wake up from her nap.'

'Yes, absolutely,' Mike said.

Even so, despite his words, I knew it had to be really hard for him to step back from heading out on a mission with us.

Tom stood up. 'Then it sounds to me as if you have a mission to prepare for,' he said.

I clapped my hands as I stood too. 'You heard the man – let's get moving, people.'

Jack offered me a lazy salute and a very wide grin. 'Yes, ma'am!'

Jack grabbed my hand. 'Oh god, Lauren, I can't wait to head to the Richat Structure.'

I squeezed it back. 'Of course, you can't. We're about to visit an archaeological site straight out of myth and legend.'

'Yeah, and I'm so in my happy place right now.'

I looked over to Jodie who was resting her hand on Mike's shoulder and felt a little twist inside.

CHAPTER SIX

WE SPED ALONG, one hundred thousand feet above the earth at the edge of space, the curvature of our home planet clearly visible below us. In the pilot's seat, Troy's broad smile had been glued to his face for most of the flight. *Ariel* spun round the gyro-stabilised flight deck, which thankfully our seats were securely bolted on to. Round us, the screens that lined the circular cockpit relayed a spinning view of the world outside.

'Are you sure all these manoeuvres are strictly necessary?' I said, starting to feel distinctly nauseous.

Jack cast Troy a grim look. 'Yes, my breakfast is threatening to make a reappearance, buddy.'

'They are, I'm afraid. I'm currently training Delphi's flight routines and I really need to shake down the flight characteristics of *Ariel*. I have to say they are nothing short of absolutely phenomenal. Anyway, the good news is that it won't be for much longer.'

Ruby seemed completely oblivious to the oscillating antics of our flight path. Her whole attention had been glued to the transparent CIC screen surrounding her. Without looking at Troy, she smiled.

'I told you, Troy, that this ship was going to be like nothing you've ever flown.'

'And it seems you weren't exaggerating.' He glanced at his altimeter that was currently reading ninety-five thousand feet. 'I'd love to go a bit higher and see what this girl can do in open space.'

'Not on this mission you won't,' I said. 'We haven't got time for a joyride, especially after I learnt my lesson with Alice last time. We need to get to that micro mind as fast as possible, recover it and then get the hell out of there before the Overseers get a lock on the latest neutrino burst.'

'Understood and of course, Captain,' Troy said as he settled the ship into level flight.

Ruby snorted and I shot her a look. 'What?'

She held up her hands. 'Sorry, it's just the first time I've heard anyone call you that. Mind you, Troy, you're a commander too.'

And so there it was – Ruby was already picking at one of my concerns about Troy joining our mission. It sounded pathetic, I knew it, but part of me was worried about him undermining my authority.

'Technically that may be true, but on the mission I fall under Lauren's jurisdiction.'

I nodded towards him, grateful for his accommodating attitude.

'I'm starting to like you,' I said.

'Yes, I'm a grower – like a bit of toe fungus.'

'And a sense of humour too,' Jack said. 'Yes, you're going to fit right in.'

He snorted before his expression became serious again. 'I bet you guys are missing having Mike here. Sounds as if he was a really integral member of the team.'

So Troy was astute too. 'He really was, but we have to respect his decision even if in the longer term I think it's the wrong call,' I said.

'You do?'

I shrugged. 'I totally understand he's emotionally scarred, but he always made a huge contribution to our missions.' I resisted adding that I would also miss the moral compass aspect he brought to our team, helping me to hang on to my sense of humanity.

'Maybe when he's had time to gather himself, he'll come around.'

'I hope so,' I said, realising for the first time just how much I meant it.

A chime came from one of Ruby's consoles and she looked at the HUD projected on her transparent CIC screen. 'Oh...' She went very quiet as she began clicking on a few icons.

'Don't you *oh* us, Ruby. What is it?' I asked.

'I've been using one of Lucy's backdoor satellite hacks to keep an eye on our destination. I've just detected a major sandstorm that's blowing in which will reach the Richat Structure any moment now.' She made a swiping movement with her hand and an image overlay appeared on the spherical cockpit screen round us. 'This is the live satellite view of the area surrounding the Richat Structure.'

We all gazed at the aerial view, showing the concentric rings of the Eye of Africa on the right of the image. But of more immediate concern was the huge cloud of orange sand billowing straight towards it from the west, eating up the desert landscape at an alarming rate.

'That looks serious,' Jack said.

'It sure is,' Ruby replied. 'Winds are already gusting to a hundred knots and it looks as if it's only going to get worse.'

'But surely our REV drive will be able to cope with that?' I said.

Troy nodded. 'Yes, it should, but as far as I'm aware we don't have any data on how *Ariel* performs when flying through a sandstorm.'

'Sounds like a question for someone involved in designing her,' Jack said.

'So let's radio back to Jodie and see what she says,' I said. 'Ruby, can you open a channel to Eden?'

'On it, Captain,' she said, grinning, then caught my eye-roll. 'Sorry, couldn't resist.'

'Why do I get the feeling I've started something here?' Troy asked.

'Yeah, I'd keep out of it if I were you,' Jack said.

'I don't mind really. At least Ruby doesn't call me "boss" anymore, which is a definite improvement.'

'You certainly earned the title upgrade after the last mission,' Ruby said. 'Anyway...' She toggled a few switches. 'This is *Ariel* calling Control. I need you to patch me through to Jodie Elliott for an urgent consult.'

Crackling filled the cabin's speakers.

Ruby checked the display on her CIC screen and tried again. 'Eden control, this is *Ariel* calling, please respond.'

The white noise continued.

'Are they receiving us?' Jack asked.

'Well, according to the diagnostics, our radio link is working perfectly so they certainly should be.'

'Maybe it's a glitch at their end,' Jack said.

'Then let's try the old-fashioned method and use a Sky Wire satellite phone,' I said, digging my handset out of the cubby hole built into the side of my seat. I put it on speaker as I punched in the secure contact details for our base. A moment later I was rewarded with a recurring beep.

'What's that mean?' Ruby asked.

'Not sure but try Tom's Sky Wire handset instead – he normally keeps his handset within reach,' Jack said.

I tried that but got exactly the same result – the same beeping tone. 'OK, I'm starting to get worried now.'

'Maybe there's some sort of problem with Eden's main comm mast in the jungle,' Troy said. 'It relays all communications to the base underground, including data. It wouldn't be the first time there was a problem with it. Once a troop of monkeys took up residence on the mast, managed to chew through a mains cable and knocked out all our comms for a week before the problem was traced.'

'Oh bloody hell,' I replied. 'OK, Ruby, you keep trying to contact them on the off-chance this is just a temporary problem.'

'Will do, Lauren. I have to say, it's great to know that such a hi-tech facility can be so easily taken out by furry things with teeth.'

'The Stormtroopers know all about that.'

'Eh?' Ruby said, frowning at me.

Jack was smiling. 'Ewoks - am I right, Lauren, from *Star Wars*?'

'Good to see my passion for sci-fi is finally starting to rub off on you,' I said.

'If you want to talk about a proper sci-fi movie, *Aliens* gets my vote,' Ruby said.

I laughed. 'Why am I not surprised?'

Troy stared at the three of us. 'Is this what it's like with you guys on a mission?'

I shrugged. 'Pretty much. So, what's your favourite movie?'

'*The Right Stuff* of course, always a bit of a go-to for a former test pilot – although I also have a massive soft spot for *The Martian*.'

'Great choices,' I replied with an approving nod.

'I sense a movie night coming up when we all get back,' Troy said.

'As long as you bring the beer,' Ruby said, grinning.

'Oh, you can count on it. I also cook a mean hotdog with all the trimmings.'

'OK, I'm so sold,' I said. 'Anyway, back to more urgent priorities. How far are we from the Richat Structure, Troy?'

'About five minutes out according to my instruments.'

'Enough time to beat the sandstorm to it?'

Ruby gestured towards the satellite view she'd now pulled up on the virtual cockpit sphere screens surrounding us. 'There's your answer.'

I turned and saw the sandstorm had already engulfed the site, obscuring it from view.

'Maybe we should hold position here until the storm has blown through,' Troy said.

'And how long is that likely to be?' Jack asked.

'According to the pressure chart I'm looking at now, probably about around ten hours,' Ruby replied.

'Damn, if we wait that long there's a good chance the Overseers will turn up, probably in an Astra TR-3B, an encounter I'd rather avoid if at all possible,' I said. 'How worried are you about entering a sandstorm in *Ariel*, Troy?'

'Well, it's something I'd avoid like the plague in a conventional aircraft as it could foul up the engines. But with this craft it's hard to say. The vectoring engines for propulsion could possibly be affected.'

'But surely if the gravity field the REV drive creates is capable of deflecting a railgun round fire at hypervelocity speeds, it can more than cope with a few grains of sand?' Ruby asked.

'My recommendation for what it's worth, particularly as time is of the essence, is to risk it,' Troy said. 'But this is your call, Lauren.'

I nodded. 'Jack, what do you think?'

'What that man just said.'

'That goes for me too, Captain,' Ruby added.

I raised an eyebrow at her and she gave me a little smirk.

'Then it's unanimous, but take it easy coming in for landing, hey, Troy?'

'One silky-smooth, airline-style landing coming right up. Ladies and gentlemen, if you'd like to raise your seats to their upright positions and stow your trays, we're about to begin our descent.'

Jack chuckled. 'Like I said, you fit right in, buddy.'

A few moments later, we'd dropped altitude far enough that the curvature of the earth had begun to flatten out on the view from outside. Like always, there was almost no sense of movement thanks to the dampening effects of the REV gravity reduction drive. It was eerily quiet too, the craft gently humming round us as we descended towards the sandstorm that rose to meet us in a boiling sea of orange smoke.

Troy flexed his fingers over the five-axis control joystick. 'OK, even though it shouldn't affect us, I'm going to say this just in case. Brace yourself, because we're about to enter the sandstorm and we have about a two-thousand-feet descent until we're safely on the ground.'

I tightened my grip on the arms of my chair as the clouds of sand rose up quickly. We plunged into the swirling top of the storm and the world turned orange as the entire virtual cockpit display was filled with nothing but swirling sand. The howl of wind beyond the protective blister of gravity protecting *Ariel* was now audible too, although there wasn't so much as a shudder from the airframe.

'OK, so far so good,' Troy said, checking over his instruments.

'Activating radar view,' Ruby said.

The display on the cabin walls switched to a 3D view and the previously invisible ground became visible again, etched out from a series of green dots stretching away beneath us.

'We've experienced severe radar attenuation because of the density of the sand out there, but at least we can partly see through it,' Ruby said, gazing at her instruments.

Troy nodded. 'Flight performance parameters are still looking nominal, although...' His brow furrowed as he trailed off.

'That's a really bad place to pause, buddy,' Jack said as he caught my eye.

The commander still didn't respond as the lines in his forehead deepened.

'Please talk to us,' I said.

'Sorry, yes. I'm seeing overheating in the trailing edge of our lateral vectoring thrusters. It suggests that some sand is making it through the gravity shield and it's starting to overload—'

Troy was cut off by multiple alarms sounding all at once as *Ariel* suddenly lurched downwards.

'Darn it...losing thrusters...trying to compensate,' Troy said as he rotated the joystick hard over.

Immediately *Ariel* pivoted round the flight deck until what had been her trailing edge was almost angled straight up to the sky.

'Trying to compensate with the opposite bank of thrusters, but they're already starting to overheat too,' Troy said, his jaw muscles protruding.

My heart was racing as dozens of bleak scenarios played rapidly through my head, most of which included the burning wreckage of *Ariel* and our bodies strewn everywhere. This would be on me – I was one who'd authorised flying into the storm, even if the others had been all for it.

'Is there anything the rest of us can do?' Jack asked, looking pale.

'Pray...because the escape pods won't be much good in this.

The parachutes they use would be shredded in seconds in this sandstorm.'

My mental image of strewn bodies grew sharper.

We all fell silent. Suddenly the metre that separated Jack and I felt like a mile. If I was about to die, I'd rather do it his arms. His eyes met mine and I could see in them that he knew. Of course he did. We both knew exactly how much we meant to each other.

The only person who looked vaguely relaxed was Ruby – a die-hard professional to the end. Her entire focus was locked on to her CIC screens. But it wasn't a good sign that she wasn't making any snarky comments about Troy's flying abilities.

The virtual dots marking the circles of the Eye of Africa were now to the east of our position as we hurtled way too fast towards the ground. Troy was unable to compensate for our lateral drift and we were straying way off-target. Despite the gravity-dampening effect of our REV drive, the wind howled round the craft and the airframe vibrated with shudders.

'Come on baby, you can do it,' Troy whispered as he pivoted the joystick backwards and *Ariel* rotated to a forty-five-degree position.

The vector radar dots marking out the ribbons of sand dunes started to grow wider apart as we closed on them. We were definitely slowing, but I could already see the dunes were too close for anything other than a crash. This was going to hurt – a lot.

'Brace yourself,' Troy said. 'I'm about to trying something.'

Adrenaline tanged the back of my throat. I hung on to my seat's arms harder, wishing that one of them was Jack's hand as we rushed towards a dune.

But then Troy pushed the throttle hard forward and the main lift engine roared in answer, audible over the scream of wind.

Despite the G-forces being partly absorbed by the REV drive, the dramatic change in dynamic forces pushed us hard into our seats as our velocity started to slow.

'Come on...' Troy said through clenched teeth as the velocity indicator ticked down.

500 knots...

300...

100...

50...

The tip of a towering dune traced out in green dots hurtled towards us.

Instinctively, I braced every muscle in my body and jammed my jaw together.

We smashed into the sand, the huge jolt of the impact slamming everybody hard against their safety harnesses as a chorus of new alarms shrieked out. Screeches came from the hull as we skidded off the top of the dune, becoming briefly airborne again as we levelled out.

Troy clutched the throttle, easing it back. 'Come, you can do it, girl...'

I caught a glimpse of the ground rushing towards us again through the static breaking apart the radar image.

Another shriek of metal on sand sent a violent shudder buzzing through my body as we skipped off the surface – once, twice, three times. Then, with a noise like the claws of a giant cat being scraped across the belly of our craft, the whole world was shaking vigorously.

Another large dune was dead ahead and the flight deck began to pitch upwards as we slid up it, the gyroscopic controls giving up on the uneven battle. Unbelievably, our speed indicator was still working.

20 knots...

10...

5...

We crested the top of the dune and my stomach dropped like the sensation at the top of a rollercoaster, the split second before the plunge. With a final long groan of metal, we came to a stop at the very top. Troy killed the alarms, but not the blinking panels of red lights. Now the only sound inside the cabin was the crew collectively sucking in lungfuls of air.

'Ladies and gentleman, we have arrived slightly behind schedule,' Troy said. 'The temperature outside is a toasty forty-two Celsius. Please check you have all your personal belongings before departing our UFO. We look forward to you flying with us again on Bat-Shit Crazy Airlines.'

Ruby shot him a withering look. 'Yeah, you fit right in, Troy.'

Jack and I caught each other's relieved expressions. Probably due to the utter relief that we were still alive, we both burst out whooping – much the bemusement of Troy, who raised a grey eyebrow at us.

CHAPTER SEVEN

My body aching with bruises, I unclipped my harnesses. 'I can't believe you managed to land *Ariel* in practically one piece, Troy,' I said.

'I've had more challenging landings,' Troy replied with a shrug.

I gave him a wide-eyed look as I stood on the steeply sloping flight deck. I had to hang on to my seat for balance.

'Well, I seriously need to buy you a drink sometime and listen to your stories of those landings,' Jack said.

'You're on. I've got a lot to tell, especially some of the carrier landings. They'd turn your hair greyer than mine.' Troy dug out a box of tools from one of the lockers.

I had the distinct impression that these two men were cut from similar cloth and were about to hit it off.

'Hey guys, you might have to save your blossoming bromance for later,' Ruby said. 'We need to check over the ship to see how bad the damage is.'

She eye-rolled me and I smiled.

'That tells us,' Troy said, shaking his head. 'The good news is that readouts from the reactor are stable as it automatically shut down during the crash. All our other flight systems look nominal – with the notable exception of six of our vectoring thrusters. That will make things tricky.'

'Does that mean we can't fly out of here?' I asked.

Troy shook his head. 'I didn't say that. Luckily we carry a certain amount of spares in *Ariel*'s hold. We can strip down the broken thrusters if necessary and rebuild them, although at a guess that's going to take a good six to twelve hours.'

'And what about being half-buried in a sand dune?' Ruby asked, gesturing to the cockpit wall beneath us.

I gazed at the flickering virtual radar display. She was right. According to that, the lower lip of *Ariel* was buried in a dune.

Jack shook his head. 'Damn it, we're going to have dig *Ariel* out to have any chance of taking off again.'

I nodded. 'We really could do with the equivalent of a tow truck about now.' I glanced across at Ruby. 'Is Eden still offline?'

She glanced at her CIC screen and frowned. 'Sorry, Lauren, still not a peep out of them.'

'Hmmm, I'm starting to have a bad feeling about this. If it was monkeys or something, surely they'd have sent somebody topside with some satellite comms to keep in touch.'

'Yes, I'm with you, Lauren,' Jack said. 'I would have expected Tom to make serious efforts to keep in contact with us during an active mission.'

'So what are you saying? Do you think there's been some sort of incident back at base?' Ruby asked.

'Possibly, but there could also be an entirely innocent explanation,' I said.

'Or an extremely bad one – like the Overseers have finally discovered our base and launched an all-out assault,' Ruby said.

'All I know is that I won't be able to relax now until we get back there and discover what the hell is going on.'

'Well, it's not as if we can fly straight back to Eden to find out, so what are your orders, Captain?' Troy asked.

Jack looked at me. 'Yes, are you saying we should abort the mission as soon as we get *Ariel* flight-worthy again, Lauren?'

'No, we're here now. Whatever is happening back home, this mission is still of vital importance. We have a window of opportunity before the Overseers turn up to investigate the neutrino burst and we have to take advantage of that.' I could feel my plan clarifying itself just by talking it through out loud. 'Jack, you'll be with me as our resident archaeological expert. We need to locate the micro mind and get it back here quickly. Troy and Ruby, you stay here and get *Ariel* repaired as fast as possible, but you'll also need to watch our backs in case the Overseers approach, having located the location of the neutrino burst.'

Ruby nodded. 'No problem. I'll keep half an eye on the CIC and will radio you if we see anything.'

'What about your fancy WASP drones?' Jack asked. 'It would be useful to have some more eyes in the sky as we head out for the site.'

'No can do, Jack, not in these wind speeds at least.'

Troy tapped an icon on one of his screens. 'That might not be for much longer. The sandstorm is starting to weaken, although it's still gusting to sixty knots at the moment.'

'Once it drops below fifty, I should be able to get the WASP swarm airborne,' Ruby said. '*Ariel*'s radar system will have to be their eyes and ears until then.'

'Then let's do this,' I said as I loaded the Empyrean Key into a small rucksack that I retrieved from a locker.

'OK, first small problem, how do we actually get outside since the exit ramp is currently buried in the sand?' Jack asked.

Troy pointed to the roof. 'Thankfully Jodie designed a hatch in the roof in case a flight crew ever had to ditch in the sea.' He flipped a switch.

One of the hexagon display panels above us in the spherical cockpit walls pivoted downwards. Behind was a closed hatch from which a ladder was now automatically lowering towards the flight deck.

I paused for a moment, looking at the team round me. I was starting to feel increasingly comfortable in charge, but I'd also learnt enough to make sure I listened to everyone's ideas and take them on board. That was the key to being an effective leader.

'Is there anything else we need to think about like suitable gear to protect us from that sandstorm?' I asked.

'Yes, we'll need to kit up with layers of desert clothing,' Jack said. 'The moment we step outside we will get sandblasted and it'll sting like hell.'

'That's an understatement. Your skin will be shredded to the bone if you're not properly protected,' Ruby said.

'Good point. Thankfully, Tom has made sure we have clothing for every eventuality. And since the forward cargo hold appears to be clear of sand, we can take the Zero motorbikes.'

'You do both realise it's going to be tough going in this sandstorm?' Ruby said.

'Then we'll just have to take it easy,' Jack replied. 'The site must be a good five klicks from here and that's certainly too far to walk, especially as we need to get to the middle of Atlantis and that ruined temple. That's easily another eleven klicks on top.'

'Then the sooner we get moving, the sooner we get back,' I said.

Troy gave me an approving nod. 'I'm liking your leadership style, Lauren. Decisive and can-do.'

'That's our Lauren.' Jack gave me one of his smiles that made my insides flutter.

Not giving anything away, I put on my most professional *I'm in charge and I've got your backs* look as I clapped my hands together. 'OK, let's do this, people.'

The wind moaned and tugged at my clothes as swirls of sand slammed into *Ariel*'s hull. In a choreographed dance the sand shimmied up it, blowing over the crest of the flying saucer's lips in billowing clouds.

Not that the stinging sandstorm gave me much time to pay attention to that. It peppered my body with a million needle pricks as I hung on to the rope ladder we'd tied to the top hatch of *Ariel*. Jack had already made down to the dune and hung on to the bottom of the ladder to prevent me being thrown around during my descent like he'd just been.

My nose was covered by several layers of a snood that I'd wrapped round my head to try to protect it, along with a clear pair of goggles, yet a smell of something like dried cinders still made its way in, drying out my nasal cavities. This part of the Sahara didn't just smell arid, it almost smelt dead, stripped of any life on its surface. The desert heat was intense and despite wearing the most hi-tech clothing that would normally wick away my sweat, I was already soaked through.

The rungs of the ladder chaffed against my hands as I clung on with a death grip, fighting for every step over the outer bulge of *Ariel*'s hull. The slope lessened a fraction as I reached the surrounding disc that housed the mercury accelerator torus ring of the REV drive.

'You can slide down the last bit,' Jack called up to me, his outline appearing and then disappearing behind swirls of sand.

'I'll try,' I called back, my words barely audible over the howling wind.

I manoeuvred my right foot off the ladder, doing the best with the tips of my toes to grip on to the grooves between the hexagonal plates of *Ariel*'s chameleon cloak. My hands gripped even harder to the ladder as I moved my left foot off and on to the tiny groove alongside the right. Jack pulled the rope ladder to one side so I would have an unobstructed run down. I peered down at the faint rainbow patterns refracted in the panels, took a deep breath and let go.

The hull sped past, my hi-tech desert combat uniform squealing with friction on the hard surface. I rolled on to my back to protect my face and slid feet first down the metallic slope towards Jack. I was unable to stop a small squeal escaping my mouth as I cannoned into his outstretched arms.

Jack pivoted round, absorbing my momentum, his hands locking under my arms and jolting me to a sudden stop before he swung me round.

'Was that squeal fear or joy?' he shouted over the screaming wind as he pulled me to my feet.

'I think a bit of both,' I replied, my voice muffled by the snood.

'It's incredible, isn't it?'

'What is?'

'This,' he said, waving at the sandstorm around us. 'To think we're about to set foot on the ancient site of Atlantis. It's seriously going to blow my mind. But can you taste something odd?'

I ran my tongue over my dried lips and tasted a distinctive tang. 'It's salty, but we're nowhere near the sea.'

'Right! Another hint that this really is the site of Atlantis. Remember those saltwater wells I mentioned? The sandstorm must be drawing the moisture up from them and throwing it into this storm.'

'It certainly tastes like the seaside, though I've never been to one with a wind that could strip your flesh away,' I said.

Jack's eyes smiled through his goggles. 'Come on then, let's grab those Zeros from the hold and go for a day trip.'

Before either of us could move, there was a skidding sound of cloth on metal and a tool bag landed at our feet – followed by couple of shovels and then finally Ruby herself, barrelling out of the sandstorm down *Ariel*'s hull. Without so much as a whimper and certainly without any help from Jack, she landed neatly on her feet with a wide grin.

'Hey, that was better than an amusement park,' she said.

'If you say so,' I replied. I gestured to the shovels. 'You're going to have your work cut out excavating the lower edge of the disc to get to those vectoring thrusters.'

'Yeah, tell me about it, but Troy will be out in a moment to help. And before you ask, I've got an alert set up on my Sky Wire in case *Ariel*'s sensors pick up anything like an Overseer craft. I thought you might need a shovel yourselves to clear away enough sand to open the hatch for those Zeros.'

'Good thinking and thanks,' I said.

I followed Jack round the edge of the craft towards the exposed belly hatch that was pointing up beyond the top of the dune. With *Ariel* sheltering us from the worst of the storm and after a certain amount of swearing on both our parts, we finally managed to excavate enough sand to gain access to the lower hatch. After even more swearing, we had two of the motorbikes out of the hold, lying on their sides on the dune.

Jack tossed me a helmet. 'The fact these Zeros are electric motorbikes will be a blessing in this sort of weather. At least we won't have to worry about the carburettors getting fouled up with sand.'

'Good point, but I'm not so keen about wearing a helmet. I'm going to suffocate from the heat inside it.'

'Don't be so sure. These are the mark two versions – Jodie had one of the Forge development teams working on ways to improve the helmets after feedback from the Machu Picchu mission. She ran me through the new features before we took off.'

'What are they exactly?'

'Put it on and you'll see,' Jack replied.

Intrigued now, I hunkered down, sheltering beneath the saucer to get out of the wind. After unravelling the snood from my face, I pulled on the mark two crash helmet. Exactly as I expected, I was met with stifling, suffocating heat.

'Bloody hell, my head feels like a potato being baked in an oven.'

'Just power up the helmet and things will be much more comfortable,' Jack told me.

I toggled on the power. Immediately a fan started whirring, but more significantly the interior surface of the helmet grew rapidly colder. I stared out through the visor on which the HUD had powered up with various diagnostics – including a display for the temperature, set to a very pleasant twenty degrees Celsius.

Jack smiled at me. 'Based on your blissed-out expression you've just discovered that these latest helmets are fitted with air conditioning,' his voice came through the in-built speakers in my helmet.

It was only then that I realised the howl of wind had vanished too. A quick look confirmed the sandstorm was still billowing past in full force.

'And they added active noise cancellation too?' I asked.

'Correct.'

'Both these features are seriously great right now. There is a team that I need to hug when we get back to Eden.'

'Maybe after a shower, hey?' Jack said.

'Oh great, you're getting as snarky as Ruby.'

'Hey, I heard that,' came Ruby's voice. 'Remember you're on an open channel, Captain.'

'Nothing I wouldn't say to your face, Ruby,' I said.

She snorted. 'Fair enough.'

Jack shook his head. 'The banter on this team just gets better and better.'

The Zeros were already partly buried in the blowing sand.

But any concerns about their capabilities in this storm from hell were swept away as the displays of both bikes powered up without so much as a complaint. The only problem I could see was a distinct lack of a map on my helmet's HUD.

'Hey, Jack, I'm not seeing a GPS marker here for our location.'

'You won't,' Troy's voice came over my helmet's speakers. 'The sandstorm is killing pretty much any reception.'

'We'll just have to do the old-fashioned thing of following a magnetic compass – fortunately the mark two helmets have that feature baked in,' Jack said.

'We're going to need to take the entire development team out to dinner at this rate,' I said.

'Them and every other person at Eden.'

'It's going to be a very expensive dinner. Anyway, what direction are we heading in, Jack? From here to Atlantis will be your roadshow.'

'Basically, if we travel directly west we should hit the outer ring of the Richat Structure in a few klicks and then we can head on from there towards the centre of the city. Even in this sandstorm, there's no way we can miss such a huge structure.'

'Then let's go for it.'

With a twist of the throttle, I took the lead on my Zero. Ruby gave us a wave as we passed her, then returned her attention to digging out the lower edge of the disc. It seemed to be filling with sand almost as quickly as she was clearing it. It would clearly be a long slog.

We'd only gone about hundred metres, the tyres frequently losing grip in the loose sand, when *Ariel* disappeared from view in the sandstorm behind us.

'Only an idiot would try driving anywhere in these conditions,' I muttered into my helmet's mic.

'Just as well we're both gold-star idiots then,' Jack replied.

'And I'm saying nothing,' Ruby said, static pops already starting to break up her voice.

The sand billowed round us and I soon found myself deeply disorientated, not helped by the fact the dunes kept shifting beneath us. Like some ancient mariner setting sail across the ocean, I clung religiously to the compass heading displayed on my HUD as I kept our pace slow and steady.

'Just about another klick and we'll be there, by my reckoning,' Jack said.

The words had barely left his mouth when a warning flashed up on my display: *Magnetic pulse detected.*

Then my HUD glitched and died as the helmet's fan whirred to silence, replaced by the roar of the storm. Not only that, but the Zero coasted to a stop, its display blank.

'What the hell happened?' Jack asked as he pulled his helmet off and examined his suddenly stationary motorbike.

'Some sort of EM pulse according to my helmet's display before it died,' I said, wrapping the snood back round my face and putting my goggles on that I'd stowed in my rucksack. 'Hang on – EM pulse, isn't that caused by a bloody nuke?'

'Well, I doubt we'd still be standing here if it was,' Jack said. His eyes widened. 'Crap, you don't think *Ariel*'s reactor suddenly let go after that crash?'

I immediately pressed my finger into my earbud. '*Ariel*, are you reading me, over?'

There was only silence in my earbud. I pulled it out and pressed the button to check the power display, but the LED stayed resolutely dark. 'Shit, it looks as if that pulse fried every-thing electronic. But if *Ariel*'s reactor has gone critical...' I trailed off as nightmare images of Ruby and Troy being torn apart filled my imagination. I covered my hands with my mouth. 'Jesus, no!'

Jack came up to me and put both hands on my shoulders, making me look at him. 'Look, we don't know that – not at all.'

'You're right, but if something has happened to those guys...'

The shoulder squeeze became a hug. 'Keep positive until we know for sure.'

'We need to get back to them to check they're OK.'

'All right, I understand, but think this through. If the nightmare scenario has happened and the containment chamber has been breached, radioactive materials will be scattered all over the desert by now. And for that reason, and as tough as it is to do so, we need to be heading away from *Ariel* and not back towards her.'

I fought to keep down a sob. 'But the others...'

Jack took me by the shoulders again. 'Even trying to locate *Ariel* in this sandstorm will be like looking for a needle in a haystack, whereas the Richat Structure is twenty-two klicks wide. We should easily be able to find our way to that if we just carry on. And right now, we need to look at our own situation – to point out the blindingly obvious, we're in the middle of a very hostile desert without any backup. We could easily die out here.'

I took a centring breath, pushing down the storm of emotions that had been threatening to spill over. 'Yes, you're right – we should carry on. We haven't got much of an alternative. Meanwhile we'll just have to pray that the others are OK.'

'Yeah...' Jack closed his eyes for a moment and took a deep breath before looking at me again. 'We'd better get ready for a tricky hike on foot.'

I nodded as I peered through the mass of boiling sand behind us, wondering what had happened back there. It was hard to imagine anything other than the nightmare scenario. But then Ruby's face filled my mind – not some sort of ethereal ghostly version, but a vision of her with a pissed-off expression as she tapped an imaginary watch. I knew immediately what my subconscious was trying to tell me. If Ruby were here and I'd been the one who'd just been taken out by a nuclear explosion, she would still be pressing ahead with the mission and would grieve later.

I sighed. 'Good point, Ruby,' I said.

Jack, who had been starting to load up his rucksack, turned to me. 'Sorry?'

'Ignore me – I'm just giving myself a pep talk.' My gaze slid from his as I unloaded the Empyrean Key from one of the panniers and started to load it into my rucksack along with the tuning fork. I just prayed that after all this there really was a micro mind waiting in Atlantis for us to discover, especially since the cost of this mission had perhaps just gone through the roof.

Loaded up, the two of us took a last glance in the direction of *Ariel*, my heart twisting. With our heads down, we set off together into the swirling storm.

CHAPTER EIGHT

OUR WORLD HAD REDUCED into a featureless orange gloom. The wind was relentless, trying to constantly grab hold of us to throw us tumbling across the dunes. Jack and I had to fight for every step as the looser material of our combat trousers fluttered like wild flags, angling our bodies into the storm to stay upright.

Clouds of sand rushed round in spiralling patterns, frequently reducing the visibility to less than a metre – even sometimes to the point where I could barely see Jack just in front of me. To make life even more difficult, the wind seemed to gust from completely different directions, as if we were standing in a tornado rather than a sandstorm.

'How much further?' I shouted, my throat feeling as if it had been scratched by a hundred claws.

'I'm expecting to see the first raised ring of the Richat Structure any moment.'

A stinging pain round my neck was starting to grow. When I raised my hand to it, my fingers came away covered in blood.

'I'm cut, Jack.'

Jack turned his back to the wind to shelter us a fraction as he leant over to examine my neck. He began to adjust the cloth of the snood covering my face, coming close to my ear to shout over the roar of the sandstorm.

'You left a gap between your clothes and the storm has sand-blasted the exposed skin.'

'Shit! The sooner this storm stops the happier I'll be.'

'You and me both, Lauren.'

In addition to the sting of pain, my whole body was starting to ache from its continued pounding by the sandstorm. A headache was slowly grinding my brain into a mushy pulp thanks to the constant howling wolf noise of the wind bellowing in my ears.

All I could do was concentrate on each step and the creeping rhythm of walking in this impossible storm.

My mind had begun retreating as the world kept disappearing around us. If a nuclear electromagnetic pulse had just ripped through the area, radiation couldn't be that far behind it, especially with the storm carrying it towards us. On the plus side, if *Ariel* was still intact and Ruby and Troy were inside the ship, hopefully they would be shielded from any brief radiation spike. But as for us, exposed out in the open, what chance did we have?

I felt off-balance in every sense, the disorienting storm only adding to my sense of building panic.

But I kept all these thoughts to myself. I couldn't afford to distract Jack from the mission and I didn't want to point out the stark fact that we might already be the walking dead...and not in the zombie sense either.

I was starting to feel as if I was stuck in some sort of waking nightmare when I spotted two low mounds ahead of us, the first feature we'd seen, apart from the dunes we'd been trekking up and down over.

Jack was veering towards them, having obviously noticed them too.

'Something interesting?' I called out over the shriek of the wind.

'Not sure,' Jack replied, dropping to his knees and beginning to scrape away the sand. Then he gasped and hung his head. 'No!'

I looked past him to see the black metal frame of one of our Zero bikes.

'Oh my god – you're not telling me we've just walked round in a huge circle?' I asked.

He hung his head. 'I'm afraid it looks that way, Lauren.'

I was already so physically and mentally exhausted that I had to fight back the tears that suddenly threatened.

'Bloody hell, enough already!' I shouted into the storm; my words instantly swept away.

Jack raised his head to meet my stare. 'I know, I know. I think our only option now is to shelter here as best as we can until the storm blows past.'

'But we'll be buried alive in this weather.'

'What other choice have we got, Lauren?'

I stared into the deep blue eyes behind his goggles. Was this it? Would this be how we died with no one ever finding our bodies out in this desert?

The sense of despair was really biting into me when I saw two dark shapes emerging from the storm behind Jack. My heart leapt. Could it be Ruby and Troy? Had they somehow managed to track us down? But then a starker thought took hold. What if these were Overseers? Had they already beaten us to the site?

My hand moved to my LRS. 'Jack, we've got company,' I hissed.

He whirled round as the figures drew closer.

But as I began to raise my pistol, Jack grabbed my hand. 'No, it's OK, Lauren.'

The sandstorm cleared for a moment, revealing two men in

long ruby robes. Their only visible features were their eyes through slits in the black fabric wrapped round their heads. They held ropes attached to two camels behind them.

Jack raised his hand in greeting and only then did the men come to a stop in front of us.

They stared as if we were two apparitions that had just materialised out of thin air – probably exactly the same expression that we had looking at them.

'We need your help,' I said.

The taller of the two gabbled something back at me in a language that I had absolutely no chance of understanding.

I turned to Jack. 'Any idea what he just said?'

'Without our earbuds to translate, not a clue. But I suspect if anyone could get us to the Richat Structure it's these two locals.'

'OK, I have an idea then.' I knelt down and started drawing concentric circles in the sand. It wasn't easy – they almost disappeared as soon as I drew them. I pointed to Jack's chest, then mine, then back to my drawing. Finally, I pointed to them. This was the extent of my foreign language skills.

The two men looked at each other and the taller one shook his head.

'He doesn't seem too keen,' I said.

'Maybe we need to offer to pay them,' Jack suggested.

I dug out the roll of gold sovereigns from my pack. We always carried gold during missions for moments exactly like this. I took a handful of coins and held it out to the men. But again, the taller of the two shook his head.

'This obviously isn't about money,' Jack said.

The shorter man knelt next to the place where my drawing had already faded away in the storm. He redrew the circle and then began to draw radiating lines round it, like an image of the sun that a child might paint. Then he pointed back over his shoulder and shook his head.

'What's that meant to mean?' Jack asked.

'I'll try to find out,' I replied.

I pointed to the image the man had just drawn and then in the direction he had. I held my hands together in the universal act of prayer and met his gaze.

His dark eyes looked deep into mine and I saw something in his expression soften. He stood up and gabbled something to his friend, who threw up his hands – the universal symbol for *what the hell did you just agree to?*

There was a lot of head shaking as the pair appeared to argue.

'Let's see if we can sweeten the deal for the reluctant one, seeing as he's not interested in gold,' Jack said. He scraped away the sand from the lumps to reveal our buried Zeros, pointed to the motorbikes and then to the men.

The taller guy gave a definite look of interest. A few moments later, after a rapid exchange of words between the two, he finally nodded.

'I think they're going to be more than a bit disappointed when they discover both bikes were fried by that EM pulse,' I said.

'Then let's leave them some gold coins in the panniers to make up for it,' Jack suggested.

A short while later we were following the two men through the scudding sandstorm, back in the direction they'd appeared from.

With the near zero visibility I was increasingly grateful for our guides. They walked ahead with an absolute certainty to their stride, although their camels kept moaning in protest at the unnecessary detour with grunts and moans and the odd bit of drool.

Things began to subtly change ahead of us.

At first I thought my eyes were fooling me. Amongst the

featureless mass of boiling sand, I started to see a glow of light in the gloom.

'Are you seeing what I'm seeing?' I asked Jack. 'Or is my imagination running wild?'

He nodded. 'No, you're good. I can see it too – some sort of phosphorous light.'

Our two guides had obviously also spotted it as the taller man was now talking to his friend in a very agitated tone. But the smaller man tugged at his friend's sleeve and, despite the growing argument, we kept going.

A sense of unreality was really starting to take hold as the light grew steadily stronger, a lighthouse beacon in the gloom. This had to be the sun object the man had drawn in the sand.

With every step my sense of anticipation grew, despite feeling pummelled and with a thirst that even constantly sipping on the tube connected to the water pack in my bag couldn't quench.

Ahead of us a slope appeared out of the gloom. The source of the light seemed to be coming from the top, just out of our line of sight. As we walked upwards towards it, I began to notice other similar lights stretching away into the desert to the left and right of us.

'This is starting to look very interesting,' I said to Jack.

'Isn't it just,' he replied. 'My guess is that we're climbing up to the outer ring of Atlantis.'

We crested the top of the slope and I let out a gasp as I took in what was standing before us.

In the middle of a field of boulders stood a glowing crystal pillar engraved with a geometric pattern of squares and circles. Behind us the men had stopped dead at the lip of the slope, watching us and the crystal rune with wary eyes.

'Those look like Angelus symbols – just like the ones back at

Skara Brae,' Jack said as he peered at the runes covering the stones.

I gestured towards the other points of light stretching away around us. 'I wonder if those other lights are pillars like this one? If so, could they be laid in a spiral pattern? You know what was buried at the centre of that back at Skara Brae...'

'Yes, Lucy's original micro mind. But I'm not sure if this is going to be the same pattern – it appears to follow the top of the first outer ring of Atlantis. And you can tell that we're standing on top of it because the boulder field around us is all that remains of the buildings that once stood here.'

I picked up one of the smaller boulders with a fresh sense of awe. 'You're really telling me this was once a mythical thriving city?'

'Not so mythical now,' Jack said. 'Anyway, isn't it about time you tried out your Empyrean Key to see if you can make contact with the micro mind via this crystal standing-stone thingy?'

'Good idea.' I carefully took the stone orb out and unwrapped it from its cloth, immediately drawing the interest of our two desert friends who came in for a closer look.

I took the tuning fork out of its pouch and held my breath as I struck it against the orb, bringing it right up to my ear. But even though I was right next to it, I couldn't hear anything other than the howl of the wind.

'Here, let me quite literally give you a hand or two,' Jack said. He cupped his hands either side of the tuning fork over my ear.

At once the note that had been ringing out of it was audible and an icon I'd never seen before appeared.

'See anything?' Jack asked.

'Yes, there's a control icon that looks like a series of concentric circles.'

'You mean as in the shape of Atlantis?'

I stared at him. 'Oh god, yes.'

'So try it already – it has to be there for a reason.'

I nodded, more than understanding his impatience. I selected the icon and flicked my wrist forward.

At once, a lance of light shot upwards from the rune and rippled outwards to the other similar pillars. As they reached them the beams of energy blazed up into the sky.

The camels let out frightened cries and began to pull on their ropes, spittle flying from their mouths, eyes bulging. And it wasn't just them that were terrified – the two tribesmen were staring at me as if I were some sort of witch. A moment later they turned and ran, disappearing into the sandstorm with their camels. And I really couldn't blame them.

'So much for our guides, but at least they got us here,' Jack said. He gestured to the beams of light. 'So this is new.'

Before I could even begin to frame an answer, more rings of the searchlights appeared ahead of us, all pointing straight up into the sandstorm like banks of theatre lights being switched on.

We peered through the storm as the illuminating rings grew smaller, seeming to converge on the heart of Atlantis.

'I think we're seeing the runes laid out along each of the concentric mounds of the ancient city,' Jack said, his eyes wide in awe. 'But any idea what's happening exactly?'

'None, apart from the fact I appear to have found the light switch.'

A humming sound began to build around us, along with a slight vibration running through the ground beneath my feet. The sand started to vibrate as if the entire ground had been turned into the surface of a drum. With a huge crackle and the smell of burning plastic, a massive bolt of lightning lanced up from the crystal rune closest to us and we dived for the floor, scurrying backwards on our elbows.

'What else have I woken up?' I called out as the stone

crackled with flickering energy intense enough that we had to shield our eyes from it.

'No idea – all I know is that we need to find some cover,' Jack shouted back.

We jumped to our feet and ran back to the edge of the slope, throwing ourselves down it.

With echoing booms that seemed to shake the entire world, every pillar launched lightning bolts skywards in one huge pyrotechnic display. The humming grew deafening and when I looked up into the sky I saw a gigantic dance of geometrical symbols dancing across it, strobing in time to the energy bursts.

And then it began to rain. But this wasn't everyday rain – small beads of molten glass were splattering down into the sand around us.

'What new flavour of hell is this?' Jack asked.

'I think that the plasma is fusing the sand into glass,' I replied as I did my best to avoid the small red-hot projectiles.

The air was starting to smell of cinnamon, heady and intoxicating, as the sandstorm cleared rapidly away, evaporated by the lightning blasts. Above us, a clear disc of blue sky gradually appeared as the lightning display faded away to nothing and an eerie silence descended.

We both clambered back to our feet to see a spinning wall of sand about a hundred metres away. It curved away, tracing the contour of the outer ring of the Richat Structure.

Jack put his hands on his head, slowly turning to take it all in. 'Holy crap, it's as if we're standing in the eye of a sand tornado.'

I took in the spectacle with a growing sense of astonishment as we climbed back up the slope. The transformation that awaited us at the top was spectacular.

The previously boulder-covered ground round the base of the pillar had been turned into glass. And it wasn't the only one. The monoliths that stretched away in a line were also surrounded by similar islands of glass.

Jack gasped. 'Oh my god!'

I turned to see what he was staring at and the air locked in my throat.

A crystal pyramid at least three hundred metres high was now sitting in the heart of the city. Light blazed from it, as dazzling rainbow patterns spun over its surface.

'Tell me that wasn't there a second ago?' Jack said as we both stared.

'Absolutely bloody right it wasn't,' I replied. 'If anything is an X-marks-the-spot, this has to be it. Based on the fact we didn't spot that on the satellite feed when flying in here, I bet the micro mind conjured it up and is lying directly under it.'

Jack nodded. 'OK, we need to hydrate. We've got an eleven-klick walk ahead of us to reach it and it's going to be one hell of a trek in this heat, especially as we're heading towards midday.'

I nodded as I took a long sip from my water tube, my gaze locking on to the mesmerising light show before us and my heart fluttering with anticipation.

CHAPTER NINE

WE WERE HEADING across the final wide dry moat of Atlantis towards the inner raised mound a good couple of kilometres wide. On it stood the semi-transparent crystal, like some sort of extraordinary ancient memorial. It was almost mind-blowing enough to take my thoughts off the sheer physical exhaustion currently wracking my body.

'What I wouldn't give to have working Zero bikes with us,' Jack said as he wiped sweat away from his forehead with the back of his arm.

'Yes, hiking for three hours in this sort of heat is no fun,' I replied.

It had been heavy going across the terrain, particularly through the boulder remains of the ancient buildings that had once stood here. We'd done our best to ration our water, but neither of us had much left. And even if we did recover the micro mind, what happened then? My heart twisted every time I thought of Troy and Ruby, but if they really had been taken out by the reactor blast - and I was too overwhelmed to even contemplate that - then we were also in a really bad situation.

The Richat Structure was a remote site in the middle of the Sahara and here we were without any form of comms. Our best hope was that Tom would eventually send out a search and rescue mission to find us. Whether we would survive that long in this extremely hostile environment was another matter.

The invisible force field round the entire site of Atlantis created by the crystal pillars was holding back the swirling sandstorm, which encircled the area, rising up to meet the blue disc of the sky above. What with that and the glowing rings of stones, not to mention the extraordinary pyramid before us, this had to count as one of the most spectacular sights I'd ever seen.

Now at last the final embankment rose before us. Threads of glass ran through it, combining and growing denser towards the top of the slope like the converging roots of a forest.

I took off the sunglasses I was now wearing to try to protect my eyes against the blinding glare of the sun overhead and wiped the lenses on my sleeve.

'This reminds me of what Lucy did to that oil rig out in the North Sea when she covered it with glass,' I said.

'I was thinking the same,' Jack replied. 'If so, we may be in the final phase of the micro mind waking up. It wasn't long after that when Lucy became fully operational and shot up into the sky.'

'That's exactly what I'm worried about. I need to make contact with this micro mind before it does that. Left to its own devices, who knows what it will do.'

'Come on then, let's go for the final leg of this marathon.'

We started up the slope, walking carefully over the threads of crystal. The higher we got, the harder it became to climb, as the slippery glass on the surface became more abundant. By the time we reached the top we were both on all fours, constantly sliding and hanging on with our fingertips to some of the raised crystal ridges.

With some considerable relief, at last we both crested the top and crawled on to level ground before standing up.

Jack's wide eyes took in the three-hundred-metre-high pyramid standing on a floor of polished crystal, broken only by the odd fissure running through it. In the pyramid itself the rainbow swirls shimmering through it were intense, every hue of colour shifting through the structure.

'This has to count as the eighth wonder of the world – and here I am without so much as a functioning camera to record the moment,' Jack said, thinning his lips.

My heart went out to him. I knew deep down how much this experience meant to Jack. Despite both of us having been thrust into the role of frontline soldiers, he was still very much an archaeologist at heart.

I squeezed his arm. 'For now, you'll just have to memorise every detail and maybe one day we can both come back here. I can be your assistant and help you study it.'

'Yes, I'd certainly like that. Here's hoping we get to have the chance one day. But meanwhile, where exactly is this micro mind that we're looking for? I'm guessing somewhere beneath that pyramid, but if so, how the heck do we get in?'

'No idea – let's go and find out if something obvious presents itself,' I replied.

We started forward across the crystal surface that was as slippery as ice. After a few topples we both got the hang of a sort of shuffling slide-step and began to close in on the pyramid.

'This is easily the size of the Great Pyramid of Giza,' Jack said, gesturing towards it.

'Interesting that it's a four-sided structure rather than the tetrahedron shape of the micro minds. I wonder if there is any significance in that?'

'Hopefully the micro mind will be able to tell us that. Seeing this here now has me wondering if the Egyptians modelled their own pyramids on this design – maybe even the Incas and Mayans too.'

'You're saying this structure could be some sort of archetype?'

'Maybe. I would certainly love to do some carbon dating to see if it predates the Egyptian pyramids.'

'Do you think this structure may predate Atlantis too?' I asked.

'It wouldn't surprise me in the slightest, but it must have been underground until you activated it with the Empyrean Key. Maybe the concentric circle embankments round us were originally built by the Angelus too. If only we had a time machine to see exactly what happened here.'

'Well, if you ever get to talk about this in public one day, your TED talk will be truly epic.'

Jack laughed. 'Won't it just.'

As we neared the pyramid, little flickers of light began to glow beneath the glass at our feet, rippling out through the ground.

'If the micro mind is awake, I'm pretty certain it knows that we're here by now,' I said.

As though someone had been listening into our conversation, a grinding sound came from the pyramid. We peered up towards its summit, hands raised to shield our eyes from the sun peeking over it. Near the zenith, holes opened like camera lenses and faceted crystal orbs slid out of them.

Then, shimmering beams of light burst from the orbs and lanced towards the ground. I instinctively readied to dive for cover, but instead of some sort of energy weapon fire, the landscape around us was transformed.

Jack and I found ourselves gawping at thousands of ghostly figures that now moved around us. If that wasn't enough, the outlines of columned stone buildings filled the plateau of the inner island of the Richat Structure, some of them disappearing into the base of the crystal pyramid that appeared to be standing on top of them. Complete with Greek-style giant statues, the scene was straight out of antiquity.

'This is similar to the Angelus hologram system we ran into beneath Machu Picchu,' Jack said, staring round us and lapping up every single detail with his eyes.

I nodded. 'You wanted a time machine, Jack, and now it seems you have one.'

He gave me a goofy smile.

We were now standing on a wide stone-floored avenue, the fused glass floor just visible beneath the rippling hologram. Through the gap between the buildings, I could see the valleys between the rings had become moats filled with virtual water, a canal system linking them together. And on each on the rings of land were ghostly bridges to connect them along with thousands of buildings. There were plants and even trees dotted everywhere, which seemed very out of place for the middle of the desert.

The men and women around us were simply dressed in toga-style wrapped clothing or sleeveless long tunics.

The avenue ahead of us was covered with stalls. The nearest one seemed to be filled with tropical birds of every description, from parrots to pheasants.

Jack stepped towards a woman with a young boy, presumably mother and child. They were choosing fish at a market stall and he just peered at them, his hands behind his neck.

'This is an archaeologist's dream come true,' he said, shaking his head.

I noticed a girl of about thirteen with flowing hair at a bakery stall, watching the two people almost as intently as Jack. The stall holder said something to her, silent in the soundless playback of the hologram, and handed her a biscuit. The girl took a distracted bite from it and a lump of biscuit landed on the ground, immediately gobbled up by a dove diving down from a roof.

I shook my head, my eyes wide. 'So this is the reality behind the legend of Atlantis. It's absolutely incredible. But I still can't get my head around the fact they built this in the middle of the desert.'

'I've had my mind blown so many times since I first met you, and once again it feels as if we're peeking behind the curtain of human history to discover what really happened,' Jack said. 'But why do you think the micro mind is showing us this?'

'Let's see if we can find out the answer to that question,' I replied.

I unslung my rucksack and took out the Empyrean Key. With a strike of the tuning fork, a circle with arrows left and right of it appeared floating over the stone orb.

'Anything?' Jack asked, looking at what I knew would be just empty to air to him.

'It's the same holographic projection controls – with rewind and fast-forward,' I replied.

'Well, my vote goes for fast-forwarding. Let's see how this movie plays out. I have a hunch that's where we'll find the answer about why we're being shown this.'

'Your wish is my command.' I selected the right-hand arrow and flicked my wrist forward.

At once the people around us moved at high speed and a holographic sun rose into the sky, closing in on the real version that burned down on our heads. Then the scene slowed to normal time, just as crowded with people as before.

'Why did you stop it?' Jack asked.

'That wasn't me,' I replied.

Before Jack could say anything else, a woman wearing a long flowing robe and a highly ornate necklace set with some sort of glowing crystal ran past us waving her hands.

I stared at her pendant. 'That doesn't look like any kind of normal jewellery to me. Is it some sort of Angelus tech?'

Jack nodded. 'Based on what she's wearing, I wouldn't be surprised if she was some sort of priestess. She certainly seems upset about something.'

By now quite a large crowd had assembled around the woman. Everything began to shake – was the hologram glitching out? I quickly realised it was an earthquake, a massive one.

'Oh my god. I think I know what this is,' Jack whispered.

'What?'

'The fall of Atlantis, eleven thousand years ago.'

His hand sought out mine as we watched the awful disaster play out in silence.

People started to flee, many crowding the bridges in their haste to escape the doomed city. Buildings were already crumbling all around us.

But it was the human tragedy that shattered my heart.

I watched with a feeling of helplessness as a column toppled over, crushing the fish stall and its owner. Tears were beading my eyes as a nearby bridge started to twist and shake violently. Dust exploded as it broke apart and collapsed into the moat, carrying hundreds of people with it. The only saving grace was that it all happened in perfect silence and we couldn't hear people's screams.

My attention was snatched downwards as the holographic ground beneath us started to drop, descending fast below the level of the Richat Structure's floor.

The ground continued to drop, now at least a hundred metres below us, giving us an aerial view of the disaster that was playing out.

Ant-like people rushed between buildings carrying their belongings. Some boarded small boats in the moats to join the flotilla making its way to the canal, trying to flee.

And then Jack pointed towards the horizon. 'Oh my god, Lauren, look.'

I felt numb as I took in what he was pointing at.

Against the wall of spinning sand to the west of us was a thin white holographic line that grew rapidly.

'A tsunami,' I whispered as Jack gripped my hand.

The white line spanning the horizon was quickly visible as a wall of rushing water.

I stared, transfixed, feeling utter horror for what these people were going through as their last moments played out.

The monstrous building wave swept over the outer rings of the city, consuming all in its path. People, buildings and even boats desperately trying to flee were all engulfed under its wild foaming wild water.

And now the wave was rising higher than even the tallest buildings. As it did so, it sucked the water from the moat and canals, leaving boats stranded in the mud at the bottom.

I spotted the mother I'd seen earlier. She stood at the precipice of where the bridge had been only a few moments before, clutching the boy to her chest, shielding his head so he couldn't see what was happening.

My heart twisted as I watched this human microcosm of the larger disaster play out. The girl we'd seen at the bird stall came to wrap her arms round the two of them – I guessed she was the boy's sister.

All I had eyes for was the three figures below us, wishing with all my might that I could pluck them out of that awful moment in history. But I couldn't.

There was a moment when the wave seemed to blot out even the sun. Then in utter silence, which only heightened the horror, the torrent of water was upon us, wiping everything out of existence as it struck.

Where the three figures had stood was now only a swirl of

water as the gigantic wave swept onwards, obliterating the rest of the city.

A small gasp escaped from my mouth as tears streamed down my face. Jack turned to me, his eyes glittering too. Finally, the hologram faded away and we stood again in the remains of that once great city, the crystal pyramid at our backs.

We held on to each other, too shocked to say anything.

But then I saw three specks in the sky, growing larger and hurtling at an impossible speed towards us.

I pulled away from Jack as the black triangular craft began to slow at around a thousand feet.

Jack turned and gasped. 'A damned squadron of Astra TR-3Bs. What the hell are we going to do now, Lauren?'

I stared at him. I was the person who was meant to have all the answers, but I was too drained for anything other than to spread my hands and shake my head as the shock of what we'd just witnessed echoed through me.

CHAPTER TEN

WE QUICKLY DUCKED down below a low, glass-covered series of boulders. I took a deep breath, trying to fire up my mind to figure out some sort of strategy as the black triangular craft lowered. Two of the TR-3Bs seemed to have shipping containers tied to their bellies with cables, whilst the third had a large dome-shaped device mounted beneath it, a glass lens visible in one side.

'What's that – a telescope or something?' Jack asked, pointing towards it.

'Not sure and I don't fancy finding out. Our only chance is to get to some cover – and fast, before they land. Just keep your fingers crossed they haven't already spotted us.'

We kept low as we rushed towards one of the fused-glass piles of boulders near the base of the pyramid and ducked behind it.

The TR-3Bs carrying the containers came in to a low hover. The cables released and the containers dropped the last few metres, landing with a loud *thunk* on their hydraulic feet that compressed to absorb the impact. Both craft immediately shot back up into the sky as a ramp burst open from each container and at least a dozen mercs in combat suits and full body armour emerged, immediately taking defensive positions.

'They've converted those TR-3Bs to become damned troop carriers,' Jack said.

'A low-tech solution for the Overseers, but it still works. The problem is that now we're heavily outgunned.'

Jack stuck his thumb over his shoulder and gestured towards the pyramid. 'Maybe we stand a better chance of survival if we try to find a way into that thing. Any idea if that magic eight ball of yours can open a door into it?'

'I pray it can.' I took the Empyrean Key out of my backpack and with a strike of the tuning fork, the control icons flared into life. My heart sunk when I saw only the holographic playback icon – there wasn't even a sign of the twilight zone icon, which at least would have meant that we could have become invisible to the attacking force.

'Sorry, nothing useful,' I said. 'I don't suppose we'll find a hidden door anywhere?'

'Actually there is a hidden stone door halfway up the Great Pyramid of Giza. If the Egyptians copied the Angelus design, maybe there's one here too...'

We both turned to peer up at the featureless surface.

'Even if it does exist, how the hell are we going to find it, let alone reach it?' I asked.

'This is where I wish we had Mike with us and his acoustic probes. He could map out the interior in the same way that he discovered Lucy under Skara Brae.'

'And he thought he held us back on our missions. I am so going to have a word with him if we make it out of this alive.'

'Yeah, me too,' Jack replied. 'Hey, look now – that last Astra with the strange dome beneath it is coming in to land.'

I turned to see the third craft descending towards the crystal plateau, its landing legs sliding out of its belly beyond the dome-shaped device. It touched down with the distinct clink of metal on glass. A moment later the specks of two people headed down the ramp from the craft.

A sixth sense made me reach for my binoculars in my rucksack. My instinct was correct –as I peered through them, my blood ran cold. I saw the unmistakable hard-chiselled face of Alvarez, an Overseers colonel. If I had a nemesis, this guy was pretty much it. But it was the person with him that really drew my attention: Cristina Garcia, my opposite number, who also had synaesthesia. She had been manipulated into working for the Overseers, whether she realised that or not.

'Surprise, surprise, Alvarez and Cristina have just turned up. You can bet she has an Empyrean Key with her,' I said.

'So we're going to be in a race with them for the micro mind – and right now they hold all the cards.'

'We could always try to steal that Astra—'

The words died in my mouth as the TR-3B silently rose back into the sky, its landing legs retracting.

Jack raised his eyebrows at me. 'It seems they've learnt from their previous encounters with you.'

'Bloody typical. They must suspect we may already be here.'

'Or expect us to arrive any time now.'

Alvarez and Cristina were heading straight towards the far side of the pyramid, flanked by one of the squads that had emerged from the containers.

'What we need is a distraction to keep them occupied whilst we try to beat them to finding the entrance,' Jack said.

I gazed at him and then an idea struck me. 'I think I know just the thing.'

I struck the tuning fork against the Empyrean Key again, selected the play icon and flicked my wrist forward.

At once holograms flickered into existence all over the plateau. I glanced across to see the mother and daughter back at the fish stall. It looked as if the hologram had been reset to the start of what Jack and I had just watched.

The appearance of what must have looked to the soldiers like thousands of ghosts was met with cries and bursts of automatic fire.

'Come on, let's try to find a way into that pyramid whilst they're suitably distracted,' I said.

We dashed past the crowds of Atlanteans between holographic buildings, running along a street that led straight to the base of the pyramid. We'd just reached the huge structure when Alvarez bellowed orders to his mercs to cease fire and the sound of gunfire fell silent. We could still just about see the Overseer soldiers through the transparent building, but the projected walls were opaque enough to make us harder to spot.

Alvarez and Cristina stood watching the holographic disaster unfold, just as we had done.

'OK, we haven't got much time to find a way into that thing,' I said.

'Working on it, but I really can't see any obvious entrance,' Jack said as we skirted along the base of the pyramid. He peered into crystal walls ahead of us and then pulled his head back. 'Can you see that building that's being projected within the pyramid?'

I walked up to it and, using my hand to shield my eyes, I peered in. Jack was right – there was a classical-looking columned building standing in the dead centre of the pyramid.

'But there are holographic buildings everywhere around us, so why is this significant?'

'Based on the legend, since the location is at the exact heart of the city, I'd say it's the temple as it originally was – and where the neutrino burst came from. An educated guess based on the statues I can just about see outside it; I'd say was dedicated to the God Poseidon.'

My gaze snapped to him. 'Its location at the heart of an

Angelus pyramid can't be a coincidence. Think of the significance of a temple dedicated to Poseidon right there.'

Jack's eyes widened. 'Are you trying to say that the micro
mind buried there might double as their god?'

'Why not – especially if one of the locals had synaesthesia
and was able to communicate with it, like at Skara Brae.'

I nodded as I caught movement in the entrance to the temple.
I peered harder, my face pushed up to the cool crystal surface of
the pyramid, to see a woman emerging from it – a woman that I
recognised.

'Hey, that's the priestess we saw trying to warn the people
about what was about to happen in Atlantis.'

'Better late than never. It does make you wonder if she was in
contact with a micro mind in there just before it happened.'

'If so, why it didn't it warn her sooner – or even do something
about stopping the tsunami, considering the technology the
Angelus have?' I asked.

'That's a good question and one we'll hopefully get to ask the
micro mind in person.'

With robes flowing behind her, the priestess sprinted out of
the wall of the pyramid like a ghost. As she passed us, I caught a
wild look in her eyes, leaving me in little doubt she knew exactly
what was coming.

'We're nearing the end of the replay if she's about to warn the
others,' Jack said.

'Then we need to scan along the base, looking for anything
out of the ordinary – however subtle,' I replied.

We continued along the edge of the pyramid, heading in the
opposite direction to Alvarez, Cristina and the mercs.

Through the shimmering rainbow patterns I spotted a long
tubular shape sloping downwards. 'Hey, can you see that Jack?
Through the crystal?'

He glanced at where I was indicating. 'Yes, that looks like

some sort of internal corridor that intersects the side of the pyramid round the next corner.'

'As in a door?'

'Here's hoping.'

We reached it at the same moment as the hologram buildings started shaking around us.

'We're getting to the main finale – we've only got a few minutes left,' I said.

'You don't need to tell me,' Jack replied, as he placed his hand where the corridor met the featureless outside wall.

Up close I could see the passageway was a hexagonal shape. But the problem was, there wasn't so much as the faintest groove to indicate the outline of a door.

Jack rapped his knuckles on the surface and a dull sound echoed from it. 'It's definitely hollow, but I'll be damned if I can see a way to open it.'

'The building at Choquequirao in Peru that contained the other micro mind had somewhere to place the Empyrean Key to enter, but as far as I can see there's nothing like that here.'

Jack interlocked his hands behind his head as he stared at the wall. 'My guess is that there has to be some sort of lock that can be opened by someone with your ability, even if we can't see it.'

Before I could reply, the holographic ground started to fall away from us as the tsunami got ready to rush in. I had a distinct spin of vertigo even though we were still standing on solid ground and I reached out a hand to steady myself, placing it on the pyramid.

When I pulled away, Jack said, 'Hey, do that again.'

'What?'

'Place your hand on the pyramid.'

I did as he asked and felt the surprisingly cool surface of the crystal. A pulse of blue light radiated from the outline of my hand, leaving an imprint of it on the surface of the pyramid, before fading away.

'Tell me that's not significant?' Jack said.

'Maybe. Let me try something.' I moved away from the invisible door and pressed my hand against the pyramid once more. This time nothing happened.

'OK, so we know that the Angelus used visual synaesthesia to control their technology,' Jack began. 'Previously your magic eight ball has been the key that unlocks all doors, so maybe try using it close to the door, in case it's proximity based.'

I walked back to the door and struck the key against the stone, but only the controls for the hologram appeared, nothing else. 'No, still not working.'

'Damn it,' Jack said, slapping his hand against the hidden door.

I bit my lip, trying to keep focused as the holographic towering wave surged past us, destroying the temple inside the pyramid and washing away the virtual buildings around us.

I stared at the crystal, willing a lock icon to magically appear. My Empyrean Key was obviously in contact with this micro mind – and on previous occasions, with different micro minds, an unlock icon had appeared above the stone orb to open doors... A thought struck me.

'Jack, what do you do when your TV remote batteries run out?'

'Usually turn the house upside down looking for spare batteries, eventually give up and then hunt around for the manual control button on the TV itself.'

'Exactly. So what if someone hasn't got an Empyrean Key, but has got visual synaesthesia. What would they do then?'

'Look for a manual control on the outside and activate it,' Jack said. 'The problem is, I'm still not seeing anything like that here.'

'You are still thinking literally, but if we look at it in terms of sound-activating Angelus tech...' Following my hunch, I struck the tuning fork against where I'd pressed my hand. I had to suppress a whoop as this time a single floating icon of an arrow pointing upwards appeared just in front of the wall. Beneath it was a glowing orb.

'Are you seeing this, Jack?'

'Nothing, but you've found something based on your lit-up expression?'

'Yes. Let's find out if it does anything.'

I reached out for the virtual orb, expecting my fingers to pass through it. But instead I felt a brush of static across my palm as if a physical object was there. With a sense of wonder, I cupped my hand to the shape and rolled it forward, just as I would with my Empyrean Key.

The arrow immediately glowed blue and a golden hexagonal line appeared in the crystal wall. The door pivoted up to reveal a corridor leading into the pyramid.

'Stop where you are and lay down your weapons!' Alvarez shouted, interrupting my concentration.

I turned around to see the colonel and his mercs by the corner of the pyramid.

Jack and I took one look at each other and darted into the passageway. Bullets pinged off the entrance as Alvarez's mercs rushed towards us, firing as they came.

'Crap, where's a door lock when you need one?' Jack said.

He couldn't see it, but I could. A glowing panel floated in the passageway wall next to the entrance, showing a door arrow pointing downward. I grabbed onto the virtual orb, but my hand passed through it this time. With my heart racing and Alvarez and his mercs less than thirty metres away, I tried again but far more gently, feeling the brush of static as the virtual synaesthesia orb registered the touch of my hand and activated the arrow.

At once the hexagonal door that had pivoted upwards into a recess began to lower.

'Stop that door closing!' Alvarez shouted from outside.

Two soldiers sprinted forward, but Jack ducked below the narrowing gap, his Glock 19 in his hand. He shot twice, dropping the first merc and making the second spin away, clutching his shoulder.

With one hand I grabbed hold of Jack's jacket and yanked him backwards as the closing door pivoted towards him, threatening to slice him in two. His head scraped against the edge as I pulled him clear. The door slammed shut, Alvarez and six of his soldiers appearing on the other side as smudged outlines through the crystal.

A new icon had appeared over the door-lock panel below the upward-pointing icon – an X.

I saw Alvarez raise his pistol and fire. I flinched, but not so much as a crack appeared in the crystal as the shot ricocheted off the surface, all in perfect silence.

'Nice!' Jack said with a relieved look in his eyes. 'But when they get Cristina here it'll be only a matter of time till she works out the door mechanism too.'

'Don't be so sure. Another icon has appeared, which I'm guessing might be a lock.'

'Then what are you waiting for? Try it!' Jack said.

'But what if I'm wrong and it opens the door permanently or something?'

'That's highly unlikely – besides, unless we find a way to lock that door, we won't be able to hold out for long. I say it's worth the gamble.'

'You're right.' I took my LRS out and placed it in my left hand, thumbing off the safety. With a deep breath, I selected the X icon and activated it. I stepped back and raised my pistol. A quiet hum came from the door, but relief flooded through me as the golden line that had been glowing round the edge of the door disappeared and it fused back into the surrounding crystal.

Jack grinned at me, turned towards Alvarez and raised his middle finger at him.

In response the colonel thudded both fists against the door in a reasonable impression of a toddler having a hissy fit.

'Very slick, Lauren,' Jack said as his grin became a smile.

'I try my best,' I replied as we turned away from Alvarez and his mercs to gaze down the sloping corridor. It had begun strobing with light, almost as if it was trying to lead us down it.

'OK, let's see exactly what it is that we've just broken in to,' I said as we headed into the heart of the Angelus pyramid towards whatever secrets it held.

CHAPTER ELEVEN

JACK KEPT CASTING a wary eye back towards the outer wall of the pyramid, the silhouettes of Alvarez and his soldiers visible on the other side of the hidden door.

But I was looking ahead at the lights pulsing past us, seemingly showing us the way.

'Talk about walking along a corridor of light,' I said. 'I just hope there aren't white pearly gates waiting for us at the end of it.'

Jack grimaced. 'Thank you for putting that idea in my head. But if death is coming for us, I suspect it will come from behind – once Alvarez manages to find a way through that door.'

'Let's hope it takes him as long as possible.'

As we moved deeper, the bright rectangle of the crystal pyramid above us grew smaller, a welcome chill enveloping us after the heat of the desert above. Ahead, a pinprick of light was growing stronger with each step towards it.

Anticipation pulsed within me – along with a certainty that we were about to find the next micro mind. But I had no idea what we'd do next because we were well and truly trapped down here. The moment we tried to escape from the pyramid, the Overseers would be waiting to pounce. For now we'd have to take it one problem at a time. I'd worry about what came next later.

As we reached the end of the corridor the corners of Jack's mouth curled upwards. 'Don't go into the light.'

I shook my head at him as we walked out of the passageway and then both stopped dead as we took in the jaw-dropping spectacle.

A huge vaulted cathedral-like chamber rose above us, multi-coloured lights pulsing through its crystal structure and cascading down onto the floor, converging on a raised dais that glowed with white light. To enhance the grand atmosphere, a soft, gentle chiming sound rose and fell – a haunting sound that had to be a carrier tone as I was already starting to see patterns appearing and disappearing, my synaesthesia triggered. Most notably this included a geometric flower shape, its angled petals folding and unfolding round the dais.

Behind that, against the far wall, was a statue made not from crystal but sandstone. It was of a bearded man holding a trident as he sat in the middle of carved curling waves.

The structure around us was so overwhelming that I didn't notice what was sitting on top of the dais until Jack pointed it out.

'Seems we've hit the jackpot,' he said.

My heart leapt as I took in the glowing blue micro mind perched on the dais. The light pulsing from the surrounding structure seemed to be pouring into it; it pulsed with luminance like a beating heart.

'I think it's fair to say that this micro mind is well and truly awake,' Jack said.

'You think? But what's with that statue? It looks so out of place with the ethereal theme down here.'

'I think it's fairly clear evidence that the Atlanteans were here at some point – that's a statue of the god Poseidon. Maybe the temple built above us was originally connected to it. It's easy to imagine the Atlanteans coming down here to worship and maybe even talk to their god.'

'In other words, this micro mind?'

'I'd put good money on it. But hopefully you'll discover that answer for certain as soon as you make contact with it, Lauren.'

'OK. If it turns out to be in a talkative mood, a conversation with a god is certainly going to be interesting. If I'd realised, I would have put on my toga.'

Jack gave me a distracting look. 'You could so carry that off.'

Next to the dais floated a transparent control orb, similar to the one I'd seen at the door, although this one had many more icons floating over it, most of which I didn't recognise.

I headed straight towards it across the shimmering floor. 'I'm assuming you can't see this control orb next to the dais, Jack?'

'No, nothing. Why? Is your synaesthesia being triggered by the sound in here?'

'Yes, very much so.' I placed my hand on the orb and once again felt the brush of static on my palm as the device detected my touch. 'This Angelus technology is incredible. Mike would have a field day over this.'

'He absolutely would – but less so the firefight outside,' Jack replied.

'Good point,' I said as I examined the icons. There was the twilight zone icon and also the star symbol for E8, which was interesting as it suggested the AI was open to us crossing over to the higher dimension to make contact with it. Having access to those functions could help significantly with trying to avoid capture. But it was the eye-shaped icon that called out to me, pulsing green as if it wanted me to select it first. Not wanting to disappoint, I rotated the orb until the symbol was in the selection box and activated it.

Beams of light shot down from crystal orbs I hadn't noticed

before round the base of the dais and a hologram appeared, floating in the air, showing a live view of the entrance to the pyramid we'd just come through.

In the hologram we could see that Cristina had now joined Alvarez and his mercs. She had the Empyrean Key that the Overseers had 3D-printed for her in her hand and she held it out towards the door. The view zoomed in until Cristina stood at a real-life scale next to us. The hologram was so clear I could even see the scowl on Cristina's face as she shook her head.

'It looks as if I did manage to lock that door after us,' I said.

'Thank god for that,' Jack replied.

Alvarez, with a suitably pissed-off expression, gestured to one of his soldiers. The man walked forward carrying a rectangular box in his hand.

'I bet I know where this going – they are going to blast through the door with C4,' Jack said.

Sure enough, a moment later the soldier was sticking not one but three plastic explosive charges on the door.

'Let's just hope that door is as tough as it looks,' I said.

'We're certainly going to find out soon enough,' Jack said.

Nervousness built in me as Alvarez, Cristina and the soldiers headed off across the plateau and hunkered down behind some of the raised glass mounds.

I gripped my hands into fists as we waited to see the results of the C4 blast.

The hologram filled with a fireball and the faint sound of a distant explosion echoed along the corridor we'd walked down. As the flames cleared on the view outside, I saw not so much as a single mark on the pyramid's crystal surface.

'Bloody hell, that's so *Forbidden Planet*,' I said as relief surged through me.

'Another sci-fi film I need to watch.'

'Absolutely – it's one of my all-time faves.'

We watched Alvarez, now practically shaking with anger, walk up to the door and give it a good kick. He withdrew a radio and began talking in it as he hurried away again.

'What's he up to now?' Jack asked.

It seemed the micro mind I assumed was controlling the feed heard us, because suddenly the view was zooming back up into the sky, locking on to two of the Astra TR-3Bs that were now descending towards the pyramid.

'This doesn't look good. Knowing Alvarez, he's just ordered a railgun strike,' I said.

'Crap. I'm not sure that even whatever material that Angelus door is made of can survive an impact from a hypersonic round.'

Just like that my tension was back as my mind began to race.

'We have to be ready for them to break through,' I said. 'But there aren't exactly a lot of places to hide. I'm going to get ready to shift us over to E8 to make contact with this micro mind. Hopefully we can persuade it to help us somehow.'

'Good idea – best be ready to transport us to E8 if it all goes south from here,' Jack said.

I nodded and headed back to the control sphere, selecting the E8 star symbol that would shift us both into the higher dimension. I hoped the micro mind's AI would be waiting with open arms, and not psychotic like Red had been back at Area 51.

On the hologram display we watched the two TR-3Bs come to a hover several hundred metres away from the pyramid. Then the pinpricks that were Alvarez, Cristina and the soldiers began to pull right back.

I held my breath, waiting for the inevitable. Both craft shook as vapour exploded round their gun ports. Milliseconds later, the hypersonic rounds struck and the whole pyramid rung out with two deep clangs as a tremor passed through the chamber.

I got ready to shift us to E8. The view of the door was obscured by a large vaporised cloud, which began to slowly clear as the sound died away. Both Jack and I stared slack-jawed at the door. There still wasn't a single mark on it.

'Bloody hell, talk about the Angelus taking their security seriously,' I said.

'That's incredible. And what I wouldn't give to see the look on Alvarez's face right now.'

No sooner had the words left Jack's mouth than the view zoomed in on the colonel, whose face was one huge snarl. We watched him spit out in silence what was no doubt a string of curses.

We turned back to the micro mind at the same time.

'Based on how helpful this micro mind appears to be, maybe it's about time we travelled to E8 to introduce ourselves,' Jack said.

'Maybe, but don't forget we'll totally be at its mercy if it does turn out to be a bit psycho like Red.'

'I think if it were it would have already tried to kill us by now.'

'That's a good point.' I nodded. 'OK, let's do this.' I raised the Empyrean Key and saw the E8 icon already flashing as if it were saying *click me*. I was about to activate it when Jack held up a finger.

'Hang on a moment...' He pointed to the hologram.

Alvarez had been talking in his headset again and now the view was zooming out sideways, looking up into the sky from a ground-level perspective. The third Astra had joined the other two craft.

'Perhaps they are going to try launching three synchronised railgun rounds this time,' Jack said.

'Good luck to them. They can huff and they can puff and still they won't be able to blast through that door.'

But rather than a railgun round, the dome with the lens on the third TR-3B was rotating its lens towards the pyramid.

Suddenly a blinding beam of energy shot out from the lens and struck the door. Immediately vapour began to rise from it.

'Bloody hell, is that thing a laser?' Jack said.

'Yes, and a stupidly big one by the looks of it.'

The beam continued and a distinct glow was starting to build round the door.

A chiming sound rang throughout the crystal cathedral. The light that had been pulsing down through it into the micro mind reversed, now shooting outwards in rapid pulses. A distant humming sound came from the pyramid above us.

'What's happening?' Jack asked.

'My guess is that the micro mind is doing everything it can to combat the attack, probably by trying to self-repair the damage the laser is inflicting on the door.'

'If that's true, based on the fact that the glow from the door is getting brighter, I think it's fighting a losing battle. Time to get our asses over to E8, Lauren.' Jack checked his Glock's magazine for ammo.

'You do know that won't be any use over in E8. The micro mind will control every aspect of the simulated reality.'

'Then call it a comfort blanket,' Jack replied.

I nodded and, with the star icon selected, I flicked my wrist forward. The crystal cathedral vanished around us in a blaze of light.

CHAPTER TWELVE

As the light began to fade around us, I let out a gasp. What I was seeing was literally the last thing I'd been expecting.

We were standing on a stone bridge over a moat with dozens of people walking past in blue and white robes. Not holographic representations, but very much flesh and blood. Jack and I were similarly garbed – I was in a white toga, Jack in an azure-blue one.

Ahead of us the inner city of Atlantis stood, but this time there was no sign of any glass pyramid, just the temple sitting in the heart of the city, a large mountain range to the east. Far more attention-grabbing than any of that were the hundreds, maybe even thousands of people moving through the bustling city around us. There were smells too, carried on the breeze, from exotic spices such as nutmeg and ginger to saltwater coming from the moat beneath us.

And then I took in what should have been desert around the city but was in fact lush prairie and even tropical trees.

Jack was gawping at it. 'Oh my god, the theory about axial shift must have been right after all.'

'Pardon?' I asked.

'There's long been a theory that once every two hundred thousand years, the magnetic poles reverse, followed by a slight shift in the earth's axis, which would result in a major climate change. It's been suggested that until around five thousand years ago, when the last shift supposedly happened, the Sahara was actually a lush and fertile region. If this is a simulation that the micro mind has conjured up, it has to be basing it on something.'

'Wow – you're saying that this is what it was really like back then?'

'Yes, and it would explain why a major city sprung up in what for us today is an arid desert region.'

'Wow, that's seriously mind-blowing.'

Just to remove any lingering doubt that this wasn't just a fancier version of the hologram we'd already seen, something thudded into my shoulder, pushing me aside. I turned to see a camel with a bridle covered in beaded decorations being led by a Arabian-looking man. He glanced back at me and spoke.

'*Samhite*,' is what my ears heard, but my mind interpreted the word as 'sorry'.

'No problem,' I replied, but the words came out of my mouth as '*makain mouchkil*'.

I turned to Jack, who stared at me with wide eyes. 'Since when do you speak Berber?' he asked in a string of foreign words that I really shouldn't have understood, but my brain perfectly interpreted for me in English.

'OK, this is certainly a new E8 experience,' I said, shaking my head.

Jack nodded. 'Not only has the micro mind apparently given us the ability to speak the native language of the Atlanteans, it also seems to have perfectly modelled the city right down to all the people who lived here, even realistically recreating the environment of the time.'

'That's not the first time though. Back in Peru, that micro mind recreated Machu Picchu, but that was very much as it is today. The huge difference though, was that apart from Cristina and myself there wasn't anyone else there. So why go to all this extra effort to recreate a fully populated Atlantis?'

'We'll need to ask the micro mind that,' Jack said.

'In that case we'd better get a move on and head to the temple. I'm hoping there's a way to enter that underground passageway from it.'

'What's the rush, Lauren?' Jack asked. 'You know time runs differently in E8. Hours could pass here and it would only be a few seconds in our world. And needless to say this is an archaeologist's dream. I could spend a lifetime exploring this city. This is literally history brought to life and a completely unique experience to interact with it in this way.'

'Maybe you're right, but that was with Lucy in charge of the show. Who knows how this micro mind will choose to deal with real world time. For all we know, Cristina could arrive here at any moment – and what if she gets to the micro mind first?'

'Damn it, you're right. Sorry, yes, excuse the natural exuberance of an archaeologist about what we're seeing right now.'

'Trust me, I more than understand,' I replied as we set off together, pushing through the crowds of people thronging the bridge.

Below us, long thin boats with raised prows and square red canvas sails glided to and fro around a busy harbour. Other boats were travelling along a wide canal that ran through each of the outer rings of the city. In the distance to the west, I could see the glitter of sunlight on what appeared to be a vast lake stretching away towards the horizon.

The view was spectacular. Seeing this, it was little wonder that the legend of its existence had refused to die. But if this was overwhelming for me, it was nothing compared to Jack's reaction.

He was drinking in every single detail, talking to everyone he could and touching everything to check it was real.

As we cleared the bridge, a young girl caught my gaze. She looked familiar, but it was only when she went up to a biscuit stall that I realised where I'd seen her before.

I grabbed Jack's arm. 'You see that girl there?'

'Yes, what about her?' Jack seemed to be more interested in two carved statues of Poseidon standing either side of the exit from the bridge.

'I spotted her before – during the hologram playback.'

'That's not that surprising if the micro mind used the same data to create this incredible simulation.'

'No, you don't understand – she's about to be given one of those biscuits things by that stallholder.'

Jack turned to look at the stall. 'I think those are actually *maamouls* – cookies made from semolina and filled with dates or nuts.'

The stallholder gave the young dark-haired girl a big toothy grin and handed her one of the *maamouls*.

'But I still don't understand the significance,' Jack said. 'She probably gets one from that stallholder every day.'

'Let's just see if she takes a bite and a big chunk of it breaks off and lands on the ground. Then a dove will be along to eat it.'

That was exactly what happened next.

'Crap, are you saying this is playing out like it did in the simulation?' Jack asked.

I nodded grimly. 'You know what that means. Any minute now, the quake will begin and when the tsunami hits we won't just be passively watching spectators, we'll be caught bang in the middle of it.'

'Then get us out of here, Lauren, and fast.'

It was then that I realised the stone orb had vanished from

my hand. 'Oh shit, the Empyrean Key's gone. We're stuck here, Jack!'

'God damn it! And I thought Alvarez was the real threat. OK, let's head straight to the temple. It's has to be our only hope of stopping this simulation before we're killed – along with everyone else.'

'Yes, but there's one thing I need to do first.'

I rushed towards the girl, who was now distractedly watching the woman and boy at the fish stall next to her.

I grabbed her hand. 'You've got to come with me – it's your only chance,' I said, my words coming out again in fluent Berber.

She looked at me with saucer-shaped eyes. 'But why?'

'Something very, very bad is about to happen and you need to get to safety. You all do.'

I tightened my grip and turned to face the people around us. I was met with concerned gazes including a woman who'd pulled her child closer into her.

'You have to all listen to me,' I called out. 'An earthquake is about to hit, followed by a tsunami which will swamp this whole city.'

The concerned looks turned mostly to ones of amusement, although I did see a few furrowed brows.

'I don't think you're selling it to anyone,' Jack said. 'Let me try.'

He cleared his throat. 'My lady was gifted the sight of prophecy from the god Poseidon when she was worshipping at the temple just now.'

I nodded, quickly picking up on the thread of Jack's idea. 'Yes, he told me I had to warn you. But you must hurry as it will hit at any moment.'

The smiles vanished, replaced by real panic in many of the expressions. People began murmuring and moving away quickly. Then in a domino effect, word rapidly spread, and soon people were fleeing towards an exit road that led up towards the lush grass of the Atlas Mountains to the east.

We began to push through the tide of people towards the temple ringed by stone columns with a larger statue of Poseidon outside it.

'You do realise that they won't be able to get to high ground in time, don't you?' Jack said.

'I thought so, but at least I'm giving them a faint chance.'

'Maybe, although I think you're losing sight of the fact this is a simulation.'

But a dark shadow was growing in my mind. This was all starting to feel dangerously real. 'You try saying that to all these people now scared out of their wits and who will probably suffer a very real death, just like we probably will.'

Jack grimaced but didn't reply.

At that moment a woman rushed out of the temple and raced straight towards us.

'That's the priestess,' I said.

Jack grabbed the woman's arm as she went to dash past us. 'Don't worry – we've already warned the people about the tsunami that's coming.'

She stared at him and then me. 'But how? Has our god spoken to you too, citizen?'

'In a manner of speaking. But more importantly, has he spoken to *you*?'

'Yes, just now in the temple.'

'Can you show us where exactly – and quickly?' I said.

Her gaze took in my simple toga. 'But you are not anointed. You cannot enter the sacred space.'

'Look, none of that matters right now. Do you want your people to survive or not? I think I may have a way to stop this disaster in its tracks by talking to your god.'

The woman held my gaze for a moment and then gave me a sharp nod.

She turned and we ran with her back along the road that led up to the temple.

There was a definite sense of panic now among the people that we were having to push through. By the time we'd reached the temple's steps, I'd been elbowed accidentally several times and a guy pushing a cart filled with clay pots hadn't spotted me and nearly ran me over.

We hurtled inside and immediately the scent of incense slammed into my nostrils in the cool, lantern-lit interior. Blue wreaths of smoke curled up from metal pots with holes in the lids, presumably the source of the strong incense that was starting to make my eyes water.

Women, many bare chested, were kneeling, their arms outstretched towards another statue of Poseidon. On an altar before the statue lay a dead goat, its throat slit by an ornate knife that sat next to it. The animal's blood was dribbling down a groove cut into the table and collecting in a gold bowl next to it.

'That poor animal,' I said as we passed.

'Sacrifice is all part of the belief system of this time, Lauren, and their way to try to appease the gods.'

A shudder passed through the building and dust began to drop from the ceiling as the temple groaned around us. The women whimpered but stoically increased the volume of their chanting towards the statue of Poseidon.

I spun towards the priestess. 'Where did you have your vision exactly?'

'In the sacred space beneath the temple. Please follow.'

We were following her as she headed towards a door at the back when a woman's bellow came from behind us.

'You!'

I turned to see Cristina standing there, her face twisted with anger.

'So it was you who dragged me here to die before the tsunami hits!' she shouted.

She rushed to the altar, grabbed hold of the knife and brandished it at us.

My hand automatically went for my LRS but of course the micro mind had taken everything we'd been carrying – even our clothes and the Empyrean Key. On the plus side, that meant Cristina hadn't brought any weapons either, but she did now have the knife.

I held out my hands as she stalked towards us. 'We didn't bring you here – it must have been the micro mind. All I did was shift Jack and me over to E8 when Alvarez ordered that TR-3B to burn a hole through the entrance.'

She searched my face. 'This wasn't you?'

Jack nodded. 'She's telling you the truth, Cristina. We're in exactly the same trouble that you are – we all know how this ends.'

With my hands on my hips, I gave her a hard stare. 'Look, as much as I know you hate me, we haven't got time for anything other than trying to survive the next five minutes. I propose a truce and we can sort our issues out afterwards – if we live that long.'

Cristina glanced between us, growled and then nodded. 'But if you try anything, so help me...'

'Understood. I promise we won't.'

The priestess frantically waved at us to follow her.

We ran through the door she was holding open for us and entered a tight spiral stone staircase, its walls covered in painted hieroglyphics. With the priestess leading we began to rapidly descend, two steps at a time.

With a distant roar and the sound of stone grinding on stone, the walls shook. This time the quake didn't stop.

Lumps of masonry fell from the ceiling and walls, smashing onto the steps as we descended.

We reached the bottom of the staircase and burst out into the now familiar crystal chamber. Just as before, the micro mind was lying on the dais in the middle.

'Oh my god, this is incredible,' Cristina said as she took it all in.

Jack gave her a look that made it clear he thought that was the understatement of the century.

The priestess headed straight for the shimmering control sphere, and we all followed. I could see it thanks to the humming carrier tone that was still just about audible over the sound of splintering rocks in the stairwell.

Christina stared at the control orb, her synaesthesia obviously like mine and the priestess's.

The woman selected a triangular icon – the same one I had previously used to summon Lucy. But when the priestess flicked her wrist, nothing happened.

She fell to her knees. 'Poseidon has forsaken us in our hour of need.'

'Not on my watch he hasn't,' I said. I raced to the control orb, but before I could lay my hand on it, the priestess let out a gasp, staring past me.

I turned to see that Cristina had stepped up behind Jack and was pressing the blade of her knife into the back of his neck.

'Back away from that thing right now,' Cristina hissed, looking straight at me.

'You don't understand, Cristina. I was just going to try to make contact with the micro mind.'

'Try it and this blade will be buried in the big guy's neck.' She pressed the tip of the dagger into Jack's skin and he grimaced.

'Ignore her, Lauren, and do what you need to,' he said.

But over his shoulder Cristina was shaking her head. 'I'm not bluffing. I'm only going to tell you to step away from that thing one more time.'

I could tell by her cold expression that she was prepared to do whatever it took to get away from this cavern.

'Have it your way.' I held my hands up and backed off.

A distant rumble suddenly grew louder fast and with a roar a huge fountain of water exploded from the doorway, gushing into the chamber. The control sphere began to flicker as the carrier tone was drowned out by the noise.

Cristina shoved Jack hard in the back, sending him sprawling into the rapidly rising water, already knee-height. She charged towards the dying control sphere, selected the E8 icon and vanished in a pulse of light.

With the water surging up to our chests, the young girl appeared, wading through the water towards me. I didn't have time to figure out how she'd managed to get down here, but instinctively I pulled her towards me, trying to protect her as Jack pushed through the water in an attempt to reach us as the current strengthened.

'I'm so sorry,' I said to the girl.

'Don't be,' she replied in perfect English, with no need for interpretation.

Then she smiled, pulled away from me and held up her arms. Everything froze, plumes of water becoming static in mid-air, individual beads hanging like pearls. Even the priestess, who'd been attempting to climb the statue of Poseidon, was now completely stationary, not a single breath swelling her chest.

The girl began to fade away before us and was replaced by a glowing ball of floating light.

I gawped at it. 'You're the micro mind?'

'Yes and I've been looking forward to meeting you, Lauren

Stelleck – and you too, Jack Harper,' the ball of light said. It had a deep male voice that echoed throughout the chamber.

'What...' I shook my head, not sure whether or not I could trust this AI after what he just put us all through. I just prayed that I could. 'Right, there'll be questions later, but for now I've got to warn you that the woman who was just here is working with an organisation called the Overseers. She will tell them exactly where your micro mind is and they'll come for you.'

'You think so?' the voice replied with a chuckle.

A hologram appeared above the level of the water. In it we could see Cristina pacing up and down a small brightly lit room without any doors or windows.

'Where is she?' Jack asked.

'Somewhere she can't do any harm until I let her go,' the micro mind replied. 'She failed the test, her anger twisting her mind. At the end she thought only of herself, not others.'

'And we passed this test of yours?' Jack asked.

'Most certainly. It's why we're having this conversation. And now there is a lot we need to discuss.'

The light pulsed and suddenly a man in a robe stood before us. He was every definition of a god, with a dark luscious beard and strong chiselled features. My gaze travelled to the statue of Poseidon behind him. Minus the trident, this guy was an exact match.

With a suitably godlike wave of his hand, the water vanished and the crystal cathedral-like structure was once again bone dry.

'My given human name is Poseidon,' he said, bowing a fraction towards us. 'Welcome to my modest abode.'

Jack and I traded awestruck gazes before returning our attention to the real-life god standing in front of us.

CHAPTER THIRTEEN

I STARED at the deity before us. Even if he was a simulation, he was still very impressive, and by that I meant a seriously hot guy – although my guard was up until I knew more. Just because this man had an easy-on-the-eye exterior, that didn't mean he would be like that on the inside. I'd dated enough men to discover that one.

'What do you mean, we pass a test?' I asked, my eyes narrowing.

'Unlike your fellow human Cristina, who only cared about her own preservation, your every instinct was to try to save my people. You even showed concern for Arianna, my alternative avatar, as the flood waters rose.'

'You mean the young girl who was just here was also you?' Jack asked.

'Yes – her persona allows me to walk among the citizens of Atlantis.'

'Like the Greek god Zeus, although in his case he often took the form of a swan to walk among mortals – and did a lot of spreading his seed, if you catch my drift.' Jack raised his eyebrows.

'Nothing like that in this case, I can assure you. I find a human girl a far more practical form for observing the everyday lives of the people here. Walking around as a god tends to draw a lot of attention.'

I nodded. 'I can imagine. You make them sound alive rather than this all being a simulation.'

'In a very real sense they are, including Themis here.' Poseidon gestured towards the priestess, still frozen climbing the statue as she'd tried to flee the incoming floodwater. 'Here in E8 I keep their memories alive after Atlantis was consumed by the flood waters. This is my attempt to atone for my sins when I so badly let these people down.'

I exchanged a surprised look with Jack. What exactly was that meant to mean? It sounded as if the micro mind had a huge guilt trip over what had happened, but what could anyone have done to stop a natural disaster? Although the very human guilt he was displaying made me more inclined to trust him.

'It sounds to me that you're being too hard on yourself, uh... Poseidon,' Jack said, echoing my own thoughts. 'Is that what we should call you?'

'If you're comfortable with Poseidon, then that's fine with me, Jack and Lauren.'

'How do you know our names?' I asked.

Poseidon responded with a very human *it's not a big deal* shrug. 'Because of the information that the micro mind you know as the entity Lucy. She has already stored a significant amount of data in the sub-stream memory that all micro minds can access.'

'You mean a bit like storing data in the cloud?' I asked.

The AI nodded. 'A very good analogy.'

I widened my eyes. 'Hang on – if you can access her memories, does that mean you're in contact with her now?'

'No, strangely. That's a mystery in itself. However, she left a briefing file in a sub-straight database that links all micro minds, but which was brought down by the Kimprak virus attack. It appears Lucy was rebuilding that matrix before she suddenly went offline.'

'That must have been when she was shot down,' I said.

'Yes, I'm seeing a last truncated entry about that, but nothing since. But there does seem to have been a spike of activity about fourteen hours ago – based on your space–time measurement.'

'That's when Red started to merge with her,' I said, drawing my teeth over my lower lip and gazing at Jack.

'What's Red?' Poseidon asked.

'The nickname we gave to the micro mind we recovered from Area 51,' Jack said.

The AI god frowned. 'That's very strange. I'm picking up no carrier signal to indicate that this Red is active. Was its micro mind damaged in any way?'

'Well, the Overseers had been experimenting on it – and it was glowing red rather the usual blue.'

Poseidon took in a sharp intake of breath. 'That means its security system was activated and it has gone into defence mode.'

'And that's not good?' Jack asked.

'Not good at all. It means the AI will treat everything it encounters as a potential threat. This defence mode is built into our core matrix to defend us from potential harm. The only way to reset Red to its normal operating parameters will be for a normally functioning micro mind to make contact with it and override its settings.'

'Is this something that Lucy can do even though she was so badly damaged?' I asked.

'Have you had any communication with her since the micro minds merged?'

'Nothing so far,' I replied.

'I see...' Poseidon's expression became drawn.

'That's really bad, right?' Jack asked.

'Possibly, but she may just be taking time to convince the other micro mind that everything is OK so that it lowers its defences.'

I thought of the hell version of Machu Picchu I'd experienced. Who knew what torture the AI had been subjected to at the hands of the Overseers? And Cristina's mental state when she'd first made contact with Red wouldn't have helped either.

'It sounds as if we need to get you back to Eden pronto to fix this,' I said.

Poseidon stared at us. 'But I cannot leave my people until I have saved them. You must understand that?'

'But this is just an advanced simulation, isn't it?' Jack said.

'You still don't understand. I'd better show you.' Poseidon waved his hand and the crystal chamber vanished around us.

We were standing in the middle of a bustling harbour at the edge of one of the moat rings of Atlantis. Poseidon in his god form was no longer with us, but Arianna was. The young girl reached out with a wide smile and took my hand.

'You'll soon see,' she said.

'Poseidon, that's still you, right?' Jack asked.

'Correct,' Arianna replied.

The young girl sat down on the edge of the harbour, clearly waiting for something.

Jack and I exchanged questioning glances before nestling ourselves beside her. She watched a boat head in, wooden boxes containing silver fish crammed on its deck. An old man with a lined face steered the boat as a young boy standing at the prow took hold of a rope and jumped on to the quayside. Within a few moments this obviously highly practised routine had moored the boat up. A short while later the boy and the old man began to unload the boat.

'I don't mean to be rude, but why are we here exactly?' I asked.

'You'll see,' Arianna replied.

A few ripples began to radiate out from the hulls of the moored boats, followed by bubbles starting to rise across the surface of the wide moat.

People around the harbour stood still as they noticed what was going on. Then a groan came from the ground as it began to shake violently. The boat rocked violently out from the harbour wall and we could hear screams from the city above us.

'The tsunami is about to hit, isn't it, Arianna?' Jack said.

The girl nodded. 'And that's why I'm here. I need to say sorry to these people and offer comfort where I can – to each and every one of them.' She stood up as the ground bucked beneath us, the buildings emitting a grinding sound as people began to throng the bridge above us...a bridge that I knew was about to collapse.

A large group of people were running down the steps towards the harbour, but several of the boats had already pushed off and were making towards the canal. Though the boat that we were standing next to remained.

The old man was beckoning to the crowd to board his boat. At least thirty people turned and ran straight towards him. The fit and young leapt on to the deck, whilst the boy helped the older ones.

Now Arianna stood up as though she'd been waiting for this exact moment to act. She broke into a run and jumped on the craft too.

I took one look at Jack and he nodded.

Together we sprinted after her, leaping on to the packed deck just as the young boy pushed off from the quayside. The old man was already tacking the sail and bringing the craft into the wind, which moaned eerily, sending a shiver down my spine.

Behind us more people had arrived at the jetty. Some tried to leap for the boat but fell short and landed in the water.

And then the water began to churn and rushed out towards the canal, dragging the boat with it in the sudden current.

Jack's hand sought out mine as screams came from above when a whole section of the bridge collapsed. People and masonry crashed into the moat, sending great plumes of water hurtling into the air.

A large shadow cast by the tsunami fell across the boat as the current sucked us into the canal. The people on the deck hung on to each other, whimpering, as an enormous wave reared up ahead of us.

Tears filled my eyes as the world roared and the tsunami rushed forward. I felt the fear radiating off the people around me like a physical thing.

It was then that I noticed, in the midst of all this destruction, Arianna walking up to the boy who'd helped people onto the boat and wrapping her arms round him.

'I am so sorry,' she whispered, somehow audible despite the fury of the thundering tsunami and the screams all around.

Arianna cried as she held the boy to her, stroking the back of his head.

Jack's hands tightened round me as our eyes locked on to each other. Then with the impact of an express train slamming into my body, the black wave crashed over the boat and the world went dark.

I drew in a ragged breath of air as my eyes opened to the gentle strobing light of the crystal cathedral. I was lying on the ground next to Jack, who was struggling up into a sitting position. Our packs and pistols were lying nearby.

Poseidon stood over us, his eyes glistening with tears. He held out a hand to help each of us to our feet. 'So you now understand?'

My mind stuttered, still trying to come to terms with what we'd just experienced. But seeing his emotion, I slowly nodded. 'You're witnessing what happened to the people of Atlantis, trying to give comfort where you can.'

Jack's gaze tightened on Poseidon. 'This is some sort of atonement for you?'

'Yes, you're both right. In fact, I have run this simulation trillions of times, so I can witness the death of every sentient being in Atlantis and live that moment with each of them to try to ease their fear in their moment of passing.'

'Trillions? That would mean you've witnessed every person's death thousands of times over,' Jack said.

'Millions and millions of times to be exact – my penance for not being able to help them that day.'

'But this isn't on you, Poseidon,' I said. 'It was a natural awful disaster. There was literally nothing that you could have done...' And then an awful thought hit me. 'Or was there?'

Poseidon hung his head. 'And now we get to the truth. I had taken myself temporarily offline to run some maintenance algorithms. When I rebooted myself, I was too late to be able to dampen the seismic vibrations that had already reached Atlantis – and I had little time left to warn the people. Everything that followed is absolutely my fault. And to think that they thought of me as their god. What sort of god lets their people suffer like that?'

The tears were running down his face now and instinctively I reached out and drew Poseidon to me, holding the broken man as Jack looked at us with soft eyes.

'You can't think like that, Poseidon. You had no way of knowing what was about to happen when you went offline. And to keep reliving their deaths is to keep torturing yourself over what happened. You have to stop doing that to yourself.'

'It is all I deserve,' Poseidon replied.

Jack shook his head. 'No, it isn't. I know what it's like to be stuck in the past. I kept reliving an awful moment in my life – torturing myself for what happened to my wife. But then this wonderful woman Lauren got me to open my eyes and to start living again.'

I felt such a surge of love for Jack right then that it felt as if a physical ball of energy was surging out of my chest towards him. I'd fallen heavily for this guy.

I gently patted Poseidon's back. 'Jack's absolutely right. I can't begin to get my head around what you've been putting yourself through. You need to start looking forward, not back. You have to stop reliving this endless *Groundhog Day*. It's doing no one any good. Especially if you're making these people go through that same awful day in their lives, again and again.'

Poseidon stared at me. 'You make it sound like *I'm* torturing *them*.'

I sighed and gave him a sympathetic look. 'All I know for sure is that you're definitely doing that to yourself. If you're looking for redemption, you have a great chance to do that now by returning with us to Eden and helping us against a very new real threat to our planet.'

'The Kimprak invasion?'

'Exactly. So are you prepared to hit the off switch on your very own *Groundhog Day*?'

Poseidon gave me a questioning look before his eyes widened. 'According to Lucy's sub-strata database, you're referring to a human film in which the main character, a weatherman played by Bill Murray, is forced to relive the same day until he gets it right.'

'That's the one. Will you please stop?'

Poseidon held my gaze. 'Time to look forward...' He slowly nodded. 'Yes, I think you're right.' He held up a hand and a shimmer passed through the world as he vanished.

The cavern around us blurred briefly before refocusing again.

'What new flavour of crazy is happening now?' Jack asked.

I looked up and saw the crystal pyramid had reappeared above us, visible through the crystal walls, and a hologram was once again floating in the middle of the chamber. Within it I could see that a TR-3B was still firing its laser straight at the hidden door at the base of the pyramid. It was now glowing white-hot.

'I think we're back in our reality, Jack.'

'You are correct, Lauren,' Poseidon's disembodied voice said from all around us. 'I am starting up my sub-systems right now, but they will take a little while to return fully online. Unfortunately, the group you refer to as the Overseers are about to burn through the outer door and gain access to this chamber.'

'Then we need to go and organise a little reception committee to slow them down a bit,' Jack said.

I grimaced. 'But tactically we won't stand much chance if we're in the corridor when they burn through the outer door. The phrase "shooting fish in a barrel" springs to mind.'

'Please do not worry about that,' Poseidon said. 'I can open up a second passageway for you to escape through. You will need to this anyway as when I become fully activated, this structure will revert back to sand and rock, and you'll be buried alive if you're still in this chamber.'

'Then that sounds like a great idea,' I said. 'Once we're up there, we can do our best to draw them away whilst you escape.'

'There is something you need to be aware of,' Poseidon's voice said. 'From what I can see there are rather a lot of these Overseers out there for you to deal with.'

'Oh, don't worry about us, we've become experts in surviving against insurmountable odds,' I said. I wasn't sure if I was trying to persuade Poseidon or Jack or myself.

'I see. Well, once I launch I will do what I can to help.'

'No, your main priority is to avoid falling into the hands of the Overseers. You need to keep your distance. Leave the rest to us.'

'We will have to see about that,' Poseidon said, giving just a hint of attitude that made me like him all the more.

'Guys, aren't we forgetting someone?' Jack said. 'Cristina is still stuck in that room in E8.'

'We can't risk bringing her back here, at least not now,' I replied.

'In that case, may I make a suggestion,' Poseidon said. 'Rather than return her here, why don't I keep her safely in E8 until this is all over?'

'That certainly gets my vote,' Jack.

'Mine too,' I added.

A chiming sound came from behind us and we turned to see a new tunnel had opened up in the left-hand side of the cathedral. 'One secret passageway at your disposal,' Poseidon said. 'And now my sub-systems are coming back online, your Empyrean Key will be able to use my full functionality should you need it.'

'Including entering the waveform version of our world?' I asked.

'If you mean the twilight zone, according to Lucy's records, then of course.'

'I fancy our chances a whole lot more with an invisibility cloak at our disposal,' Jack said.

I nodded. 'Then let's do this. Good luck to you, Poseidon.'

'And to you, my friends,' the AI replied.

His micro mind crystal began to glow more strongly as Jack and I grabbed our kit and sprinted towards the new passageway.

CHAPTER FOURTEEN

We stood before a crystal door similar in design to the one we'd used to first enter the pyramid. I unlocked it with a strike of my tuning fork and a flick of the control orb.

'OK, here goes nothing,' I said as we stepped outside, my Empyrean Key in hand.

Everything was just as it had been before. The buildings we'd seen so vividly brought back to life over in E8 were now just a boulder field stretching away, underlining the scale of destruction that had happened here. In the far distance the sandstorm looked considerably thinner but was still being held back by an invisible wall surrounding the site of the ancient city.

'I never thought I'd be so relieved to see a pile of rubble and desert,' Jack said.

'Yes, in other circumstances you'd be in your element visiting Atlantis as it used to be,' I replied.

'Absolutely, but not when witnessing its destruction time after time and the effect on the people who lived there.'

'I know. I can only begin to imagine what Poseidon's head

space must be like. I'm surprised he hasn't gone insane, if that's a thing AIs can do?'

'Maybe only in the sense that he should have forgiven himself a very long time ago.'

I took a moment to look into Jack's eyes. 'I guess we all carry guilt in some form or other – but just like we told Poseidon, it's all about looking forward.'

Jack reached out and gently cupped my face in his hand. 'It most certainly is.'

'God, will you stop looking at me like that? We're meant to be on a mission but right now all I want to do is kiss you.'

Jack gently chuckled. 'Yeah, we need to keep focused – so let's go and kick Alvarez's ass.'

I held up the Empyrean Key, struck it with my tuning fork and selected the three wavy lines icon. The world shimmered and morphed into a ghostly version of the twilight zone. The ground and our bodies blurred as the particles making up our reality were turned into waveform versions of themselves. The pyramid next to us, along with the stone orb in my hand, were the only solid objects in this fluctuating universe of energy.

Within the crystal walls of the pyramid, the true beauty of the light show was spectacular. Infinite patterns of geometry danced and spun in constantly shifting shapes, every colour imaginable cycling through them.

'Wow, that's pretty psychedelic,' Jack said, gazing at them.

'If you ever wanted to know what my basic visual synaesthesia looks like when triggered by a sound, that's it, but on steroids.'

'To see the world as you do is always astonishing,' Jack said as we started to head round the pyramid.

The TR-3B was blazing its laser canon into the hidden doorway as we rounded the corner. In the twilight zone the craft was a ghostly version of itself and we could see partly through the hull to the spinning plasma in its gravity-reduction drive. There was a two-person crew inside – a man and a woman.

Further out from the pyramid, Alvarez and his soldiers were watching the proceedings from the cover of the glass boulders.

'Let's make a start on this arse-kicking by giving those soldiers the shock of their lives,' I said.

'Amen to that,' Jack said.

Weapons in hand, our fingers did their usual trick of partly merging into the stocks as here in the twilight zone thanks to the particles being in their waveform state, edges weren't so much a thing. We made our way towards the nearer of the two squads – although we couldn't actually shoot anyone whilst in the twilight zone. That meant their bullets couldn't hurt us either, but only as long as we were here.

'Looks as if Alvarez deliberately split his soldiers up so they could create a crossfire situation for anyone trying to escape the pyramid when they finally melt through the door.' There was a certain amount of begrudging admiration in Jack's tone.

'I'd expect nothing less from the Colonel, although it will boil down to shooting first and taking prisoners second.'

We were closing on the squad and Alvarez when a female soldier came running up him.

'Still no sign of Cristina Garcia, Colonel,' we heard her say to him. 'She seems to literally have disappeared off the face of the planet.'

'They must be holding her prisoner, probably somewhere in that damned pyramid structure.' He positioned the mic closer to his mouth. 'Hear this – I will ensure the soldier who rescues Cristina is given a million US dollars. She has to be saved at any cost.'

Lots of affirmatives came back from the soldiers gathered around him.

Jack grinned at me. 'If only they knew where she actually was – that would give them pause for thought.'

I gave him a vague nod. Not for the first time I'd noticed real concern in Alvarez's tone towards the woman he had abducted. Maybe the stone-hearted knucklehead had developed a soft spot for her. But no, that couldn't be it. His interest had to be entirely professional – he saw Cristina as a useful asset and nothing more.

'So how are we going to play this?' Jack asked.

I gestured to a nearby pile of fused glass rocks that had once been an Atlantean building.

'We take cover behind there. When out of sight, we drop out of the twilight zone briefly to shoot, then drop back, move and repeat, taking out as many of the bastards as we can. But remember our priority is simply to buy Poseidon enough time to launch. Once he's done that, we can take our chances heading out into the desert.'

Jack grimaced, closing his eyes for a moment before reopening them. 'And what about Ruby and Troy?'

I felt a surge of guilt. I'd been so busy with things here that I hadn't had a moment to think of our friends and whether they were alive or dead. My imagination leapt to the worst scenario, filling with an image of a ceremony where their names were being added to the memorial wall back at Eden.

A lump formed in my throat. I wanted to reach out and squeeze Jack's arm. But of course, in the twilight zone my fingers would only bury themselves into his flesh.

'Let's just pray they make it out of this alive. Meanwhile, let's go and make Ruby proud of us. You know she would have wanted us to kick Alvarez's arse.'

Jack's expression became determined. 'Hell yes.'

We crouched down behind the boulders and I shifted us back with the Empyrean Key. At once the world grew solid again.

I checked the magazine for my LRS, Jack doing the same

with his Glock 19.

'Ready?' I asked.

Jack nodded. 'As I'll ever be.'

'OK – three, two, one, go!'

We both popped up from our cover and opened fire.

All that practice on the firing range paid off when Jack immediately dropped a burly guy carrying some sort of huge machine gun.

I took aim at another guy who was blocking my line of sight to Alvarez. A cool laser-focus kicked in as I pulled the trigger. But despite my battle-hardened exterior, I still winced inside when blood sprayed from the guy's left temple as my bullet exited his skull and he toppled to the floor.

I ignored that as best I could and hung on to the strange calm I experienced now during firefights. Once, I would have agonised over each and every death, and later I would even wonder if they were Overseer stooges. But being forced to cross the line from my old life as a radio astronomer to effectively a frontline soldier meant part of my brain had been permanently rewired. It was necessary for me to survive in this new reality. But at what cost to my soul?

I shifted the sight of my LRS a fraction to the right, lining up for a kill shot on Alvarez. Our eyes met and I paused for a split second – enough time for him to start throwing himself to the ground as I pressed the trigger. My bullet whizzed over his head.

And then, as Ruby would have said, *the shit got real.*

A hailstorm of return fire peppered the boulders, sending glass shards flying and forcing us to duck down for cover.

'Time to move,' I said.

'You'll get no argument from me,' Jack replied.

I struck the tuning fork and a moment later we'd shifted into the twilight zone. I gestured towards another outcrop of boulders on the right flank of the first squadron.

We ran towards it, the solid ground vibrating beneath our feet like rubber in this alternative reality, making us stumble several times. When we eventually we reached the outcrop, Alvarez's mercs were already darting forward towards our original position, firing.

'Classic special forces training: take the fight to the enemy rather than waiting to be picked off,' Jack said.

'That won't work out well for them,' I replied as I shifted us back to our world.

This time we dropped three of the mercs between us before the second squad pinned down our new position with sustained fire. We were far from invulnerable here – brought home when a flying shard of glass bounced up from the floor, slicing my cheek. I dabbed my hand towards it and drew it away to see blood dripping over my fingers.

'Jesus, are you OK?' Jack said.

'Yes, just a flesh wound. We need to haul our arses again – but I have a new idea. Have you got a normal grenade in your bag?'

'Of course.'

'When I say, pull the pin on it and then we'll move.'

'Not the other way round?'

'Oh, you'll see.'

Bullets smashed into the ground all around us as the second squad closed the distance, several glass slivers slicing my combat jacket as we hunkered down behind our cover. But even though a coil of fear was building in my abdomen, I waited until I could hear a soldier's boots clinking on the glass before I struck the tuning fork.

'OK, Jack, pull the pin and drop the grenade now.'

He gave a shocked look. 'At our feet? Seriously?'

'Seriously.' I selected the twilight zone and shifted us just as the shadows of the soldiers fell over our hiding place. 'Do it now!'

Jack knew me well enough to trust me implicitly in a situation like this. He yanked the pin and dropped the tubular canister of explosive on to the ground.

'Run!' I shouted, even though I knew the blast shouldn't hurt us in the twilight zone.

We sprinted as fast as the oscillating terrain would allow. I glanced back to see the blurring grenade become a physical object as it reappeared in our world, out of the range of the twilight zone field being generated around the Empyrean Key.

The squad had only a fleeting moment to register the grenade appearing out of thin air right among them. The next moment an explosion ripped through them, the shrapnel shredding limbs and torsos and killing at least four of the squad outright.

This time I couldn't help but shudder at the carnage. I obviously wasn't quite the hardened solider I thought I was. Maybe that was good thing.

'You bastards. I'll make you pay for that!' Alvarez bellowed, his eyes searching for his invisible assailants.

I was just about to retort with 'in your dreams', despite only Jack and I being able to hear my words, when it seemed the whole landscape erupted at once with explosions. What was left of the soldiers fell back towards Alvarez's position.

Something blurred from the sky, smashing into the ground less than a hundred metres to our left. Shock waves rippled out even in the twilight zone, throwing us both to the ground.

I rolled on to my back and saw the two other TR-3Bs silhouetted against the sky as their railgun rounds blasted down across the landscape.

'They can't hurt us here, even with that aerial bombardment, whilst we're in the twilight zone, right?' Jack said with uncertainty in his voice.

He had a point – as I looked round I could see holes opening in the waveform universe, energy flowing around them.

'I can't be sure,' I replied honestly.

A blinding flare of light came from the base of the pyramid. My blood iced as I glanced back to the pyramid and saw the hidden door collapse in a pool of molten crystal. Already a group of four mercs were running towards the entrance, led by Alvarez. The barrage of continuing fire meant we had absolutely no chance of reaching them in time. Worse still, the laser turret of the third Astra was turning in our direction, sweeping like a scythe across the landscape.

'Crap! What do we do now, Lauren?'

I turned to Jack. 'Take out as many of the bastards as we can. All we need to do is buy Poseidon the final time he needs to get airborne. Have you ever seen *Braveheart*?'

'Oh hell, you don't mean the bit where he storms the English position?'

'That's the one. Get ready to shift back and go out in *Bonnie and Clyde* style.'

I pushed down the fear threatening to paralyse me and, doing my best to cling on to my sense of detachment, shifted us back.

We ran forward, roaring like two demented Scottish warriors, firing as we went.

We had the element of surprise on our side that meant we winged at least two more of the mercs before the laser-turreted Astra honed its laser in on us.

In a final act of desperation, I emptied the magazine of the LRS at Alvarez and the four soldiers running towards the steaming doorway, the melted crystal cooling. But they were too far away and every bullet of mine missed.

Three other squad members were bringing their weapons to bear on us as Jack grabbed my jacket and yanked me to the ground. No time for final words, no time even for a final hug, only time left to die.

But then I heard a high-pitched whining sound and first one, then two of the soldiers dropped. A dozen WASP drones zipped straight towards the last soldier firing on us, its motors at max over our heads. The guy didn't have a chance. The two battle drones peppered him with enough bullets to shred his body into a bloody pulp. The guy slumped backwards to the ground.

Jack and I watched in stunned silence as dozen more of the drones began to swarm the TR-3B. It frantically swung its laser round, trying to lock on to the fast-moving targets, but with no success.

And then, like an avenging angel, *Ariel* herself burst out of the spinning sandstorm wall. Her miniguns were already spooled up and firing as she came.

Exhilaration and relief surged through me at the same time. Ruby and Troy were okay!

A stream of tracer fire struck the TR-3B, slicing straight through its cockpit compartment. The craft lurched and tilted before sliding towards the ground at a forty-five-degree angle. It ploughed into the moat with a sickening crash of metal. A moment later, with a boom of explosion, a fireball rose into the sky from the wreckage.

Ariel spun on her axis in a victory roll, shooting through the rising fireball as she engaged her chameleon cloak. The last thing we saw of her was the ship hurtling straight upwards to engage two other TR-3Bs now diving down to meet her.

Jack and I exchanged slack-jawed looks as the WASP drones flew in a defensive hovering ring around us, their weapons aiming outwards.

'You guys are alive!' Ruby's voice boomed from the speakers mounted on each craft.

'So, evidently, are you,' I replied, fighting back the need to laugh hysterically. 'We thought that EM pulse was *Ariel*'s reactor letting go.'

'Nah, nothing to do with us. The source of the pulse seemed

to come from that glass pyramid, based on its coordinates. What is it?'

'I'll tell you another time, Ruby. For now, please send your WASPs inside it before Alvarez and his mercs reach the micro mind in the chamber below.'

Jack grabbed my arm. 'I don't think that will be necessary, Lauren – look.' He was pointing towards the crystal pyramid. It appeared to be folding in on itself like a huge piece of origami. The air started to rush in towards it, making my ears pop at the sudden pressure change in the air. Around us the WASP drones angled their motors to the horizontal position as they fought to maintain position in the growing gale.

'What the hell is going on?' Ruby said over the roar of the wind.

'I think that's a sign Poseidon has fully powered up his systems,' I replied.

'Who?'

'Oh, you'll see.'

As the structure grew increasingly smaller, it glowed brighter and brighter. Just before it vanished, a single tetrahedron crystal shot up from it, like a rocket lifting off a launch pad into the sky.

A pulse of blinding light came from all around us as the ground groaned and shook. Every one of my senses overloaded as we were thrown to the ground. The cracking sound was defeating, forcing us to clamp our hands over our ears as the smell of burning flooded my nose.

As the light began to fade, I looked up to see rocks that had been catapulted into the sky raining down on us like a stone hailstorm, taking out at least two of the WASPs in the process. As the roaring grew louder the hard glass softened beneath our feet, the ground reverting to sand. That same phenomena was happening everywhere around us as the crystal and glass surface melted away.

The last remnants of the sandstorm swept in as the invisible wall that had been holding it back vanished. It swirled over us in a face-stinging barrage as Jack and I stood up. Where the pyramid had stood was now nothing apart from a huge square of pressed-flat, boulder-free sand.

'What happened to Alvarez and his men?' Jack said.

'Presumably buried alive when the pyramid disappeared above them.'

I gazed towards the burial site, thinking about Alvarez, a person who had caused so much misery. 'I can't say I'm going to shed many tears for him – or for any of his mercs.'

We both instinctively ducked as two explosions came from high above us. A moment later, pieces of twisted metal plummeted down from the sky, trailing fire on to the mountainside behind with distant booms as they impacted. The WASP drones that had survived rose up in formation to get clear of what was left of the sandstorm, their motors screaming on maximum power.

My heart clenched. 'Oh, my god, Ruby and Troy!'

But Jack grabbed my arm and pointed. 'No, look!'

The WASP drones seemed to vanish one by one and I caught a slight shimmer in the air as a large invisible disc descended rapidly downwards, the sandstorm still swarming around us.

Static washed over my skin as the cloaked shape came in to a hover right before us. Then a ramp appeared in mid-air and utter relief surged through me as the interior of *Ariel* became visible through it.

'Will you haul your asses up here? I've detected another squadron of TR-3Bs coming in hot,' Troy's voice boomed out through an external speaker on the craft.

Jack and I didn't need to be told twice. We sprinted up the ramp towards the safety of *Ariel*. With her REV drive quietly humming, she began to rise up again.

CHAPTER FIFTEEN

Ruby and Troy had stared at us with increasingly shocked expressions as we'd briefed them on what had happened in the Sahara during the flight back to Eden. Ruby had fist-pumped the air when we'd told them that Alvarez had been buried alive. It was certainly hard for me to get my head around the fact that someone who had always made our lives so tricky was finally gone.

The virtual spherical cockpit showed Poseidon's glowing micro mind flying in tight formation with us, against the background of the star-filled night sky. Much to my relief he'd appeared moments after we'd taken off and had stuck to us like glue as we rushed to flee the site of Atlantis before the next squadron of TR-3Bs arrived.

'So, you've heard our story, but what happened with you guys?' Jack said. 'You had us worried when that EM pulse occurred.'

'*You* were worried? We were convinced you'd been taken out by some sort of blast from the Richat Structure site, especially when we couldn't contact you,' Ruby said.

'That was because everything electronic we had with us got fried, including our handsets,' I explained.

Troy nodded. 'Luckily for us, *Ariel*'s shielding absorbed the pulse, so no damage was done. Ruby would have sent her WASPs out to look for you, but the sandstorm was still gusting too strongly. So we kept everything crossed that you were OK and worked as fast as we could to get the damaged vectoring jets replaced.'

'And those repairs were a bitch of a job,' Ruby said. 'It took us hours to dig out the damaged thrusters, not to mention replacing them in the middle of a sandstorm, but somehow we pulled it off and here we all are.'

'I would expect nothing less than a miracle from you guys,' I said.

Ruby grinned. 'Yeah, so what's new?'

I gazed out at the virtual landscape of clouds scudding beneath us as we hurtled back towards Eden at Mach 6 speed.

'Any radio contact with base yet?' I asked.

Troy thinned his lips as a concerned look filled his face. 'Nothing at all, Lauren. All communications still seem to be down. They aren't responding on any of the emergency frequencies either.'

'That really doesn't sound good,' Jack said. 'Knowing Tom, I would have expected him to have found a way to re-establish contact with us by now.'

With the mission behind us, I allowed myself to focus on the sense of anxiety that had been building inside me.

'Are we saying that we should consider something may have gone seriously wrong?'

Jack gave me a straight look. 'I think it's safest to assume exactly that and proceed on that basis – though we'll pray it isn't the case. That way we won't get caught with our pants down.'

'So what does a cautious approach look like in practice?' I asked.

'I say we should go in fully stealthed-up, then we can do a reconnaissance sweep to see if we can spot anything obvious from the air,' Troy suggested.

'And maybe you could use your WASPs for a closer look, Ruby?' I said.

'That would make sense and would certainly give us more eyes on the ground,' she replied.

'And if we do see a problem?' Jack asked.

'We'll cross that bridge if and when we come to it,' I said.

Jack raised his eyebrows at Troy. 'In other words, welcome to one of Lauren's famous seat-of-her pants plans.'

'Right...' our pilot said, frowning slightly.

'Nah, you should trust Lauren's instincts when the shit hits the fan,' Ruby said. 'Her crazy ideas have saved us in the past.'

I appreciated the vote of confidence, especially coming from Ruby. I gave her a small nod, which she returned. Yes, we really did get each other these days.

'So how long until we arrive at Eden?' Jack asked.

'We have about four thousand miles left to travel, so about fifty minutes at this speed, give or take,' Troy replied.

'In that case I'll make myself useful and use the Empyrean Key to contact Poseidon so he can patch into our systems ready for when we arrive,' I said.' Meanwhile, I suggest everyone else gets some shut-eye – we still have no idea of what we're heading into and need to be sharp. And, Troy, I include you in that. I suggest you let Delphi take over the flying.'

'Roger that, Lauren,' he replied.

'What, no in-flight movie?' Ruby asked.

'You'll be lucky if you get a warm towel on this particular airline,' Troy quipped, making Ruby snort.

'Wake up, sleepy head, we're directly over Eden,' I heard Jack say.

It felt as if I was surfacing from a very deep pool as I opened my eyes.

Around me the virtual cockpit display showed a nightscape dotted with stars above and the jungle far below us.

Immediately I was wide awake and sitting up. 'Have we received any incoming communication yet?'

Ruby looked up from her CIC screens. 'Not a thing, Lauren, and I'm starting to get a bad feeling about this.'

'In that case we need to tread extra carefully – until we know exactly what it is we're dealing with. Is our chameleon cloak turned on?'

'We're fully stealthed-up,' Ruby replied. 'I've even activated our ES shield just in case.'

'Good, so it's probably time to send down one of your WASPs to scout out the situation on the ground.'

Ruby nodded. 'Already preparing one now.'

'I'm liking your cautious approach, Lauren – much better than going steaming in,' Troy said.

'In my experience it's always best to be paranoid when you're facing an unknown situation, at least until you have a chance to assess the situation properly.'

'Absolutely, I couldn't agree more,' Troy replied.

Jack smiled at me.

'What?' I asked, wondering if I had a string of sleep drool hanging from my mouth.

'Just that on every mission you're sounding increasingly like a military commander, that's all,' Jack said.

'Apparently that's all part of the job description, but I'll take that as a compliment.'

'You should, because I agree,' Ruby said, peering over the top of her screen at me.

'Well, thank you both for the vote of confidence. It means a lot.' And it did, although inside I still had a fair amount of impostor syndrome swirling round.

I toggled the radio switch on the arm of my chair. 'Poseidon, did you hear all of that?'

'Yes, I did. I will just follow your lead, Lauren. However, if there is anything I can do to help, just ask.'

'I certainly will when the time comes.' I scanned the sky around us. 'Where are you?'

'Currently about twenty metres away from *Ariel* and fully cloaked, as you can probably guess.'

Ruby finished activating a bank of software buttons on her screen.

'Right, the first WASP is primed and ready to launch on your command, Captain,' Ruby said.

For a moment I didn't realise she was talking to me until she looked straight at me, waiting for an answer. Yep, I was definitely suffering from impostor's syndrome.

'Oh right – please go ahead,' I said, feeling more than a little bit self-conscious, not helped by the tiny smile I spotted curling the corners of Jack's mouth before he managed to suppress it.

'WASP away,' Ruby said as she activated a pop-up window on the virtual cockpit showing a view of clouds whipping past.

'And the feed from WASP One is live,' Ruby said. 'Where shall we send the little guy to first?'

'It's a he, is it?' Jack asked.

'Well, just like a real wasp, the sting of these drones are real sons of bitches, so yeah, definitely a guy.'

Troy chuckled and shook his head.

'Let's send that WASP down to just over the jungle canopy to see if we can see anything out of the ordinary – especially around the launch silos and hidden entrances.'

'And what sort of *out of the ordinary* are you looking for?' Troy asked.

I looked at him and then the others. The time had finally come to voice the niggling knot of worry that had taken hold in my stomach.

'I want to check there's no sign of a firefight,' I said. 'We have to assume worst case that the base has been compromised in some way. As we discussed, it may have even come under an Overseer attack.'

'Hang on, I'm not sure that makes any sense,' Ruby said. 'I'd expect to see my CIC screen swarming with enemy traces by now, but I'm seeing absolutely nothing unusual, even with our new microwave sensor array.'

'Maybe so, but I'm with Lauren on this,' Troy said. 'Better to assume worst case and then be pleasantly surprised.'

Jack nodded. 'That makes sense to me too. Besides we won't have much longer to wait either way. It's almost there.' He gestured towards the live feed from the WASP's camera, showing the night-time jungle growing steadily closer.

My shoulder muscles slackened when I didn't see any rising columns of smoke.

'So far so good,' Jack said, also looking relieved.

'I'll take it in for a look at the main launch bay entrances next,' Ruby said.

The view swung round as the drone went into a shallow dive towards a small hill covered in dense trees – the position of the silo we'd departed from the previous day.

As the WASP closed in, Ruby dropped it through a gap in the canopy. Suddenly the view was swooping between the trunks as the drone zoomed between them. She switched the night-vision mode on.

'Hey, that's like the speeder-bike chase scene in the forest from that *Star Wars* movie you made me watch, Lauren,' Jack said.

'Bonus points if you can name which movie in particular?'

He pulled a face. '*Return of the Jedi*, right?'

I beamed at him. 'You are so my man.'

'Guys, trying to concentrate here,' Ruby said as she swerved the WASP round a large trunk and began to slow it down. 'OK, we're approaching the outside of Launch Silo 1.'

I peered at the jungle floor crowded with leaves and bushes. 'I can't see anything.'

'That's generally the idea,' Troy replied. 'If you didn't know what you were looking for, you could be standing right on top of the launch bay door and you wouldn't know it was there until it started to open. You see that large vine hanging down from the tree on the right of the screen?'

'Yes?'

'It's actually a disguised antenna used to receive remote commands to open it.'

'That's one serious piece of camouflage,' Jack said.

'And that's the general idea, like the rest of Eden.'

I turned a thought over in my head. 'Considering it's closed and there's no obvious sign of firefight on the surface, have you got any way to open it, Ruby?'

'Yes, I can relay a signal to the WASP unit to do exactly that.'

'Good, then do it and let's find out what's happened down there,' I said.

Ruby nodded. 'Sending command signal now. I'm also turning on the WASP's external mic.'

Immediately the cockpit was filled with the sound of cicadas, the night-time soundtrack of the jungle.

But Ruby was frowning at her CIC screen. 'That's weird – the open command protocols aren't working.'

'Maybe we're looking at a base-wide power failure then?' Jack wondered.

'That's unlikely when it's powered by multiple underground hydro-power stations,' I said. 'I can imagine one of them going down, but not all of them.'

'So what the hell is going on?' Ruby asked.

Before I could throw out any sort of theory, I saw a series of flashes of light between the trees on the video feed from the WASP. It appeared to be coming from the top of a hill across the valley.

'Hey, isn't that Morse code?' Jack said.

'It most certainly is,' Troy said. 'Just give me a moment and I'll translate it.' He grabbed hold of a tablet and stylus from a cubby hole by his seat and started to write.

'What if it's an Overseers military unit on the ground that's signalling to another unit?' Ruby said.

My blood turned to ice. 'You mean they may have infiltrated the base already?'

She shot me a tight look. 'That could explain a lot, especially the sudden comms blackout.'

A rumbling sound came from the speakers and a crack of light appeared as the silo door began to roll back, revealing the launch shaft.

'Please tell me that was you, Ruby?' I said.

She held up both hands. 'Nothing to do with me.'

'Maybe this is a good sign and it means that someone has detected the WASP drone hovering outside,' Jack said.

But Troy looked up from his tablet and shot us a grim look. 'I don't think it's that. I've translated that Morse code. It says, "Watch out, base taken."'

'Shit, Ruby, get your WASP out of there,' I said, leaning forward in my seat.

'Already on it,' she replied, way more calmly than me.

The camera on the drone pivoted downwards as it rapidly climbed. A circle of light appeared beneath it in the jungle as the silo door slid back.

At first I thought I was seeing things as it seemed like hundreds of black seeds were rising up from the silo entrance.

'Delphi, enhance image and zoom in on drone video feed,' Ruby said.

The view closed in on three of the specks, revealing them to be WASP drones, their short-barrelled weapons aiming straight upwards. Tracer rounds sped up into the sky round our WASP in a blaze of fire.

'Crap, they've got a lock.' Ruby frantically threw the drone in every direction, trying to evade the incoming fire.

With a burst of static, the video-feed window went dark. On the virtual cockpit, we could see a brief bloom of orange far below, marking the explosion of the drone as it was taken out.

Nobody spoke for a moment as we all processed what had just happened.

It was Ruby who finally broke the silence. 'What the fuck is going on down there? More importantly, what the fuck are we going to do about it?'

Three sets of eyes turned to me as one, all obviously expecting some sort of coherent plan.

But all I could do was just stare blankly back at them as I tried to gather my thoughts.

Jack jumped into the stunned silence that had filled the cockpit. 'Hang on, if those were all WASP drones, there must have been at least a hundred, but how? As far as I'm aware, I think there were only a dozen or so in production when we left – weren't there, Ruby?'

She nodded. 'Yes, the plan was to start putting them into production sometime in the next month, but nothing like in those numbers.'

Troy drummed his fingers on the arm of his flight chair. 'Maybe what we should be asking is not how but *who* is controlling those things?'

'Exactly,' Jack said. 'Whoever took down Ruby's drone must have recognised it as one of their own, but deliberately targeted it anyway.'

I stared out at the bank of clouds sliding beneath us as my thoughts started to crystallise. 'That Morse code warning must have been sent by someone who escaped – who probably has all the answers to these questions...' My words trailed away as a horrifying thought struck me. I opened a channel to Poseidon.

'You know you were telling Jack and me about that security protocol in Red being triggered by the Overseers, hence him turning that colour? Extrapolating from that fact, you don't think that might be anything to do with what's just happened and why our base has gone silent?'

The others stared at me open-mouthed.

'I'm afraid I was just considering that very possibility,' Poseidon replied.

Jack stared at me. 'What, you think Lucy might be responsible for all of this?'

'Not necessarily her, but rather Red taking over her systems and then through her, hacking straight into Eden's security systems and seizing control of the base.'

Troy was nodding. 'Yes, shooting down our drone just now could be construed as Red defending itself from something it sees as a potential threat.'

'But if a rogue micro mind is in control of the base, what about all the people in there?' Jack asked, his face pale.

My blood was now Arctic cold. 'There's only one way we're going to find out the answer to that and that's to head down there and locate the person who signalled to us. If anyone knows what's happened, it has to be them. Then we'll put together a plan to recapture the base. What do you say, people?'

'I have to say I'm starting to like your seat-of-the-pants style of planning,' Troy said. 'Adaptive and logical, if not a little risky.'

'Everyone gets brainwashed into thinking like that sooner or later.' Ruby spread her hands wide and shrugged. 'Welcome to the madhouse, Troy.'

CHAPTER SIXTEEN

With Poseidon having assured us that he was sticking to us like glue, Troy started to slowly descend *Ariel* through the bank of clouds.

'I can't help but think about the fact Eden has a new railgun defence grid ready to smear us across the sky if we get spotted,' I said.

'Will you please relax, Lauren? The new ES shield is online, so they won't have any target to lock on to. You saw for yourself how effective that was against the new sensors in the training exercise.'

'I know, but a training exercise is one thing – a real-life mission is another. I'm going to feel happier when we're on the ground and all in one piece.'

'Now that attitude I understand,' Troy said with an approving nod.

The cloud thinned around us and we were suddenly met with an interrupted view of the jungle, hundreds of metres below. There wasn't a light to be seen anywhere beneath us – no more Morse code. But somewhere down there we knew at least one person had made it out of Eden. But what about the others? If Lucy, or at least Red acting through her, had gone rogue on us, just how bad could it be? What would we find exactly? The corridors running with the blood of everyone else who'd been living down there – including my closest friends such as Mike and Jodie?

I fought down the lump in my throat. I had no intention of voicing these thoughts right now, but I could tell everyone else was thinking something similar, based on the tight expressions on their faces and the unusual quiet in the cockpit.

Ruby was the first to break the silence as she looked up from her CIC screen. 'Hey, I'm seeing something on the optical scope. Delphi, enhance the view now and put it up on the main view screen.'

'Enhancing,' Delphi replied.

A window appeared on the virtual cockpit showing a zoomed-in section of the jungle. Hundreds of red dots of light could be seen dancing around the leaf canopy like a swarm of fireflies.

'Are those what I think they are?' Jack said.

'Switching to thermal night-vision mode just to make sure,' Ruby said.

The individual points of light became stubby-winged WASPs. The view panned out to reveal not just hundreds of them, but thousands, flying all over the jungle.

'Crap, we seem to have stirred up a hornet's nest with Ruby's drone,' Jack said.

'Don't you mean a wasp's nest?' she replied with thin lips.

'Whatever we want to call it, those drones appear to be patrolling the jungle,' I said. 'It'll make this even trickier.'

Jack peered at them and shook his head. 'I still don't get how the hell they produced so many in such a short amount of time?'

'If the rogue micro mind has access to all of Lucy's systems, that will include access via her hacks to all the 3D printers. Working on the assumption that Red took control of the base when we lost contact so suddenly with Eden, the AI has probably been producing them non-stop ever since.'

'Oh, this day just gets better and better,' Ruby muttered under her breath.

'On the plus side, at least they seem to be clustering round the silo entrances,' Troy said, glancing across his screens. 'There only appear to be a few groups patrolling further out, including where that Morse code signal came from.'

'Can you find us a suitable landing site near to it?' Jack asked.

'Unfortunately not. I would normally suggest a halo drop at this point, but with that many drones in the skies you'd be spotted long before you got anywhere near the ground.'

'But there has to be a way to get us down there,' I said.

'There is,' Troy replied. 'I can bring you in real close and then you can rappel down from *Ariel* for the last hundred.'

My stomach did a slow flip. I still had a healthy fear of heights, but I wasn't about to let the others down over something like that. As always, I tried to lean into my fear.

'Then that's just what we'll have to do,' I said. 'Jack and Ruby, you'll be on the ground mission with me. Troy, you'll need to be on standby in case we need to urgently evacuate.'

Troy nodded. 'You've got it, Captain.'

My training and mission experience started to kick in as we assembled all the required gear for an assault mission. I was more aware than ever of the knot of fear inside me. It seemed the more experienced in the field I became, the more a feeling of vulnerability had started to creep in. At least part of that was probably down to being increasingly aware of my responsibility to keep everyone alive. One of the many perks of being the one in charge.

I gazed down at the jungle. How we could gain access to

Eden, especially under the beady eyes of all those killer drones, I'd no idea – but somehow we'd find a way. We had to.

Troy banked *Ariel* over and swept us down towards the hill-side where the signal had come from.

It was then that all hell seemed to break loose.

It sounded like a hundred thunderclaps all going off at once right on top of us. It was like we'd suddenly been dropped into a Second World War blitz as projectiles streaked up into the sky on the virtual cockpit walls and burst into explosions at varying heights around us.

The ship shook with the shockwaves, but Troy was already reacting, pushing his control yoke hard forward and sending us into a dive towards the ground.

'Shit, does that mean our ES isn't working?' I asked.

'No, it most definitely is – we'd have been blown out of the sky already if not,' Troy said. 'But that darned AI has obviously guessed we must be out here and is using the defence grid like anti-aircraft guns, hoping to get a lucky shot in.'

'But surely our gravity shielding will protect us?' Jack asked.

'From a single round, yes, but if Red converges the railgun fire on us and we're hit by more than two rounds, it's likely it'll be overwhelmed,' Ruby said as her eyes darted around the tactical display tracking the incoming shots.

'Then do whatever you need to do to get us down to the ground in one piece,' I said, dropping back into my seat and strapping myself in harder as the ship whirled around us through every orientation.

'Consider it done.' Troy's expression was icy calm, as if this was an everyday school run for him. 'This is me doing what I was born to do – much more so than growing potatoes in a biodome.'

Explosions blossomed across the sky, lighting up the clouds above with orange hues. The virtual cockpit was now lit with dozens of rectangular overlaid boxes that marked a myriad of points all over the jungle.

'I have a target-rich environment,' Ruby said. 'Permission to use our JASSM-ER air-surface missiles, Captain.'

'Request denied,' I replied, knowing Ruby was talking about the weapons *Ariel* had been fitted with before this mission. 'If you take a single shot you will give away our position.'

'Ah, good point.' Ruby released the weapon targeting joystick she'd been gripping. 'Shame we can't let loose with those JASSM-ERs.'

'Yes, but we can't risk giving away our position.'

'Fair point.'

An explosion ripped through the air just beneath us, but Troy's reactions were laser-fast. Even as the shrapnel cloud blurred past us, our astonishing pilot used his skills to roll *Ariel* round the explosion in a corkscrewing dive. However good Delphi's combat AI routines became, Troy would be a tough act to follow.

The jungle rushed towards us and a thousand metres dropped to less than a few stomach-churning hundred. Troy pulled the joystick hard back and the flight deck tipped briefly before the gyros had a chance to level it again. Despite the gravity-dampening effects of our REV drive, we were all pushed hard into our seats as the ship shot sideways over the jungle towards the hill.

My heart pounded in my chest as I struggled to suck in a breath.

'Now that was fun!' Troy said with a wide smile.

His exuberance was only matched in the cockpit by Ruby's grin.

'You flyboys,' she said.

'And an interesting definition of fun.' Jack wiped the beads of sweat that had popped out all over his forehead.

'You're telling me,' I said, swallowing down the bile that had filled my mouth as we began to slow.

'ETA two minutes,' Troy called out.

'OK, let's do this as fast as possible before those WASPs spot us.' I unbuckled my flight harness and crossed to the equipment rack on slightly shaky legs.

The three of us pulled on our tactical helmets. They were similar in function to the Sky Dreamer Corp's motorbike helmets we were very used to wearing, but with extra shielding, and in addition to the night-vision HUD system, these had also been fitted with thermal vision. They even had the equivalent of a Sky Wire built in.

Ruby had her Accuracy International sniper rifle slung over her shoulder, as she grabbed a plastic moulded backpack.

'What have you got in there, Ruby?' I asked as I helped myself to a Heckler & Koch MP5 submachine gun fitted with a suppressor from the weapons rack, which would augment my LRS's firepower.

'A couple of my own WASPs. They could come in handy in the shitstorm I suspect we're about to be dropped into.'

Jack had grabbed a Benelli M3 tactical shotgun from the rack. 'Could be useful to take out one of their drones, if we get spotted,' he said when he noticed me watching him as I put on my rappel harness.

'Good choice,' I replied, slightly marvelling at the fact that not only did I know the name of the weapons everyone was using these days, but I also appreciated their different tactical contributions in a firefight. A lot had changed.

'OK, people, we're twenty seconds out. Get ready,' Troy called.

With a hiss of hydraulics, the ramp began to lower and the three of us clipped our harnesses on to the ropes we'd fastened to one of the bulkheads. Fear was doing laps in my stomach as we began to walk backwards towards the edge of the ramp.

'Ten seconds...' Troy shouted.

The tree canopy whipped past the belly of *Ariel* less than a few metres away. I cast a silent prayer to any deity who might be interested in what we were up to and tightened my grip on the rope.

Ariel came to complete stop, almost silent apart from a very quiet hum from the REV drive. Directly beneath us was a small gap in the canopy. On the plus side, the ground was less than thirty metres away. On the negative, it was still thirty bloody metres!

'Go, go, go!' Troy called out.

Ruby and Jack rappelled off the ramp first and I went a split second later.

My stomach rose to my mouth as I plummeted down the rope that hissed through my carabiner. With my gloved hand I stretched the rope out behind my back, slowing my descent as leaves slapped past. Then I was through the canopy with the ground rushing up to meet me. I killed the acceleration and came to a perfect soft landing, to my own surprise more than anyone's. Those few seconds had felt like a lifetime. Ruby gave me an OK sign with her thumb and forefinger.

Jack and Ruby were already stepping out of their harnesses and I started to do the same. By the time I looked up, the ramp was closing, hiding the interior of the ramp bay. Then any hint of *Ariel*'s presence disappeared as she completely vanished.

'Take *Ariel* out to a safe distance but get ready to tear back here if we need you,' I said into my helmet's in-built mic system.

'Roger that and good hunting, guys,' Troy replied.

I spotted a slight shimmer in the air moving at high speed towards the horizon. And just like that we were on our own.

I pulled up the tactical map in my helmet's HUD, marked

with the position of our mystery contact. It was about three hundred metres directly ahead.

'Poseidon, are you still with us?'

The air rippled four metres away in answer, making the three of us jump as the micro mind thinned its stealth field for a second.

'Does that answer your question?' he replied with more than a hint of amusement in his voice.

'Don't sneak up on us like that. I could have damned well shot you.' Ruby shook her head at the AI.

'Sorry, I'll keep that in mind next time.'

'Anyway, let's make life easy for ourselves and shift over to the twilight zone,' I said.

Poseidon made a coughing sound. 'Ah, that's maybe another thing I should have mentioned.'

I turned to stare at the micro mind. 'Go on.'

'Because of the proximity of the other micro minds, if you attempt to do that, there will be a significant energy spike detectable across E8 and Red will be able to direct the drones under his control to exactly where you are, hidden or not in the twilight zone.'

'Oh bloody hell – are there any other bombshells you'd like to drop on us?' I asked.

'No, that's all of them,' he replied with a matter-of-fact tone.

The three of us traded head shakes. With our weapons forward and Poseidon bringing up the rear, we set off towards the marker on our HUD maps.

The cicadas were even louder on the ground than they had been over the WASP's feed. I caught far too many spiders watching us with way too many eyes, not to mention some gigantic insects scurrying away through the undergrowth. The humidity was oppressive, and I was starting to wish we were using those helmets with air conditioning that we'd had in the

Sahara when I spotted a single red light moving over the tree-tops a few hundred metres out. It was heading straight towards us.

'Hostile coming in fast,' I whispered into my headset.

The three of us dropped down on to our knees, Jack aiming his M3 shotgun towards it as it closed on us.

My heart thundered in my chest as the enemy WASP drone sped past about a hundred metres away. I felt sure that this beady little red-eyed drone would spot us with all the night-vision tech the WASPs were equipped with. I sighted it along the barrel of the MP5, ready to shred the drone with bullets and risk the consequences.

But the drone flew past without incident, speeding away over the jungle.

'That was too close,' Jack said.

'Too damned right.' Ruby nodded. 'Our luck is going to run out at some point. Lauren, I suggest we send one of our WASPs ahead to scout the area and check what's waiting for us up on that hill.'

'Good idea – do it,' I replied.

Ruby opened her hard-case backpack revealing two stowed WASPs inside, their wings folded into their sides. She pressed a button built into the case and a green light glowed on one of the drones. The craft's wings rotated into a vertical position ready for take-off.

'OK, sharing a live feed from our WASP to your HUDs now,' Ruby said.

A small window appeared in my helmet's glass screen displaying the view from the drone's camera as it looked back at the three of us.

Ruby took out a small pebble-shaped control unit from the case and pressed the built-in joystick forward with her thumb. With a slight whine, the crafts rose up from her backpack into a hover, turned one-hundred-and-eighty degrees and then sped away up the hillside.

I watched on my HUD as Ruby controlled the WASP. It sped between the tree trunks. A small green box pulsed on the tactical map that had been reduced to a small window, showing the drone was closing in on the location of the Morse code signal.

'Thirty metres, twenty...and we're there,' Ruby said.

The view from the drone stabilised and she slowly rotated the WASP for a sweep of the area. It revealed absolutely nothing.

'Switching to thermal mode,' she said.

A false colour image appeared on my HUD with only cool blues displayed.

'OK, I'm still not seeing anyone—'

The words died on her lips as the video feed broke apart and we heard the distinct hiss of a suppressed bullet in the distance.

'Fuck, it's been ambushed!' Ruby said.

'Then we need to get out of here. This is looking like a bloody trap,' I said. 'Follow me!'

We turned to run back the way we'd come when the ground seemed to erupt with figures leaping up, their weapons aimed straight at us.

In a split second my brain registered the ghillie suits all the soldiers were wearing and the strange foil camouflaged capes draped round their shoulders.

'You all so need some training on moving stealthily,' one of the disguised figures said in what was undoubtedly Tom's voice. 'We could hear you approaching like a herd of small bloody elephants through the jungle.' He pulled off the hood of his ghillie suit to reveal his face.

Poseidon dropped his stealth field and shimmered into exis- tence behind us. Tom's soldiers turned their guns towards the floating, glowing AI micro mind.

'Stand down,' Tom ordered and his squad immediately

obeyed. His gaze swept over Poseidon. 'A successful mission, by the looks of it?'

'You could say that. We'll brief you later. But what the hell has happened here, Tom? We're guessing something to do with Lucy?'

'It's everything to do with Lucy. I'm afraid she's gone full-blown killer computer on us.'

'Jesus, just tell us that everyone is OK?' Jack said.

'Mostly, although I did lose a handful of security guards when she took over every single system in Eden. She used hacked WASP drones and Mircats to take hostages and herd people into the recreational caverns before sealing them in. Niki and I, and the security team, did what we could to slow the drones and bots down, but they quickly overpowered us. I lost a dozen people during our escape to the surface before Lucy had a chance to seal all the exits.'

'So Mike, Alice and Jodie have been taken hostage?'

He shot us a grim look. 'Unfortunately, yes.'

'Jesus, I can't believe this is happening,' Jack said.

'Well, unfortunately it is and now we need to do whatever it takes to regain control,' Tom said.

'We've got some C4 charges with us so we can blast our way into one of the sealed hangars,' I said.

'You'll get nowhere near them – Lucy has the whole area locked down with those damned WASP drones of hers.'

'Can we stop referring to the entity who is doing this as Lucy?' I asked. 'This so isn't her doing. We learnt from Poseidon that the red micro mind we recovered from Area 51 was in security mode.'

'Poseidon?' Tom asked, giving me a questioning look.

I hitched a thumb over my shoulder towards the floating micro mind. 'Our new friend there.'

'Sorry for not introducing myself sooner,' Poseidon said

through my helmet's speakers, setting them to broadcast. 'Yes, Lauren is correct. When the compromised micro mind that you've called Red merged with Lucy, the first thing it would have done was take over her subsystems. That would have been made considerably easier than normal because she had been heavily damaged. Then, in an effort to protect itself, it would have dealt with anything it viewed as an imminent threat – namely yourselves, I'm afraid.'

'Those damned Overseers have a lot to answer for,' Ruby said, shaking her head.

'We haven't tried to launch a mission yet because Red is so entirely in charge of every aspect of Eden,' Tom said. 'I knew we would end up throwing lives away without a way to shut him down.'

'But what about the C4 charges around the Cage?' I asked.

'We attempted to remotely detonate them, but they had already been taken offline,' Niki said. He looked sideways at Tom. 'If I were in charge I would have gone in already.'

'Only because your daughter is one of the hostages down there, clouding your judgement. But if we had tried that tactic without a clear way of being able to stop Red, it would have ended up being a bloodbath. And you won't be much good to her if you get yourself killed, will you?'

Niki didn't answer as he scowled back at Tom, but he didn't argue the point either.

'So you have been waiting for us to get back with the micro mind to stop Red?' Jack asked, looking between the two men.

'Yes. Although I don't know how much longer we would have waited. We had started to give up on you coming back, in all honesty. I'm so relieved to see you – in many ways.' Tom turned towards the floating micro mind. 'Poseidon, can you help us win back control of the base from Red? I certainly hope so, since I've been basing everything on the answer being yes...'

'Yes, I can assist you with that,' Poseidon replied from helmet's speaker. 'However, it is ultimately only you yourselves who can sort this out.'

'How so exactly?' I asked.

'You will have to get me into close proximity with the other micro minds, then I will be able to transport you to E8 where Lucy's core matrix is situated, Lauren. It will be up to you to talk Lucy down and get her to realise that her systems have been taken over. Do that and she should be able to regain control.'

Ruby crossed her arms. 'So let me get this right – you want us to stroll into a base that is swarming with WASPs and killer Mircats, break into a heavily fortified lab and place you next to Lucy?'

'I didn't say it would be easy, but basically, yes,' Poseidon replied.

I held up a hand to stop the torrent of abuse I knew Ruby was about to unleash on the micro mind, before turning back to Tom.

'OK, that's our plan then,' I said. 'But the real question is whether there's the equivalent of a back door we can sneak through – one that isn't on any of the schematics for Eden that Lucy and therefore Red would know about?'

Tom forehead ridged. 'There is, but you're really not going to like it.'

CHAPTER SEVENTEEN

With Tom and ten of members of his team, we picked our way very carefully over wet boulders beside a large stream. Tom had given each of us a foil-lined cloak, telling us that the quickly adapted survival blankets not only masked any thermal signature to an infrared camera but also blocked radio signals. That was why Poseidon hadn't detected them until they'd leapt up and ambushed us.

In theory, we were then invisible to the patrolling drones. But after the thirty-minute hike into the hills, my nerves were on edge from several close encounters with WASP drone patrols. Tom had insisted we remain absolutely quiet as we trekked, something I wasn't going to argue with as that was how we'd given away our position to them. But the jungle insect soundtrack was becoming so loud it was almost oppressive – and it made listening out for any hint of a motor whine getting louder distinctly harder.

In the lead, Tom paused and held his clenched fist up, the military signal for us to freeze. We were fifty metres from a small cliff into which the stream we'd been following disappeared through a mossy cave entrance. Large creepers hung down over it like a net curtain, the space beyond an inky black even to the image intensification of the night-vision system in my combat helmet.

Tom flashed his torch four times towards the entrance.

A light flashed back from the cave and Tom made a chopping forward signal with his hand. Our squad started moving again in a line.

'What is this place, Tom?' I whispered.

'A hidden store for our equipment and weapons – one of the many layers of safety measures that Niki insisted were put in place should Eden ever be taken. Of course, never in our wildest dreams did we think that would become a reality.'

I turned to Niki. 'Thank god for your overabundance of caution.'

My boots made slight ripples in the water as we entered the enveloping darkness of the cave. All I could hear for a moment was the soft gurgle of the stream, the dripping of water and the breathing of the team around me. A slightly acidic smell filled my nostrils, mixed with the scent of dank air.

Poseidon killed his stealth field and a ripple passed through the air as he uncloaked.

A dim light about fifty metres inside flared into existence, faint but bright enough to give our night-vision systems enough to make out our immediate surroundings.

At least a hundred people stood ahead of us, most dressed in security guard uniforms and all carrying weapons. With hushed whispers they walked forward to surround us, but all their attention was on Poseidon, many of the barrels pointed towards him. Trust in a micro mind was obviously running thin after the stunt that Red had just pulled.

Tom held up his hand for silence. 'As you can see, Lauren and her team have been successful and have recovered a micro mind from the Atlantis site. Thanks to them we have a real chance to retake the base.'

The tension that had been present in many of the faces faded away, replaced by a few smiles. Then everyone was stepping forward, patting out backs and shaking our hands. Despite the darkness I could see the spark of fresh hope in their eyes. These people had obviously gone through a lot and we represented their best hope to take back what had once been a safe place. I felt the huge weight of responsibility press down a little harder on my shoulders.

Tom crossed to a pile of ropes and climbing gear, beginning to sort through it.

I gave him a wary look. 'Please don't tell me we're going to need this stuff for this backdoor of yours?'

'I did say you weren't going to like to, Tom replied. 'We'll follow the stream underground to where it meets a river that powers one of our hydro plants and from there gain access to the base. Unfortunately, it's going to be a tough descent involving some very narrow passageways, and some of the cavern we will be going through will be completely submerged.'

Ruby grinned. 'Oh, I love potholing.'

'Yes, that sounds like an absolute riot,' I said in a flat tone. In the darkness I felt Jack squeeze my shoulder in an attempt at reassurance.

Poseidon's voice came through my helmet's speakers. 'And are these passageways suitable for me to traverse through?'

'I'm afraid you can't come this way with us – some of the sections are too small,' Tom replied. 'But once we've eventually regained control of Eden, we'll open one of the silo doors for you.'

I wasn't exactly thrilled at the idea of leaving Poseidon behind, but I could also see there wasn't much choice. 'Poseidon, are you good with this?'

'Yes, I can see the sense of it. I'll be waiting to help the moment the silo door opens.'

I nodded and turned to Tom. 'How come you have all this kit here? Surely you didn't have time to grab it when you escaped Eden?'

Tom shook his head and gestured towards a couple of shipping containers at the left of the cave. 'It was all in there – in this outdoor store. This is where some of the team love to pothole from, so it contained full climbing gear – along with the weapons cache as the container was already here.'

Niki gave me a toothy grin. 'Yes, we have everything we need to make this an absolute breeze.'

'Oh, I wish it was going to be as easy as you make it sound,' I replied as the seed of a plan started to grow in my mind.

Ruby shook her head. 'Just like you always do, Lauren, before we head off on an impossible mission.'

'Fair point,' I replied with a shrug.

Rocks scraped into the top of my pack as I crawled flat on my belly beneath wet limestone rock. I was following close to the heels of Ruby's boots as she wiggled like a well-oiled eel through the confined space.

'Jesus, I would have lost a few pounds if I'd known we had this ahead of us,' Jack said just behind me.

'Just as well none of us suffer from claustrophobia,' I added.

'Who says I don't,' Jack said, his tone tense.

'Oh, bloody hell, you should have said something.'

'Let's just change the subject. I'm doing my best not to think about it here.'

'Sorry, yes,' I said. Ruby's heels disappeared ahead of me as she reached the next cavern.

I shimmied out of the passageway and stood up just behind her to join the group already assembled there. I was partly blinded by the head torch that Tom had strapped to his combat helmet – he was trying conserve power until he really needed the helmet's night-vision system, as we all were – our spare batteries were limited.

'All good?' he asked.

'That depends on your definition of good,' I replied, trying to ease some of the tension out of my neck with my fingers. When the dazzle had faded from my eyes, I looked round at the large cavern. A dozen of the security team were already picking their way down a steeply sloping wet boulder field towards a sheer ledge. The noise of fast-running water echoed from somewhere far below us.

Jack crawled out from the low tunnel behind me, the body armour panels of his combat suit streaked with limestone and mud.

He stood up, his legs shaking, and sucked in a big lungful of air. 'Thank god that is over. Tom, please tell me that's the last of those damned rabbit holes we have to crawl through.'

Tom turned briefly towards us, dazzling me again with his head torch, before he realised and angled it towards the ground. 'Yes, things open out from here. We have a cliff to get down and then at least one underwater cavern to get through.'

Ruby was already halfway down the boulder field by the time Jack and I started on it. The torches of several members of the security team bounced around the cavern as they anchored ropes for the coming descent. I shifted the weight of my pack on my shoulders, feeling the friction marks after the scrabble through the often-suffocating cavern system. Even though I didn't suffer from claustrophobia like Jack did, I wasn't afraid to admit I'd been near to a panic attack a couple of times when I'd managed to get myself wedged thanks to my pack. But at least so far the descents hadn't made my head spin too much.

Jack and I both slipped several times as we traversed the boulders. Ruby must have had suckers for feet, as she had already reached the bottom of the slope and abseiled over the edge by the time we arrived.

Niki headed towards us, handing Jack and me a harness each. 'Make sure these are securely tightened. It's a long way to the bottom.'

I gave him a stiff nod as we took them from him.

I didn't know quite what my brain was thinking, but for some reason I found myself glancing over the edge – definitely a very bad idea. My abdomen clenched as I took in the cliff. It had to be at least two hundred metres down to the bottom. Just to heighten the sheer knee-trembling drop, the group who'd already descended looked like tiny ants as their torches flicked around, illuminating a flowing river behind them.

'Bloody hell, that is a ridiculously long way down,' I said.

Jack casually walked to the edge and glanced over. 'Oh, that's easy compared to what we've just done.'

But I really felt as if we were on the edge of an abyss. I found myself having to fight back the urge to vomit as we clipped on to the rope and stood at the edge.

'Race you,' Jack very unhelpfully said just before he disappeared over the edge, his barely contained "whoop" rapidly fading into the distance beneath me.

I took a last look at the rest of security team behind us as they made their way towards the top of the cliff and then made myself shove off without another thought.

The rope hissed through my hands as the cliff face shot past centimetres away from my head, my torch illuminating patches of moss that seemed to be thriving everywhere in this underground environment.

A movie moment flashed through my mind – the *Bill & Ted's Bogus Journey* scene where they plummet down a dark shaft to hell. This experience somehow felt much worse.

I glanced down to see a rocky beach, the people on it already rushing towards me. I shoved my hand out, killing my speed. And then the waiting hands grabbed on to me as I landed harder than I meant to. I had to bend my knees to absorb the impact.

'Wow, that was one seriously fast descent, show-off,' Jack said to me, his grin even wider than it had been at the top.

I just gave him the *look* as I unclipped my harness with slightly shaking hands.

Then I headed with Jack towards the beach where, watched by Tom, two of the security guards were already in the water, being swept away down the river towards a tunnel that dipped even deeper into the earth.

'This experience is starting to increasingly resemble a horror movie,' I said as we watched Ruby with the cased WASP strapped to her back, rifle clutched in her hands, disappear into the churning white water at the entrance of the tunnel.

'OK, now I'll brief you on what to expect,' Tom said, approaching us. 'Just let the river, which is fairly shallow at this point, carry you down to the bottom where it splits. Whatever you do, make sure you take the right-hand fork. You can easily climb out of the river there and it's a short walk from there to Hydro Station 5.'

'And if we take the left fork?' Jack asked.

'You'll be carried straight out over a waterfall into deep water and sucked towards the turbine blades where things will get very, very messy.'

'Best not go that way then,' I said with a shudder as I far too clearly pictured the food-blender results of a turbine blade on a human body. 'OK, let me go first, Jack, so I can get this over and done with.'

He stepped aside. 'Be my guest.'

I took several deep breaths, trying to slow down the clatter of my heart that banged away like a drum. 'Here goes nothing.' I waded out into freezing-cold water.

The current was powerful and straight away started pulling hard at my legs. Beneath the spotlight of my head torch I could see the embankment drop away into deep, slate-grey water just ahead.

I glanced back at Jack who was already wading in behind me. 'See you on the other side.'

He gave me a thumbs up as I took a half step forward and the water came up to my chest. Immediately the current grabbed hold and swept me away. I kept my head on the surface, but as I spotted the rock roof arcing down ahead of me, my stomach dropped in anticipation.

With a roar of white water, I crested the top of the slope and then I was rushing down over it, the river pummelling my body from every direction like a very bad spa experience.

Face-numbing icy spray crashed into my face as the river's roar became raw and almost primordial in the confined space of the tunnel, as if it was replicating the sound the earth made when it was born. I was continually being pulled beneath the surface, coming up and gasping for air only to be plunged beneath it again.

Rocks sped past, many smacking into me, no doubt leaving a bruise memento for the following day – if by some miracle I lived through the next thirty seconds.

I was kicking hard, fighting away my panic and keeping my head up, when I saw a junction approaching. Torches and lanterns shone from the right-hand passage, a booming alley leading away to darkness on the left.

The junction rushed towards me and I kicked hard with everything I had to force my direction. I was spat out into the calmer water of the right-hand passageway and I moved into an awkward version of the crawl to reach the others, including Ruby, who had all gathered on a rock ledge sloping out of the water.

The current began to slacken off and I felt my body sliding over jagged rock. At last my feet were able to find purchase and I stood up to find Ruby grinning at me. But her expression froze as she stared at something over my shoulder.

I turned round with a sense of dread. Sure enough, Jack was being swept past the junction, towards the left-hand tunnel, his eyes closed and head lolling to one side.

I tried to wade back to him, but Ruby grabbed on to me. 'You won't reach him because of the current. Follow me!'

She sprinted away down the right-hand tunnel. In three strides I was up on the ledge and running after her. Jack was about to get swept over the waterfall and... Bile filled my mouth at the unfinished thought.

Somehow I increased my pace and overtook Ruby, my arms pumping the air, lungs burning. I had to do whatever it took to save Jack, or I would die trying.

I hurtled out into a well-lit cavern. The river was roaring below me through a deep channel, into the spinning turbine blade at the far end. But all I had eyes for was any sign of Jack. Ice crackled through my spine. What if we were already too late? But then I saw his head, his eyes still closed as he was sucked inevitably towards the turbine.

No time to think, only time to do. I raced towards the railing that ran along the edge of the walkway carved into the rock.

'Don't, you'll be killed!' Ruby shouted from behind me.

I ignored her, pulling off my pack in one motion and leaping over it. I had a split second to tuck my arms close to my body and put my feet together to point down towards the water. I hit hard, the air exploding from my lungs, but I kicked, I fought with everything I had, and I broke the surface again.

Jack was less than five metres away from me. In three powerful strokes I'd caught up with him and hooked my arm round his chest. But the reality of the situation hit home as I tried to swim towards some rocks at the side of the channel. The current was too powerful; we were being sucked in by the spinning turbine, its blades beating the water with a rhythmic *thwacking* sound.

I hung on to the love of my life, fighting against our deaths in the impossibly powerful current. I was starting to weaken. And then an eerie calmness came over me. I held Jack tighter, preparing to give in to the inevitable...

A rope came snaking down and splashed into the water just ahead of us.

'Grab on to it!' Ruby shouted from somewhere above.

I reached out as we were swept towards the rope. If I missed...

Focus, Lauren!

Fresh determination roared through my body. I reached out and caught the rope with the tips of my fingers. It hissed through them, but I locked my hand round it. The current pivoted us hard round on the rope, pulling it taut and practically yanked my arm out of its joint as we were slammed into the rock wall. Another line dropped into the water next to me, Ruby rappelling down it to join us, quickly grabbing on to Jack.

'Tie yourself to the line and then let go, Lauren. I've got him!' she shouted over the thunderous water.

I had to force my hands to let go of Jack from my death grip.

But Ruby was as good as her word. She already had the rope round him and was nodding to the group of people who had gathered above us. Then she and Jack were being hauled up into the air.

My fingers shook in the icy water, but I managed to force them to loop the rope round my chest and somehow tie a knot.

It bit into my body as I was hauled up with short jerks. I hung there like a broken puppet, spinning in the air. But metre by metre I was pulled up until the walkway came into view. Then strong hands grabbed on to me, yanking me over the railings and on to the path. I rolled to my side to see Ruby crouched over Jack, compressing his chest.

'Come on, you bastard, don't you fucking dare!' she shouted.

Tears had started to bead my eyes when a torrent of water spewed from Jack's mouth. His chest jerked under Ruby's desperate attempts to keep him alive. Darkness pressed into my mind. If he died, I couldn't go on... Suddenly a racking cough shook his body and Ruby rolled him on to his side as he spewed up water.

A sob broke my lips, the soldier in me forgotten. I reached out and rested my trembling hand gently on his head as his shuddering coughs subsided and his eyes met mine. 'Don't you dare ever do that to me ever again, do you hear me, Jack bloody Harper?'

A feeble smile filled his face. 'Yes, ma'am.'

I pulled him into a fierce hug as Ruby and the others pulled back, watching us.

'Thank you,' I mouthed to her over Jack's shoulder.

She nodded at me, and it was only then I noticed the tears in her eyes before she turned away. Ruby might have been as hard as the rock of this cavern, but right then I knew just how much she cared about all of us. The feeling was entirely mutual.

CHAPTER EIGHTEEN

SOMEONE HANDED ME A HOT DRINK, though I had no idea where they'd got it, as Jack injected himself with a shot of adrenaline.

'What the hell happened back there, Jack?' Ruby asked as she crouched by the two of us.

'The last thing I remember is getting sucked beneath the surface for a moment and a rock catching my head beneath the rim of my helmet. The next thing I knew, you were on top of me, giving me chest compressions. You saved my life, Ruby.'

She shook her head. 'No, I just got to tie the ribbon on that particular present. The person you should be thanking is Lauren. She risked her life, diving into the water right in front of the turbine to save you. She's the real hero here.'

Jack's eyes locked on to mine. 'You risked your life for me?'

'I didn't exactly have a lot of choice in the situation,' I replied with a small smile.

'I wouldn't have hesitated if the situation was the other way around.' His gaze lingered on me.

'God, you guys are so cute together,' Ruby said, shaking her head at us. 'I would say get a room, but...' She flapped a hand at the turbine thundering with water.

That encouraged a smile from both of us. I saw Tom break away from a group he'd been talking to and headed towards us.

'We need to discuss our options to try to retake the base,' he said. 'But, Jack, I think you should sit this one out after what you've been through.'

I nodded. 'I totally agree. You should stay here, rather than head into the base with us and catch your breath after nearly drowning. I'm also worried that you may have some sort of concussion.'

But Jack was already standing and shaking his head. 'No, I'm good and besides, there is absolutely no way I'm sitting this out. I just gave myself a shot of adrenaline and now I'm wired for action.'

'And if I tried to order you?' I asked.

Jack gave me a straight look. 'Probably best we don't test that theory out for the sake of our relationship.'

I let out a mock sigh. 'You.'

'But you love me anyway, yeah?'

'Something like that.'

Normally I wouldn't put our relationship on show like this in front of the others, but in the circumstances I was beyond caring. And that was despite the eye-roll I caught Ruby giving Tom. We followed him back towards the large group assembled on the bridge over the churning turbine beneath it.

Niki was at the centre, getting people to check their weapons after the white-water ride. He saw Jack and gave him a thumbs up and a nod, though there was clear tension in his face. This was of course particularly personal for him – Jodie, his daughter, was one of the hostages. I suspected he'd tunnel through the solid rock with his bare hands to save her if he could.

Tom clapped his hands. 'Right, everyone, we need to start

talking about the next step. I have some ideas, but I'd like to hear yours first.'

Niki was the first to speak and he gestured towards the heavy rotating door locked in a closed position. 'I say we plant several C_4 charges on that and blow through it. Then we can be straight in the base and head for the hostages in the recreation area of Eden.'

But Tom was already shaking his head. 'There are a number of problems with that approach, Niki. If we just charge in there, guns blazing in a confined space, we'll present a target-rich environment for those hacked WASP drones. We'd be throwing lives away for likely little gain, plus we don't know exactly where the hostages are being held.'

'I hate to ask this, but we do know that everyone is still alive in there?' Jack said.

Many people in the group shot him shocked looks, especially Niki.

Tom held up his hands. 'I know it's upsetting, but it's a good question – one that needs to be asked. But if we look at it logically, what advantage would it give Red to take over Lucy and then through her the base, and then kill everyone? Absolutely nothing. Whereas keeping the hostages alive makes perfect sense as it gives the AI major leverage against us.'

A woman spoke up from the back of the group. 'What if they start shooting people when we get inside?'

'That's exactly what I'm worried about – we need to tread very carefully until we're in a position to save all of them,' Tom replied.

I raised my hand and Tom nodded towards me. 'In that case it sounds like our first priority is to scout out the locations of the hostages. Is there any way we can enter the base without being spotted? Air-conditioning ducts, something like that?'

'Yes, and that's part of the reason we've come to this location,'

Tom replied. He pointed up at the pipework mounted to the ceiling above us. 'There is a duct directly above that will give us access to the industrial areas of Eden. Unfortunately, we won't be able to reach the recreational areas – this duct and the ones it's connected to go nowhere near them.'

'So you're saying there's no way to reach them?' Jack asked.

'The only direct route from here is through one of the larger wiring conduits, but they are far too small for an adult to squeeze inside.'

'What about a WASP drone?' Ruby called out. 'I still have one left with me.'

Tom shook his head again. 'Great idea, except the moment Red spots it with one of his own drones, that damned AI will almost certainly be able to hack it in the same way it has all the rest. If that happens, it's likely Ruby's WASP will lead the rest of the swarm straight to us.'

'How about rigging up some sort of remote-controlled explosive device on it?' I suggested. 'The moment it looks as if its position is compromised, we can blow it.'

Tom scratched his chin. 'I can't see why that wouldn't work, although we'll need to be quick to act if it looks as if it's even vaguely in danger.'

'Oh, I'll turn it to dust long before I let that happen,' Ruby said.

'And I have another idea to increase the odds in our favour,' I said. 'Why don't we send a small assault team in through the air ducts into the industrial area? They could deliberately cause a diversion, then whilst Red is dealing with them, you can blow the door here and enter with the main assault team.'

Tom nodded. 'Now that I like the sound of; a two-pronged attack working in parallel with a reconnaissance mission to find out where the hostages are. Who did you have in mind for this reconnaissance and rescue squad?' He gave me a knowing look.

'Who do you think?' I glanced at Jack, who nodded.

'And what about me, Captain?' Ruby asked.

'Your role, at least to start with, will be to stay here and control your WASP drone. But I've no doubt you'll find a way to get directly involved in the firefight.'

'Oh, you can guarantee it,' Ruby replied with a smirk.

'Hang on,' Niki said. 'As capable as you and Jack are, I for one would be happier if it was a three-person team. You don't know what you'll be running into. And if it's a diversion you want, I think some carefully placed C4 charges will be needed. For that I'm your man.'

'Then we'll gladly have you on board, Niki – if you're OK with that, Tom?'

'I am. All right, I think we have a plan. Once we have the hostages secured, we can then move on to open up a silo and let Poseidon in to deal with Red.'

We all nodded.

His gaze swept out to everyone gathered there. 'The people trapped in Eden are depending on us. We can do this. So let's get a move on and save some lives.'

I noted the certainty that Tom put into his message and how everyone responded to it with smiles and nods. But I also knew that however good a show he was putting on for the team, he had to be worrying about the extremely low odds of us pulling this off. Everybody here knew how risky this would be. But that knowledge wouldn't stop us trying.

Just an hour ago I'd been crawling through a rock tunnel; now I'd traded it for a metal equivalent. I was shuffling through the air duct, my knees and elbows already complaining from the friction burns despite the protection of my combat suit. Jack and Niki were just behind me, with Jack probably getting a very nice view of my bum as I wiggled along in front of him.

At the rear, Niki was trailing out a wire directly plugged into his Sky Wire which was linked back to another handset Tom was currently holding in the turbine room. Tom had insisted on the physical wired link connected directly to our Sky Wire handsets so we had totally secure comms that couldn't be hacked into by Red. Since our combat helmets relied on a wireless link, we'd been forced to leave them behind.

Ruby, still back in the turbine hall, was connected via another wired tether to her WASP drone. One of the tech team had rigged up a temporary connection on it using a port that was normally used for system updates.

Theoretically, these steps would make it harder for our presence to be detected, but we were about to find that out if that theory held.

Chilled air ran over my body, coming from fans buried somewhere in the ducting system. But I was more focused on the whirs and bangs now coming from the other side of the metal over which we crawled. Just ahead of me shafts of light appeared through a vent. I pulled up the photo I'd taken of Tom's schematic of Eden and its systems to check where we were.

'OK, it looks as if we're somewhere over Factory Hall 1,' I said. 'I'm going to take a look through the vent and see what's happening down there.'

'Just try to distribute your weight either side of the vent when you get to it,' Niki said. 'Unlike what might be shown in the movies, they're really not designed to take the weight of somebody crawling over them.'

'That's just the fact I need in my head when there's a fifty-metre drop to the floor below.'

'Don't worry – I'll grab on to your ankles if you start to slip through,' Jack said.

I didn't need to look round to know he was grinning. Ignoring the idiot, I shimmied up to the vent, making sure I was putting absolutely no weight on it as I peered down.

The view I was met with made me gasp. The XA103s that had been in production when we left had been cleared to one side of the production floor. Mircats were trundling around everywhere, at least a few hundred of them – far more than we'd had when we left the base. But their numbers paled into insignificance compared to what they were helping to make with the 3D printers. WASP drones were being produced at a breakneck speed and I watched dozens of them reach the end of the production line, their LEDS initially blinking green. Then a Mircat waved a silver box device over them, their lights turned red and they took flight to join the hundreds that were already crisscrossing the air over the production floor.

'Hey, don't keep us in suspense – what are you seeing down there, Lauren?' Jack whispered.

'Sorry, let me call this in, then you guys will get to hear at the same time.' I pressed the button on my Sky Wire. 'Tom, are you there?'

'Affirmative, I'm receiving you loud and clear. Any update for us, Lauren?'

'Yes, we've just reached factory hall one and the news isn't good. It seems our psycho AI Red has been very busy. Every 3D printer seems to be in operation. and they are producing WASP units as fast as they can make them. Based on the rate of production and extrapolating from that, I wouldn't be surprised if several thousand of the WASP drones have been created since Red took charge. There are also a hell of a lot more Mircats down there than before.'

'That sounds like bad news for our chances of being able to overwhelm them,' Tom replied.

'Not necessarily – if we strike now. Is there a place nearby that we could draw those units into? We could set off a C4 explosion to draw them in, then once they arrive to investigate, we ignite a second round of explosives to take out as many units as we can.'

'You're talking about creating a kill zone,' Niki said from behind me.

'I guess I am.'

'Classic tactic,' Jack said. 'That could definitely work.'

'Tom, can you see a suitable location for a trap on your maps?' I asked.

'Hang on... Yes, I've found somewhere ideal. If you take the next right fork and head along it for another three hundred metres, there's a vent into a transformer room that powers Factory Hall 1. If you set a C4 charge on a timer there, not only will it severely curtail Red's ability to produce more hacked WASP units, there's also a structural beam supporting the roof. You can set a second timer to blow that once you've withdrawn to a safe distance and it will crush any units that have gathered in there.'

'Right then, leave that to us,' I replied. 'But before I sign off, how's Ruby getting on?'

'I'll pass the Sky Wire over so you can ask her yourself,' Tom said.

There was a clicking noise and Ruby's voice came on. 'I've done a sweep of all the labs and haven't seen anyone, Lauren. But to back up what you were just saying to Tom, I've seen a crazy amount of WASP units patrolling the corridors. Mircats too – dozens of them, all armed with assault rifles. Before you ask – no, I haven't seen lots of dead bodies strewn everywhere.'

'Oh, thank god for that,' Niki said.

'I've almost reached the first of the recreation caverns. It won't be long till we hopefully know which one they are all in.'

'As soon as you know, let us know,' I said.

'Will do,' Ruby replied.

'OK, over and out for now.'

I clipped the Sky Wire back on to my webbing belt.

'Time to go and make ourselves a wasp trap, guys,' I said over my shoulder.

'What, you brought a jam jar and some honey water?' Jack asked.

'Metaphorically, yes,' I replied.

Still being careful to spread my weight either side of the vent, I shuffled away along the ventilation ducting.

'Goddamn, you weren't kidding about the number of WASP units down there,' Jack said as he passed over the top of the vent behind me. 'How the hell are we ever going to defeat all of them?'

'That's going to be the final part of our plan. I didn't mention it to Tom since I knew he'd try to stop us as it's so risky.'

'Ahem,' Niki said from the rear. 'What makes you think that I won't stop you? I do technically outrank you as this is a base security issue.'

'Because it's our best chance of saving the lives of a lot of Tom's team.'

'Then tell me what it is?' Niki asked.

I finally gave voice to the idea that had been steadily growing in my mind since we'd left the others. 'We're going to find the off switch for this military coup to stop it quickly in its tracks, bringing forward the bit of Tom's plan where Poseidon is let in. I had a quick look at the schematics of the base before we set off and I've worked out a way to get to the launch bay. Once we reach it we're going to climb to the top and manually open the hatch with the override that Alice ordered to be fitted to the silo doors after Lucy locked them all in during our Area 51 mission. Once we've done that, we'll call in Poseidon, who we've already asked to keep an eye out for any silo door opening. He'll fly down into the silo, we gain access to the lab, he merges with the other micro minds with our help and Lucy regains control of the base before anyone else gets hurt. Bish bash bosh, and the job is a done. Retaking the base will get done twice as fast and, more importantly, this will save the lives of a lot of people in Tom's assault team.'

'Hang on, that sounds dangerously as if you've thought this through,' Jack said. 'What happened to making it up as you go along?'

'Oh, don't you worry, to coin a phrase, there are so many holes in this idea that it almost looks like Swiss cheese.'

'Now that's more like the Lauren we all know and love.'

'Speak for yourself,' Niki muttered from the back as we continued along the ventilation shaft that would eventually lead us to the transformer room.

CHAPTER NINETEEN

I LET GO of the edge of the vent and dropped down into a large room. Rows of large transformers stood before me, all quietly humming away behind a caged-off area secured with a very large and serious-looking padlock. There was a large warning sign on the cage door showing an electrical bolt striking a person, leaving anyone with little doubt of the consequences of meddling around with any of the equipment inside. But that was exactly what we were going to do.

Jack dropped down next and winced as he landed awkwardly. 'Ow, cramp.' He immediately began stretching.

Niki was last to emerge, trailing our comm line behind him from the Sky Wire handset. He headed towards the cage and tried the gate. It rattled on its lock. 'Damn it, we'll need a master key to open that.'

'You think?' I said. I dug into the bottom of my pack and withdrew my small canvas pouch.

'What have you got there?' Niki asked.

Jack was nodding and giving me an approving look. 'Your trusty lock-picking kit.'

I nodded. 'Ever since the Peru mission, I don't leave home without it.'

I opened the pouch and quickly inserted the tension wrench followed by a suitable-sized pick into the lock.

Whilst I worked, Niki moved to the edge of the room and slapped his hand against one of the steel beams that traversed the wall and ceiling.

'What are you up to, Niki?' Jack had his Glock out, standing guard by the door to the corridor.

'Just looking at these structural support beams, trying to work out how many we will need to blow to bring the ceiling down in here.'

As he continued to survey the room, I squeezed the tip of my tongue between my teeth whilst I jiggled the pick in the lock. With a satisfying snap, I felt the first pin click into place.

'How's it looking?' I asked as Niki rejoined me.

'I think about four charges should do it,' he said. 'I'll also set a charge to blow the steel lintel above the door. That'll trap Red's WASP drones and Mircats in here so they can't escape when we bring the roof down on their heads.'

'Sounds good,' I replied. The second pin clicked in the lock as the technique started to come back to me. 'We're going to have to coordinate closely with Tom on setting the timer for blowing the charges.'

'Absolutely,' Niki replied. 'We won't have much leeway either way.'

The third and fourth pins of the lock clicked into place. I was definitely on a roll.

Jack had his ear to the door and cast a glance towards me. 'How much longer, Lauren?'

'Just give me a second...' I felt the final pin dropped into place and withdrew the pick. 'I gestured to Niki. 'All yours.'

He headed over and turned the handle. I felt a surge of elation as the gate swung open.

'Very slick,' Jack said with an approving look.

'I have a lot to thank Tom for, with all that training he put me through.'

Niki nodded. 'Well, it's certainly impressive. He turned to Jack. 'Time for us to go and place those C4 charges. Better call in.'

I took the Sky Wire from him and moved to the door to take over guard duty as they headed into the caged area. 'Tom, are you there? We've reached the transformer room and the guys are setting the C4 charges, over.'

Tom's voice came straight back. 'That's excellent news. I also have an update from Ruby. She wants to talk to you, Lauren. I'm putting this handset on speakerphone as she rather has her hands full controlling her WASP.'

There was a click over the line and Ruby's voice came on. 'Captain, I've managed to locate the hostages. They're being held as we suspected in the gymnasium complex, heavily guarded by at least three hundred WASP drones and a dozen armed Mircats.'

I grimaced. 'The odds don't seem great for attempting a rescue without losing any of the hostages.'

'I agree,' Tom said. 'To make matters even trickier, we've also discovered that Alice, Mike and Jodie are being held in a separate area to the rest of the hostages.'

Niki's head snapped round from the transformer where he'd been placing the last charge. 'Where exactly are they?'

'In Alice's home,' Ruby replied. 'I managed to get my drone into the ducting vent that runs through the top of her cavern. The bad news is that Red has another thirty WASP units patrolling the grounds, no doubt to keep Alice, Mike and Jodie well away from her lab where they could cause plenty of trouble. It's a classic strategy to separate the leadership from the rest of the group so they can't get busy organising an escape attempt.'

Tom's voice cut in. 'I'm also seriously concerned that if we try to free the rest of the hostages, there is every chance Red may order the execution of Alice and the others.'

'Oh, come on, surely Red wouldn't go that far?' Jack said.

'You try telling that to the families of the security guards who were killed when that damned rogue micro mind first took over the base,' Tom said. 'Remember we're not talking about Lucy here. We have no idea just how far Red will be prepared to go to defend himself against something he views as a threat.'

'It sounds to me as if we will have to delay things slightly so my team can secure Alice and the others before we attempt anything else,' I said.

'And how do you propose to do that?' Tom asked. 'The ducting for that chamber is mounted fifty metres up in the cavern's ceiling. If you try to slip down from a vent on a rope you can be certain you'll get spotted by the patrolling WASP drones.'

Then I knew exactly what to do. The route I'd chosen to get to the silo also ran under Alice's house. But first I had to wrap a small lie around the truth of our extracurricular plan.

'About that, Tom. I was studying the schematics and think I may have found a way to reach her house,' I said. 'Of course, that will mean delaying our attack a bit. But I fear the guys really aren't going to like how I'm going to suggest we get there.'

Jack and Niki gave me very suspicious looks as they planted the last of the C4 charges.

Jack, Niki and I crawled along the sewer pipe. The smell was beyond awful and I was doing my best not to be sick in my mouth.

'You really weren't kidding when you said we wouldn't like it,' Jack muttered behind me. 'After this I'm going to smell like a latrine for a week.'

'Will you listen to yourself? Just think about all the lives we're going save.'

'I know, I know,' Jack grumbled.

'What more do we know about what we're heading into, Lauren?' Niki asked from the back.

'From what Ruby has been able to see from her WASP drone located in a vent in the roof of Alice's cavern, the drones and Mircats seem to be keeping out of the house itself. The sewer manhole cover that we'll be emerging from is right next to one of the outbuildings of Alice's house, according to the schematic. We'll have a ten-metre dash to make it into the house out of sight of those drones.'

'For a seat-of-your-pants plan, Lauren, it might be a gag-inducing one, but it's up there with some of your best,' Niki said. 'Especially as we can then carry on to the silo once we know Alice and the others are secure.'

'I just hope it goes smoothly. Although my hair might never recover – I may have to cut it all off in an effort to get clean after this.'

'I think it's inspired,' Niki went on. 'I'm so going to add crawling through sewers to the standard training programme.'

'It seems it's not just Tom who has a small streak of evil in their DNA,' Jack quipped.

Our head of security chuckled as I spotted a chink of light in front of us.

'OK, I think that's the manhole cover just ahead,' I said. 'How much time have we got left to get to the hangar after this, Niki?'

'The C4 charges are set in the transformer room for forty-one minutes from now, which should give us plenty of time to get to the silo after we've finished here.'

'That sounds doable, but we can't just leave Alice and the others,' Jack said. 'One of us is going to have to stay back to defend them when the crap hits the fan.'

'I'm happy to do that if you are both happy to complete the rest of the mission without me?' Niki suggested.

I didn't need to be able to see his face to understand his determination, I could hear it in his tone. This wasn't so much a request but a statement of fact. It wasn't a surprise – we were talking about his daughter here.

'That sounds good to me,' I replied. 'But first things first, let's check things out before we go storming in there, especially as we ran out of wire a way back and have no way of getting updates from Ruby.'

'So you want one of us to scout ahead?' Niki asked.

'Actually, I've got something less risky in mind.'

I unclipped the Sky Wire and connected the flexible optical camera - a permanent fixture in my lock-picking kit - to its USB port. Then I stood up in the small space beneath the manhole cover.

I slowly lifted one side of the metal cover, opening up a small crack and slipping the end of the camera through the gap.

Compared to the normal simulated views of the cavern's virtual walls, what I saw on my Sky Wire display was quite a serious contrast.

Stark white light flooded the large cave from the blanked screens overhead. Around the lake the ducks had huddled together into one group and were watching one of the Mircats warily as it trundled past them patrolling the grounds, a heavy machine gun clutched in its pincers. The same was true for the rest of the wildlife that Alice kept down here. The cows were keeping as far away as possible from the WASP drones buzzing overhead and there was absolutely no sign of the chickens – presumably they were taking shelter in the hen house.

I swivelled the end of the camera round towards the house. For a moment I didn't think anyone was in there. But then a shadow moved behind the kitchen window blind.

'Looks as if somebody's home,' I said.

'Any of those WASP units close enough to spot us running for the house?' Niki asked.

'Hang on, let me check,' I replied.

I slowly rotated the camera through three-hundred and sixty degrees. There were plenty of WASP drones further out, especially round the door to the lab, where I presumed Lucy and Red were.

'No, I think we're good.'

Jack was now standing next to me in the small shaft and pointed towards the camera screen. 'It's pretty obvious that Red expects any attack to come from the lab.'

'That's AI logic for you,' I replied. 'I mean, who would be stupid enough to crawl through a sewer to get in here?'

'Exactly,' Jack said with more than a hint of irony in his voice.

'OK, as the coast seems to be clear, we can—'

Jack put his fingers to his lips as a whining sound came from above us. I tensed as he unholstered his Glock, wiping off the unspeakable detritus covering it and aiming its barrel at the small gap beneath the raised manhole cover.

Niki had already unslung his Heckler & Koch MP7 submachine gun.

Millimetre by millimetre I slowly rotated the camera scope upwards, revealing a WASP drone hovering directly above the manhole. It was close enough for me to be able to see its red eyed camera rotating round in its gimlet, its short-barrelled weapon tracking exactly where it was looking.

No one said a word. I couldn't even hear anyone breathing.

Should the WASP choose to rotate its thermal vision camera downwards, despite the metal between us and it, we knew there was a good chance that it would pick up the heat signatures of three humans hiding beneath it. One false move and I would get us killed.

I pushed down the swirl of panic and breathed through my nose, trying to settle myself into a cool military focus. I couldn't allow anything to get in the way of us achieving our objective.

I attached a suppressor to my LRS and flicked the safety off. Nothing but a kill shot through the WASP's central processor would be enough to stop the drone broadcasting our position to the rest of the swarm – and more importantly relaying that information to Red. It would be a surprise attack – but I'd only do it if we had absolutely no other choice.

But my body surged with relief as the WASP's motors began to whine louder and it slid away through the air towards the corner of the house. I waited until it disappeared before letting out the long breath I'd been holding in.

'OK, get ready to move on my mark.' I did one last sweep of the immediate area with the camera and then nodded to Jack. 'Go!'

In seconds he'd carefully lifted and manoeuvred the manhole up and sideways to rest on the path. I pulled myself up first and immediately took up a kneeling position in the shadow of the outhouse I'd emerged beside, giving cover to Jack and Niki as they climbed out of the sewer.

With our backs pressed against the building, we edged towards the corner of the outhouse, weapons raised and ready.

There was less than five metres of ground between us and the railing of the porch. With a quick dash, Niki would be safely inside to guard the others. He was getting ready to sprint across when a whining came from the opposite side of the outhouse, getting louder quickly.

I pivoted on my foot, ready to take the shot as soon as the WASP emerged. But Niki had grabbed one of the silver-backed camo blankets he'd used so spectacularly when ambushing us in the jungle.

'I'll deal with it – just shoot the bastard when I give the signal,' he whispered into my ear.

'OK, do it.'

He darted to the far corner and waited like some sort of ancient gladiator in the arena, brandishing his net.

The moment the nose of the drone started to clear the building, Niki threw the blanket over it. Just like an angry wasp suddenly trapped in a jam jar, the drone's motors buzzed frantically as Niki wrestled it to the ground.

He gave me a sharp nod. 'Now!'

I aimed my LRS straight at the centre of the vibrating bundle and pulled the trigger. A bullet hole punched through the camo blanket and the whining motors stuttered to a stop. Smoke started to billow from beneath the bundle.

Niki picked the smouldering package up, raced towards the manhole and threw it down into the sewer in one fluid movement. Jack was a split second behind him. Just as flames licked upwards, he dropped the manhole cover into place, cutting off the fire. He leant down on it as a muffled bang went off in the sewer as its lithium battery let go.

I scanned the sky, ready for the attack, but nothing came for us.

I slumped into myself as relief rushed through me. We all stared at each other.

Jack raised his eyebrows at Niki. 'Taking a WASP out with a blanket, I mean, seriously? There was so much that could have gone wrong with that plan.'

But I'd already got my head around Niki's move. 'No, because it was foil backed. You knew, didn't you, Niki, that the foil would block any attempt for it to call for backup?'

'Let's just say I hoped it would work. It seems these seat-of-your-pants plans are just a little bit catching,' Niki said, suppressing a smile.

I shook my head at him, but over his shoulder I spotted two more WASP drones curving towards the house.

'Looks as if our little buddy may have been missed already. Niki, get into the house now.'

He nodded and sprinted past me, vaulted the veranda railing and disappeared through the back door. I was about to leap back down into the sewer when I heard the growing trundling sound of a Mircat from the other side of the outhouse.

In that split second I knew there would be no way both Jack and I could get back down into the drain in time.

Instead, I pointed at the porch and Jack nodded, already on the same page as me. Together we vaulted the railing just as Niki had done and hurtled through the back door into the kitchen. I quickly closed the door behind us and peered through a gap in the blind. A second later the Mircat appeared, heading towards the corner of the outhouse where we'd just taken out the WASP. Jack and I gripped our weapons, ready for wherever this was heading. The Mircat was joined by two more WASP drones looking for their vanished companion.

'Bloody hell. I thought Niki smelled bad enough,' Mike said from behind us.

We turned to see Alice and Mike staring at us from their wheelchairs. Jodie, despite the crap covering Niki, already had her arms clamped round her dad's neck in a fierce hug.

The head of security turned and stared at us. 'What happened to you two heading on to the launch bay?'

'The phrase "shit happens" springs to mind,' I said with a shrug.

Niki gave me a straight look and snorted with laugher.

CHAPTER TWENTY

ALICE STARED AT US, shaking her head. 'I mean, I hoped against hope that you might turn up, but how on earth did you manage to get past all those WASP units to get into the base?'

'It's a long story and unfortunately we're on the clock here,' I replied. 'To tell you what you need to know now: when the C4 charges that we set in the one of the transformer rooms blows in the next –' I glanced at my watch – 'thirty-eight minutes, creating a distraction, Tom will lead an assault team to rescue the hostages.'

'But, Niki, you said something about heading towards the silo?' Mike said, wheeling his chair towards us.

'That's right – but not me. I'll stay here to guard you, whilst Jack and Lauren head back via the sewer to the launch bay next to the lab.'

'And what exactly will you do when you get there?' Jodie asked.

'We're going to manually crank the launch bay open to let in a micro mind called Poseidon that we recovered from Atlantis,' Jack said.

'Now we really have to leave.' I looked at Jack. 'Niki can explain the rest.'

'Wait,' Alice said. 'Before you go, you need to see this. Jodie?'

Jodie crossed to the kitchen table and spun round a laptop screen to show us lines and lines of code. 'I'm been writing a firewall patch for the WASP drones and Mircats operating systems. If I can get close enough to one of them I'll attempt to upload the software patch, which will stop Red being able to control them. I've also designed the patch to act as a virus that will spread rapidly throughout the swarm and Mircat network using their secure communication system, allowing us to be able to regain control of the base.'

'I should have expected nothing less from you, Jodie – brilliant stuff as usual,' I said.

'Yes, she is constantly amazing,' Mike said, beaming at her.

Jodie blushed. 'The patch is very nearly there. About ten more minutes I reckon.'

'This could make the whole mission a lot easier,' I said. 'But what about capturing the first one to update it?'

'I can do that,' Niki said. 'I have another foil camo blanket in my pack that I can use to snare it.'

Jack managed a grin. 'It sounds as if this plan of ours is on much more solid ground.'

'Good luck,' Alice said. 'Our prayers are with you.'

'For all of us,' I replied.

Jack tapped on his watch. 'Time is ticking, Lauren.'

I nodded. 'OK, see you on the other side of this, people.' It took considerable effort not to add 'hopefully' to that statement as Jack and I headed for the door.

It had taken a while to crawl along the sewer and find the right manhole cover, but at last we'd made it. After having once again scouted that the coast was clear with my flexible camera scope, we emerged beneath the partly finished hull of the *Pangolin*. Tools lay abandoned everywhere, no doubt left where they'd fallen when the base had been overtaken by Red and his robotic stooges.

We emerged slowly from under the shadow of the craft and I scanned for any threat. It seemed to be clear. The door to Alice's lab containing the Cage with the micro minds was sealed tight.

But we wouldn't know for sure the micro minds were in there until we stormed the lab, guns blazing. And no doubt Red would have them guarded by a whole swarm of WASPs. But what if Red had already moved the micro minds to a different location? I didn't know what we'd do if that was the case, although it would be hard to see the AI doing that, since the lab was one of the most secure areas within Eden. All I could do was keep everything crossed and hope the universe would have our backs on this.

'I better get the C4 charges set up on a remote trigger to blow that door,' Jack said. 'If this all goes to plan we'll need rapid access into the lab before Red can summon up reinforcements – once we've taken down whatever is waiting for us.'

'Hopefully that will be a moot point, if Jodie's firewall virus works out.' I glanced up towards the closed door, high overhead in the launch silo. 'What's our ETA until the transformer charges blow?'

'About twelve minutes,' Jack replied. 'Five minutes after that, Tom will kick off the main assault when the second charge brings the roof down – hopefully on a lot of WASP and Mircat heads.'

'Whilst you're placing the C4 to blow the door into the lab, I'd better get climbing to the new manual override control at the top of the silo. I wish Jodie had installed them at ground level.'

'You can put in an official complaint the next time you see

her,' Jack said. 'You're sure you're OK doing that climb? I know you have a thing about heights.'

'It's a phobia – and phobias are things that one needs to get past.'

'All right, but only if you're sure.'

'I am, Jack, but thanks for caring.'

He flashed me a smile. 'Always.'

I handed him my MP5 submachine gun. 'Hang on to this for me.'

'Will do,' he replied as he grabbed it. Then he dug out the C4 charge that Niki had given him – along with clear instructions on exactly how to place it for maximum effect on the door.

He headed away and I placed my hands on the ladder built into the side of the silo.

OK, lean into your fear, Lauren Stelleck...

With a deep breath, I began to climb. Ten metres off the ground became twenty, and a strong sense of déjà vu flooded through me. That feeling only increased the higher I got. And then it hit me why.

I was transported back to my time at Jodrell Bank, the radio telescope facility I'd previously worked at – and specifically the night there that had changed my life for ever.

My partner in crime Steve Dexter and I were on duty when the Lovell dish had glitched out. We'd thought it was a problem with one of the axial motors, causing a power failure, so Steve and I had been forced to climb the ladder up to the top. But really we had no idea what had caused the power spike and we would later discover it was due to the dish capturing a signal containing the data for another Angelus AI called Sentinel.

Back then my legs had been like jelly during the climb, pretty much like now, but it was also getting easier the higher I got. I felt increasingly calm and focused...and that wasn't a mean feat especially since I was literally covered in shit.

Not for the first time I wondered what my old colleague Steve would say if he could see me now. Maybe he wouldn't be quite so impressed at my current state. And I wondered what had happened to Sentinel. I'd asked Lucy many times over if she'd ever heard from him, but she always said that she never had, although she'd always quickly changed the subject. That just left me even more intrigued about what the other Angelus AI was up to. Maybe, if we were forced into the nuclear option of destroying Lucy, we could find a way of making contact with Sentinel to see if he could help us. But that option was right at the bottom of my list because having to end Lucy's existence, even if it would be like unplugging a coma patient in order to be kind, would be like murdering a very real friend.

My thoughts had kept me preoccupied enough that when I glanced up again, the roof was only ten metres above me, a very pleasant surprise.

I glanced briefly down at the empty landing pad that *Ariel* should have been sitting on, a long, long way beneath me.

With a tug of vertigo, I quickly looked back towards the manual override box and the crankshaft handle sticking out of its side. To complicate matters further, because hanging on to a ladder two hundred metres above a launch pad wasn't enough, it was mounted to the silo wall on a tiny ledge about five metres from the ladder. I would so be having a word with Jodie about getting it remounted at ground level.

In any normal situation I would have clipped myself on with a carabiner, but there simply wasn't any time for health and safety.

Heart thumping, I stepped out on to the ledge, gripping the ridge of metal above it, and edged out. Instinctively my toes clawed inside my boots on the lip as I hung on with a grasp of steel. Suddenly my new-found confidence when it came to heights didn't seem quite so certain. One slip and I really would be a bloody pulp on that landing pad...

Really not helping yourself here, Lauren, I told myself.

By the time I arrived at the manual override box my mouth felt as dry as it had back in the Sahara. With the drop sucking at my heels, I reached out and grabbed the handle that sat in the three o'clock position.

OK, that's the hard part over. Although even my eyes were still clinging to the wall for imagined extra grip.

I pulled at the handle. It didn't move.

Seriously!

I tried again with the same result. I figured I needed to put more weight behind it, so with sweat dribbling down my back as I hung on to the panels of the shaft with my right hand, I reached out with my left and pulled with everything I had.

It didn't move even a millimetre.

There was only one option left. A distinct chill ran through my body despite the comparative heat of the launch silo.

My stomach dropped way past the tips of my toes as I forced myself to push off the ledge and grab the lever with my right hand too. I swung out into the air.

'Shit!' I hissed between my clenched teeth.

But with a groan and a slight shudder, the handle suddenly rotated down, and the silo roof above opened at least a centimetre.

I treaded thin air like someone drowning in the sea, but somehow managed to swing myself back and clawed my toes back on to the ledge.

It took an even bigger mental push to force myself to let go of the handle with my right hand and let it flail about for a second in a state of sheer bloody panic, before I grabbed the lip of metal and pulled myself back to the wall. If someone had told me I had kissed the metal at that point, I wouldn't have been surprised, but all I would remember later was focusing on turning the freed crank handle as quickly as I could.

The silo roof began to slide back, though its progress was so slow it was worse than watching paint dry. Gradually, a thin slit of star-filled sky started to appear. But then everything seemed to go wrong at once.

A shout came from Jack far below me, followed by the unmistakable blast of a shotgun being fired. Even more worryingly, I heard the staccato bark of return shots.

Tracer fire lanced across the bottom of the launch bay, coming from the direction of the door to Alice's lab. I fumbled for my LRS as the firefight intensified, orange glows lighting the landing pad below. A WASP drone unit appeared at the bottom of the shaft and its red-eye camera swivelled up straight towards me.

I aimed and fired, but my bullet only sparked off the ground as the drone's wings rotated into a vertical position. The WASP rose fast upwards and a muzzle flash came from its barrel.

I let go of the crank and managed to throw myself to the side as the bullet ricocheted off the section of wall where my head had been a split second before.

I took a steadying breath, centring myself, ignoring the adrenaline that was coursing through my body. I breathed out, aimed straight at the WASP's body and fired.

My bullet sliced straight through the drone, knocking it sideways. A flash came from its own weapon again and the bullet smashed into the manual override box, tearing a hole through it with a piercing sound.

The WASP spiralled down, its engines dead. But before it hit the ground, a massive bang and a flash of white light came from the bottom of the landing bay. As the WASP smashed into the floor with a distant crump, I realised the gunfire below had stopped.

My heart clenched. 'Jack!' I called out before I could stop myself.

But the image that had threatened to take hold of my imagination was swept away as the big guy himself staggered into view from the direction of the *Pangolin*, blood dripping from a cut in his shoulder, but very much alive.

'Oh, thank god you're OK, but what happened?' I called down to him.

'I got surprised when the lab door opened and a WASP came charging through. I'd just managed to take it out when its buddies followed. I had no choice but to blow the charge I'd just set round the door. I took shelter in the *Armadillo* whilst the blast wave hit and took out the drones – and three Mircats in the lab.'

'What about Lucy?'

'From what I can see, she's still in one piece. But she's glowing like a supercharged ruby, so I'd say Red is still very much in charge of their merged micro minds. Anyway, you need to get that silo door open so Poseidon can get down here fast. You can guarantee Red has more reinforcements on the way.'

'Working on it,' I replied.

I reached out and grabbed hold of the crank handle once more but saw its mangled gears where the armoured bullet had punched through it. Sure enough, when I tried to move the handle, it was jammed solid.

'Shit, it's broken, Jack.'

He placed his hands on the top of his head. 'Oh Jesus, what are we going to do now?'

My mind whirled, desperate for an answer. 'Hey, have you got any more C4 left on you?'

'No, that was the last of it.'

Panic started to run laps around my stomach, but I couldn't afford the luxury of losing it. Too many people depended on us thinking our way out of this problem.

Jack tilted his face towards me, his eyes wide. 'We need to contact Troy on-board *Ariel* and ask him to use her miniguns to slice a hole in the silo door big enough for Poseidon to get through.'

'And how are we going to do that when the radio is...' I trailed off as a thought struck me. 'We could use Morse code like Tom did to contact us from the ground.'

'Great idea. Have you got a flashlight on you?'

'Yes, it should be on my belt.' I felt along, located the pouch and took the torch out.

'Good. Now set it to its highest setting. I'll talk you through exactly what you need to do to send Troy that message. Just pray he's keeping an eye on *Ariel*'s sensors.'

'Something tells me he'll be doing exactly that.'

The walls suddenly shook as I heard a distant explosion rumbling somewhere in the base.

'That's phase one of our plan kicking in with the transformer being taken out to draw those WASP units into the room,' Jack said as he looked as his watch.

I nodded. 'OK, that will split Red's attention for a while. Here's hoping that second charge takes out as many of those little flying buggers and Mircats as possible.'

'It also means we have less than five minutes before Tom launches his main assault,' Jack said. 'We need to shift our butts.'

'On it.' I aimed the torch towards the gap in the roof. I tried an exploratory burst of light and a beam lanced out like a spotlight into the sky. I just prayed it was powerful enough to be spotted by a UFO hovering at a considerable altitude.

'It's working, Jack,' I called down.

'OK, now do the dots and dashes exactly as I tell you and we'll just have to pray that Troy spots it before Red's reinforcements get here to end our party.'

CHAPTER TWENTY-ONE

I PRESSED the final Morse code dash on the torch's button that Jack had been calling up to me.

For a minute there was nothing, but then my heart lifted as a single light blinked back at me from high overhead.

'Well, something up there just responded,' I shouted down to Jack. 'We'll soon know if it's Troy or not.'

'Keeping everything crossed down here,' Jack replied.

Whoever it was fired off a series of dashes and dots back at me that I quickly relayed to Jack.

'Get back down here fast!' Jack shouted. 'Troy's coming in hot and fully stealthed-up with Poseidon in tow – there are hundreds of WASP units pouring in on your position. The moment he makes the shot and takes out the roof he's going to give away his position. It's quickly going to get interesting up there.'

'Got it,' I replied. I was climbing back down the ladder when a whining sound seemed to come from every direction at once in the jungle above.

Like a scene out of a horror movie, red camera eyes appeared at the slit of the door and a split second later the firing started.

In a hailstorm of bullets, sparks flew off the metalwork all around me.

'Lauren, get the hell out of there!' Jack shouted.

I still had a good fifty metres to climb down the ladder, but I pushed my fear away, grabbed hold of the sides of the ladder with my feet and hands, and slid down. The heat in my hands built rapidly, despite my gloves, and my palms started to burn as tracer fire blurred past me.

I hit the ground hard, but absorbed the impact like a parachute landing, rolling away before the drones could get a lock on me. Jack did his best to return fire with my Heckler & Koch MP5.

A massive explosion came from the roof as it crumpled inwards. A deafening shockwave roared down the shaft, crashing into the ground and expanding sideways to fill the hangar. It threw Jack and me through the air. Winded and lungs burning, my ears numbed to silence, I crawled with Jack into the cover of the *Pangolin* as twisted pieces of burning metal rained down on us, clanging on to the hull of the half-constructed ship.

I swallowed hard to pop my ears from the pressure wave and gradually the roar of battle grew louder again as my hearing began to return.

WASP units criss-crossed the air in the ragged hole above us where the silo door had been a moment before, but a chain gun rattle quickly shredded them to pieces.

Jack tossed me back my MP5 as he slipped his Benelli shotgun off his shoulder.

'We've got to get to the lab!' I shouted over my lingering deafness.

He nodded, wiping the blood from his ears. Every muscle in my body aching, we clambered out from beneath the belly of the

Pangolin, dodging the WASP units crashing down around us like meteors.

The broken doorway that had been taken out by the C4 charge lay on the floor to one side. Wreckage of more WASPs and Mircats was scattered everywhere. We sprinted into the lab. The sight that met us was chaotic. Benches and equipment had been thrown everywhere by the blast. One of the few things that still seemed to be working was the bank of monitors, currently showing feeds from security cameras around the base. But I barely registered any of that because my attention was drawn to the middle of the room.

Much to my relief, the fused micro minds were sitting within the Cage, the glass walls of which were cracked but incredibly had held. However, the last time I'd seen the crystal structure, there'd still been blue swirls rippling through the ruby. Not any more. Now there wasn't a hint of anything other than a deep, dark blood colour. My heart clenched in my chest. Did that mean Lucy was completely lost?

Jack headed over to inspect the C4 charges that had been set up around the Cage. 'These still look intact, but I'll have to connect new timers to them.'

'Do it, but blowing them is still an absolute last resort.'

'I agree, but we may have no choice if things don't work out how we hope when Poseidon merges with them.'

My attention snagged on one of the monitors' displays. They all had the same feed from a camera pointing at the transformer room where we'd set the trap. One of the transformers in the middle of the room was little more than a pile of jagged metal that billowed smoke. On the next camera view at least a hundred WASPs and a dozen Mircat units were crowding down the approaching corridor and rushing into the room to examine the chaos.

'Now keep your fingers crossed the next part of our plan

works out,' Jack said as he looked at his watch. 'Five, four, three, two, one...'

A flash of white light lit up the monitors. There was a brief glimpse of the ceiling collapsing in on top of the drones and Mircats. A split second later a boom vibrated around us.

I allowed myself a brief smile. 'At least that part of the plan has come together.'

'And hopefully the next phase will too with Tom kicking off the main assault,' Jack said. He glanced at his watch. 'In three, two, one...'

Another distant rumble came and this time my smile was a grin. 'Brilliant. Now if Poseidon can do his bit then we'll be able to say this ended up being a better day than maybe any of us had been expecting.'

The phrase 'me and my big mouth' was the next thing to spring to mind.

A pulse of light blazed from the launch silo, followed by a volley of rounds ricocheting off one of the landing pads. Then barrelling through the door came Poseidon, pursued by two WASP drones.

I opened fire with my MP5, shredding the drone on the right with a gunslinger's instinct.

Jack was almost as fast, blasting two cartridges from his Benelli that hit the other WASP, sending it cartwheeling into the Cage and leaving another large crack in the glass before it crumpled to the floor.

'Cover the door, Jack,' I said as I raced to the Cage door and yanked it open. 'Poseidon, we're on the clock here. You need to get inside and do your stuff.'

The speakers around us crackled and Poseidon's voice filled the lab. 'Understood. I will begin my attempt now, Lauren.'

A gentle shimmer of white light passed through his blue exterior as he started to glide towards the open door of the Cage.

Any hope that we were on the verge of ending this died when Red suddenly rose from the floor into a hover, bursts of plasma arcing out from him and into Poseidon. It seemed he wasn't going to take this lying down – but neither was the AI in our corner.

Lightning bolts lanced out of Poseidon and straight into Red. As both micro minds exchanged blasts of raw energy, static washed over my skin and a smell of burning filled the air.

I clenched my hands into fists.

'Lauren, oh Jesus, look!' Jack shouted, gesturing towards the monitors.

I turned to see the security camera feeds had switched to one of the main wide corridors that led to the gym complex, presumably being controlled by Red. Hundreds of WASP units had engaged Tom's forces in a firefight so intense that the security guards were pinned down behind support pillars as they exchanged fire. Then the view changed again to another bank of cameras.

It took me a moment to register what I was looking at before I recognised it. It was the main lab area directly above our heads. Hundreds more WASP units were flying towards the shaft of Alice's lift office that stood in the middle.

My blood chilled as I heard the whine of motors getting louder fast from the bottom of the shaft where Alice's office had been lowered into the lab.

They were coming for us.

Sure enough, gunfire started to rip through the office's ceiling as the descending army of WASPs opened fire, dropping down the lift shaft towards it.

Jack shook out all the grenades from his bag, spare cartridges and magazines too, piling them up next to us in our position behind one of the overturned lab benches. 'Lauren, we've got to seriously think about destroying Red.'

'But that will mean taking out Lucy too!'

'And she would be the first to tell you that you should sacrifice her for the greater good. We can fall back with Poseidon to fight again another day.'

'But all those hostages – Mike, Alice, Jodie, and every single person in Eden. If we escape, they all die.'

Jack held my gaze and nodded. 'Right there is one of the many reasons why I love you so damned much. OK, we'll try to hold them off until the last moment in the hope that Poseidon can still defeat Red. But if he can't, we won't have any other choice, Lauren.'

'Although I hate it with every fibre of my being, you're right.'

Jack nodded, kissed my forehead and jumped up to trail a detonator wire to the C4 charges mounted around the Cage. We'd both be killed in such close proximity to the blast, but it was a price worth paying if it meant saving everyone else across the base.

I reloaded my MP5 and stacked my spare magazines ready for use for my LRS.

As hundreds of points of light started to pepper the metal ceiling of Alice's office, we used the lull before the final battle to add some rubble and chairs to our impromptu barricade.

But then, with a groan, the office ceiling collapsed in a shower of debris. With a whine of motors, the first wave of WASPs swept through the opening into the office. Their bullets began shredding the office door and it didn't so much open as disintegrate before us.

Then these deadly drones were upon us.

My body was humming with adrenaline as Jack and I took turns to blast the drones as quickly as they emerged from the office. Pure reaction and muscle memory were driving me in a desperate attempt to survive. Our bullets poured into the machines as they emerged from the door, turning the lab into a kill zone.

I managed a quick glance towards the Cage. Poseidon was slowly edging forward towards Red. My mouth tanged with bile when I saw that little bursts of red light had started to appear over him too. Was the battle between the AIs already starting to swing in Red's favour? It wasn't surprising, I guessed – he had the processing power of three micro minds to Poseidon's one. But that was his fight and this was ours.

My attention snapped back as Jack took out two drones with a single blast of his shotgun.

I grabbed hold of one of his fragmentation grenades. 'Do you mind?'

'Go for it,' he replied.

I pulled the pin and wound my arm back as if I was going for a baseball throw. I launched it with all my might, straight through the shattered doorway into the office.

We both ducked down behind our barricade as an explosion ripped through the office and shrapnel peppered the lab around us. I grabbed the opportunity to slam a fresh magazine into my MP5 as Jack reloaded too.

We peeked together over the barricade to see flames and smoke filling the office, but more importantly the shattered remains of dozens of WASP units lying everywhere.

'You should be playing in Eden's baseball league with those pitching skills,' Jack said with a grin.

'Who'd have thought?' I spared a glance at the monitors to see another wave of drones pouring into the lift shaft above Alice's office. The odds for us living through this were rapidly shifting from bad to impossible.

'There's a second wave coming, Jack!'

He grimaced. 'I thought as much.'

We both trained our weapons on the doorway.

This time Red seemed to have learnt from his previous tactical mistake. Rather than sending his drones rushing for the door, as they dropped into the office through the shattered roof he held them back and let their weapons shred the office walls apart. There'd be no kill zone this time around.

Jack glanced at me and I understood that look. We were about to be overrun and we both knew what we had to do. Without saying a word, he grabbed hold of the detonator for the C4.

'Poseidon, we've lost this. Get the hell out of here!' I shouted.

A howl of static burst from the speakers. 'I'm sorry, but I can't, Lauren – I'm trapped. You have no choice but to blow the charges with me in here.'

Tears instantly filled my eyes. No more Lucy, no more Poseidon. Our best chance to save the world would be lost.

Jack looked at me with such compassion and understanding in his eyes that I felt the fear that had been swirling up inside me start to subside. I drew on his strength. I would and could do this.

Sections of the office wall began to collapse as the drones continued to cut multiple exits out.

I flinched as we squeezed the C4 trigger together.

Nothing, not so much as a whiff of smoke, came from the charges set around the Cage.

The speakers crackled and a man's hollow laugh echoed round the room. 'You should have realised that the first thing I would have had my drones disable was your ability to destroy me.'

Red, it had to be him.

Jack stared at me, disbelief filling his eyes.

'We go down fighting then, Jack,' I said.

He nodded. 'To quote that *Blade Runner* movie you so love, it's "time to die".'

The surge of love I felt for my blond Viking was off the scale. But we had no time to do anything other than level our weapons towards the office wall that was collapsing.

And then I heard the unmistakable sound of a door tube grinding open behind us. I spun round to see the one that led to Alice's cavern opening.

'Fuck, Red's bringing the WASPs and Mircats from Alice's cavern!' I shouted.

'Shit, a dammed pincer movement!'

Exactly as I feared, the door finished revolving open and at least thirty WASPs poured out of it. I was getting ready to take out the one at the front of the pack when I realised they didn't have red lights but green.

Green? Green!

I batted down the shotgun that Jack was raising towards the WASPs rushing at us from the cavern.

'Friendlies!' I called out as the green-eyed drones hurtled over us like the battle crazy swarm that they were. Not only did Ruby appear from the doorway with a WASP controller in her hand, soaking wet, but Mike emerged too, not in a wheelchair but walking on his carbon fibre leg as if he'd been doing it all his life. It wasn't the only new thing about him – the guy was carrying Niki's MP7 and spraying bullets, Rambo-style, towards the enemy drones.

With small detonations, red-eyed WASP after WASP tumbled out of the air. Ruby's control was incredible; the ally drones danced about, completely outmanoeuvring the enemy controlled ones as they flew in deliberately close to them. Each time they buzzed past, their red lights turned to green to join Ruby's ever-increasing swarm.

Mike reached us first, running on his prosthetic leg. He ducked into the cover of the lab table, Ruby following seconds later.

'Bloody hell, Mike, look at you!' I said.

'Yeah, seems like I take to things like a duck to water when you shove a submachine gun in my hand.'

'I meant you wearing the prosthetic leg.'

He grinned at me. 'Oh that. Needs must, but I have to say it's damned great. I really don't know what I was so screwed about before.'

I nodded as the hostile fire fell away. Niki appeared, shielding Alice right behind him.

'I told you to stay back until the coast was clear,' Niki said, glowering back at her.

'I'm not hiding myself away when my people are in danger,' she replied. It was exactly the reaction I would have expected from her.

Ruby had been squinting at the control panel of her WASP controller unit, but suddenly punched the air and whooped. 'Take that, you little bastard!'

A thud came from behind us as a red-eyed drone smashed into the wall, its body peppered with bullets.

She gave us a thumbs up. 'And just like that we have control of the immediate area.'

'But what about the hostages?' Alice said.

'On it,' Ruby replied. She flicked a couple of controls and the green-eyed swarm fell into a line formation, speeding through the hole in the office roof and away up the shaft.

Things had swung in our favour, but I knew this was far from over.

I was immediately on my feet and heading towards the Cage. My heart clenched as I saw that the blue light in Poseidon's micro mind had seriously dimmed, giving way to the tide of red surging through it. And if he lost, everything we'd just gained would be a temporary respite in this battle.

I bashed my hands on the glass walls. 'Poseidon, can you hear me?'

'Yes, but I'm barely hanging on,' he replied through the lab's speakers. 'Whatever I try, I can't get through to Lucy.'

I grabbed the Empyrean Key from my bag.

Jack stared at me as I returned to the Cage. 'Hey, what are you going to do?'

'Whatever it takes to save Lucy and Poseidon – and this whole damned world of ours.'

I struck the tuning fork and held it close to my ear. As the icons flickered into existence I was already selecting the star symbol for E8 with the Empyrean Key. I flicked my wrist forward and just like that, the lab and the others vanished around me.

CHAPTER TWENTY-TWO

As the light of the lab faded, I found myself standing alone in a cobbled square that was familiar. I took in the ornate stone buildings and numerous spires, not to mention the imposing domed Radcliffe Camera building, and I knew exactly where I'd been transported to in E8. Oxford, the place I'd grown up under the guardianship of my real Aunt Lucy.

But this was unlike any version of Oxford I'd seen before, even here in E8. An oppressing darkness was closing in and rather than sky there seemed to be a dome of black held back only by a shimmering boundary of energy. Beyond it, shadows swirled, and occasionally I could see dark dots moving through it like flocks of distant crows.

If that wasn't a big enough transformation of the city, thick snow lay on the ground and an icy chill was already sucking the heat from my body.

My thoughts whirled as I tried to make sense of what I was seeing. Was this some sort of manifestation of the battle between the micro minds playing out in this higher dimension?

'Hello, is anyone there?' I called, my breath steaming in the freezing air.

No response came, just the sound of the wind moaning between the buildings.

Whatever this was, something was definitely off in this altered version of Oxford. If Lucy was still alive - and my being in this city suggested she might be - on previous visits she had recreated my aunt's rooms in Christ Church College. But I wasn't there now.

I cut across the square into a narrow street that would lead me out on to the main road.

The wind's touch was bitterly cold on my skin, making me long for a thick ski jacket instead of my combat uniform with its anti-wicking fabric.

I reached the high street and headed along it.

The road was deserted, not a car to be seen in what would have been a bustling street back in the real world. But that wasn't the only thing that was different. Many of the shop windows were broken and others had been boarded up. Some of the roofs of the tall buildings had sagged inwards. The entire front of a four-storey building had collapsed to a pile of rubble. It was like an earthquake had hit the city...no, more than that – like a huge amount of time had passed and the city around me had decayed. Could this be a glimpse of the city I loved so much in the future?

The chill wasn't just in my body but in my mind now, too. If this was Red's attempt to deliberately freak me out, then he was doing a very good job of it.

I had to drive my feet through the snow drifts that were piled up against the edges of the buildings and spilling into the middle of the road, turning hard stone edges into a soft rolling landscape.

Sticking to the middle of the road, I reached the junction where the Carfax Tower stood, a real favourite with the tourists thanks to its views of the dreamy spires around it. But without its lifeblood of tourists it only added to feeling of desolation.

I turned down the street of St Aldate's, which would take me directly towards the college.

The same frozen decay was here too – even a double-decker bus lay on its side, its rusted frozen body sticking out of the snow like the bones of a dinosaur skeleton.

By the time I finally reached the gates to the college I was completely weirded out. A hell version of Machu Picchu that Red had created for Cristina had made some sense, at least considering she'd been cut up with grief about the loss of her husband and child. But what was this version of Oxford for me?

I headed through the college gates as the wind began to strengthen, driving flurries of snow into my face.

The trees of the college park were stark twisted stumps, the pristine lawns buried under a thick blanket of snow. No doubt the River Thames that ran past the bottom of the grounds would be frozen solid too. For a simulation, I was finding this alternative version of Oxford increasingly disturbing.

But then my heart leapt when I saw a hooded woman standing at the college entrance, staring at me.

'Lucy, is that you?' I called out.

The figure turned and ran into the college.

'No, stop! It's me, Lauren!'

I began to run after the woman, but she'd already disappeared into the quad beyond. Suddenly the wind strengthened and I was stumbling through a blizzard so intense I could barely see the ground, let alone the college buildings around me.

With driving strides, I started up the steps towards the archway entrance that was just visible through the flakes smacking into my face. I staggered through it and into the quad where the walls at least gave me some shelter from the snarling wind.

A trail of footprints led across the quad at an angle – not towards the door to the stairwell that led up to Lucy's rooms, but peeling left in the direction of the cathedral within the college.

But why would Lucy go there?

I headed through the snow, tracing the footprints that were rapidly disappearing in the blizzard. I reached the heavy oak door covered in a large, tree-like pattern and with black iron scrolled hinges, crusted with ice.

I opened the door. I had plenty of memories of the cathedral, even attending Christmas carol concerts here with Aunt Lucy back in my old life. But the vaulted space before me was almost pitch-dark now, the only faint illumination provided by the low storm light coming through the stained glass windows.

'Lucy, are you in here?' I called out as I walked down the aisle.

A slight scuffling noise came from somewhere near the altar.

'Oh, thank god you're here. Are you OK?'

The only answer was the howl of the blizzard outside.

I passed between the rake-backed wooden seats where the choir would normally sit, hymn books scattered everywhere.

'Please talk to me.'

Again nothing.

I was just about to approach the altar when a shadow caught the corner of my eye. I began to pivot as a person hurtled towards me, instinctively bringing my arms up in a defensive cross to protect my head as they swiped something down on it. A heavy candlestick slammed into my forearm and I felt one of the bones splinter, sending a sickening shudder through my body.

Despite the explosion of pain, I dropped down and kicked upwards, my foot hitting the figure hard in the solar plexus. They crumpled to the floor as I sprang up. Nursing my injured arm, I reached for my LRS but found it missing. If Red was responsible for this sim, it seemed he didn't want to give me any sort of advantage in this fight.

As the figure turned their face towards me, I finally processed who my attacker was, taking in the hard eyes framed by dark hair.

'Cristina, stop this!' I said as she clambered back to her feet.

She swept the hair out of her eyes. 'And let you kill me in this hellhole? I suppose this is your idea of payback, Lauren Stelleck.'

I held up my hands, trying to placate her. 'I promise none of this is anything to do with me. But it does have everything to do with the micro mind that Alvarez and his people were torturing.'

Cristina glared at me. 'That thing was an alien device sent to our planet to destroy it – like the one your people stole from Choquequirao. Alvarez told me about how you've been collaborating with these aliens to take over our world.'

If my arm hadn't been throbbing like hell I would have put hands on my hips in a stance of pure indignation. 'That is so back to front it isn't funny, Cristina. It's almost as big a lie as the one he told you about us murdering Gabriel and your baby boy.' The tactical side of my brain had obviously shut down. That was exactly the wrong thing to say in this situation.

'Liar!' Cristina snarled. She rushed towards me, swinging the candlestick towards my head to finish what she'd started.

Even with an injured arm I didn't miss a beat, spinning round on my left foot as I dropped low, taking Cristina's legs out with my sweeping right foot.

She crashed to the floor, the candlestick skittering across the floor.

Ignoring the pain rattling through me, I leapt on top of her, using my knees to pin her down by her shoulders.

Cristina struggled and screamed beneath me, but I just let her exhaust herself, just as Niki had once done with me during an unarmed combat training session.

Eventually, after a good couple of minutes of her panting hard, her struggling subsided and she glared up at me.

'God, I hate you so much, bitch!' she hissed.

I groaned. 'Will you bloody listen to me? Alvarez lied to you.'

In answer, Cristina spat straight into my face. It took every fibre of self-control not to smack her hard across the cheek with my good arm.

Instead I glowered at her. 'Stop this now! Do you see me trying to cave your skull in with a damned candlestick?'

For the first time I registered doubt behind her eyes.

'Why should I believe you?' Cristina asked, baring her teeth.

'Because it's the truth,' a man's voice replied before I could.

A pulse of light came from behind me and I turned to see Poseidon standing there dressed in the robes of an ancient god, definitely a chilly option considering the near Arctic temperature outside.

'And who the hell are you – a reject from a frat party?' Cristina said.

That was rewarded with a slightly bewildered look from our resident god. 'No, I'm another micro mind. My given human name is Poseidon. And as I speak to you with part of my consciousness, the larger part of my mind is trying to stop one of my brothers, who you have had dealings with, from destroying the micro mind that Lauren knows as Lucy.'

'And why should I care about that?' Cristina asked, glaring at Poseidon.

'Because, Cristina Garcia, I have inspected Lucy's data records and they show you helped facilitate this dire situation by working for Colonel Alvarez to help him torture my brother, twisting his mind.'

'But the colonel is trying to save the world,' Cristina protested. 'It's all of you who are trying to destroy it.'

'That is an outright lie you have been fed by Alvarez. He has manipulated you.' Poseidon spoke with a bit of reverb, making him sound extra godly.

'Yeah right,' she said.

'Will you bloody listen to yourself?' I said. 'Just step back and try to look at this objectively. Who was it that abducted you in the first place?'

'That bastard Miguel Villca, the police commander. But as Alvarez told me, that was done to protect me. And then you, bitch, turned up and murdered my family. Let me up and I'll claw your fucking eyes out!' she screamed, spittle forming on her lips.

'That version of events is a complete fabrication and I can prove it,' Poseidon said, his voice back to a more normal human tone.

We both turned to stare at him.

'How?' I asked.

'Because Lucy was actively investigating what really happened before she crashed. She uncovered the police report that listed you as missing, Cristina. And then she found this.'

A portal appeared in the air. Through it we could see a police officer interviewing a woman sitting at a desk in a small room.

'This is security camera footage from the police interview with Cristina's neighbour, Alessa Huaman.'

Cristina looked at the image with wider eyes. 'Yes, that's her, but how are you doing this? It looks as if I could actually step into that room.'

'Knowing micro minds and how they manipulate reality in E8, you probably could,' I said.

She ignored me, her attention only on what was happening in the interview room.

The young policeman leaned across the table, his hands together. 'Are you sure you don't know the whereabouts of Cristina Garcia?'

'As I keep saying, her husband Gabriel was telling everyone that your damned boss, Villca, abducted her.'

The officer scribbled something on his pad and nodded. 'And what about the whereabouts of Gabriel and the baby boy?'

'He told me he was taking his son somewhere that the chief of police and the people that he was really working for wouldn't find them.'

'And would you happen to know where that might be?'

'As if I'd tell you with the amount of corruption going on around here. The important thing is they're safe and well. That's all you need to know.'

Cristina's eyes widened as a small gasp escaped her mouth.

'I see...and what about the Westerners who were seen in their apartment?'

'They did what the police should have done – they tried to track Cristina down and rescue her.'

I felt Cristina go limp beneath my knees as the portal vanished.

'This isn't a lie or some sort of trick?' she whispered, looking up at me. 'You're trying to tell me that my beautiful husband and son are alive?'

I nodded. And just like that tears filled her eyes, making my frustration with her ebb away. 'I promise you this is no trick. I for one couldn't be happier for you.'

She began to sob. I clambered off her and pulled her into a hug. 'Whatever it takes, we'll make sure you are reunited with your family. That's a promise.'

Cristina lifted her head and nodded. I felt the wetness of her tears that had already soaked through the shoulder of my combat jacket.

'I hate to rush you, but to make that happen, we need to stop Lucy being taken over by my brother. Her defences are failing as we speak and she's not the only one. I'm battling him with the bulk of my processing power, but it's just a matter of time before I too am overwhelmed. You need to go to Lucy before it's too late, Lauren.'

I pulled away from Cristina. 'Sorry, duty calls. You stay here.'

Her expression cleared as she shook her head. 'No, I'm coming with you. I'm going to do whatever it takes to make this right. I can't believe I let that bastard Alvarez manipulate me to the point that I believed his lies.'

'He's a devious son of a bitch so I wouldn't beat yourself up too much. But any help in this mad situation would be much appreciated.'

'You've got it...' She gestured to my arm. 'And I'm really sorry about that.'

I shrugged. 'As Jack would say if he were here right now, crap happens. It's what you do next that matters.'

Cristina gave me a small smile and nodded. It was like a switch had been thrown, all the tension between us evaporated.

I got back to my feet, being careful with my arm. 'OK, Poseidon, let's go and...' My words trailed away as I turned back to see he had started to disappear.

His eyes clung to mine as his face twisted in agony. 'Sorry, my systems are being overwhelmed. You must hurry—' His voice cut off as he flickered away to nothing.

Cristina stared at the spot where he'd been standing. 'What the hell do we do now?'

I turned to her. 'We need to find Lucy and fast. I have a very good idea of where to look.'

She nodded and together we set off at a run to the door, every step sending a pulse of agony through my shattered arm.

CHAPTER TWENTY-THREE

CRISTINA and I climbed the old staircase towards Aunt Lucy's apartment. Knowing some sort of consciousness had gone to the effort of recreating this twisted dystopian version of Oxford, logic suggested that at least an element of Lucy still existed somewhere this simulation. And what better place to look than in her rooms, where I'd first encountered the AI.

As we reached the door that led to her rooms, I stopped. 'OK, now we've no idea what we're heading into here. It could be extremely dangerous.'

'And?' Cristina asked.

'So you don't have to come with me.'

Cristina shook her head. 'Oh, but I do, Lauren.' She gestured through the window towards energy dome that seemed to be hold the swirling darkness beyond it at bay. 'I'm pretty sure a lot of this is down to me. And I need to try to put as much of this right as I can, if only so I can live with myself afterwards.'

'I understand, but only if you're really sure?'

'I have never been more certain of anything,' Christina replied with a sharp nod.

A wave of relief passed through me. At least I wouldn't be facing whatever this was alone.

'Then let's do this.' I placed my hand on the door handle and opened it.

We entered Lucy's study to find it covered in a thick layer of dust. Frost-covered spiderwebs had turned the furniture into woven works of silk art. Chairs and bookshelves had been knocked over, their contents scattered everywhere. Several of the window panes were broken and wind moaned through the gaps, rustling the ragged curtains that were crusted with a fine layer of glittering ice.

My eyes travelled to the desk. A framed photo of a younger me and my aunt had been swept off, lying shattered on the floor. I made the softest *oh* sound from deep in my chest, like someone who had returned home to find it ransacked by a burglar.

Cristina's hand was on my shoulder, squeezing it gently. 'This place means a lot to you?'

'It means everything to me,' I replied. 'This is where I grew up with my real Aunt Lucy after my parents died. The micro mind modelled herself on the person who stood by me through everything. And that AI version of Lucy has become a real friend.'

'Then let's do everything we can to save her,' Cristina said.

As my eyes adjusted to the faint light, I could see a slight blue luminance coming from the ajar bedroom door.

'Lucy?' I called out.

But as I'd half expected, there was no response. I took a deep breath as we headed towards the door, steeling myself for whatever was inside.

My heart lifted when we entered the bedroom and saw Lucy lying on her bed, her eyes closed. But then I realised her lips were blue, her eyelashes crusted with ice like the curtains. On a maybe more positive note, the faint light we'd seen from the other room was emanating from her body in a blue aura.

A hundred emotions crowded my mind as I rushed to Lucy and tried to pull her to me. But her body was as unyielding as rock.

Tears filled my eyes. 'Lucy, wake up! It's Lauren.'

No sharp intake of breath; no gaze snapping open for her to look at me. No look of recognition with the words, 'What took you so long?'

Cristina gazed down at Lucy, her expression puzzled. 'This is like that tale of Sleeping Beauty.'

I smeared my tears away with my injured arm. 'If only this was as easy as her eating a poisoned apple and us finding a prince to wake her.'

I knelt by the bed and placed my hand over Lucy's frozen ones clasped together on her stomach, looking as if an undertaker had prepared her for a final viewing.

'Come on, Lucy. I know you're in there. Just give us a sign, a hint about how we can help you?'

Once again there was absolutely no response. Despair was growing inside me when a deep rumble like distant thunder came from outside.

Cristina crossed to the window and gasped as she looked out. 'Lauren, you're going to want to see this.'

I stood up and joined her. As I took in the view through the window, cold dread spun up through me.

In the sky the dome of energy started to flicker, before dying away completely. As if they'd been waiting for exactly that moment, the shadow birds that had been swirling beyond it now flew down towards the city, carried within a wave of boiling black fog. Soon I could see that the creatures were little more than vapour, made from a denser version of the black gas that was forming the fog. Even their wings were barely streaks in the air. Yet their black beaks and claws looked as solid as obsidian.

'What in the name of the mother of Jesus are those things?' Cristina asked, her face growing pale.

'A nightmare,' I said as I glanced back at Lucy still lying motionless on her bed.

When I returned my gaze to the window, the black fog was boiling down into the courtyard, carrying thousands of the shadow birds into it.

Instinctively, Cristina and I took a step back. Through the murk outside we could just about see the flock of birds swarming together. They knotted and slowly a vague form began to build from them. But the next moment, the fog grew impenetrable and we lost sight of whatever it was.

'What's happening out there?' Cristina asked as she clenched her hands on the windowsill.

'Whatever it is, I'm pretty certain that this is the start of the end game,' I replied.

I realised then that something in this sim was probably listening to us, as Poseidon had back in Atlantis. But in stark contrast to that experience, I suspected this was only Red, playing with us like someone taunting mice in a lab maze, especially when a red pulse of light came from the middle of fog and settled down to form two red, burning-coal eyes within it.

My mouth went dry. 'Holy shit, that can't be good,' I whispered.

Cristina made the sign of the cross on her chest as we both watched, almost hypnotised by the two points of light as they headed towards the door below us. As they drew closer, the eyes looked directly up at us and Cristina grabbed on to me.

My blood iced as I took in the face around them. It was a blank, featureless swirl of shadows, the body beneath it nothing more than wisps of darkness that undulated in slow motion, like black dye flowing slowly through a water current. Then the phantom figure lowered its gaze and leapt forward. A crash of the door to the courtyard made us both jump and I had a horrible feeling that the figure from nightmares had just entered the stairwell.

'What is that thing?' Cristina said, her voice strained.

'It has to be your rogue micro mind that we call Red. And I'm absolutely certain that he's coming to murder Lucy.' What I didn't add was that it almost certainly included us too, especially as neither of us had an Empyrean Key, so there was no way to escape whatever fate this entity had in mind for us.

Cristina shot me a wild look. 'But how can we stop it, Lauren? There has to be a way!'

'I'm not sure we can, but maybe we can slow it down. Come on, I have an idea.'

I rushed back into the study and started to haul the heavy desk towards the door. Within moments Cristina was helping me build a barricade across the doorway as the footsteps on the stairwell got louder. By the time we'd thrown a sofa against the door, the whole room was shaking with each heavy footfall.

Cristina's shoulders rose and fell fast with her breathing. 'Whatever that thing is, I'm not sure we can keep it out for long.'

'I know. Really our only hope is to wake up Lucy to fight that thing.'

I rushed into the bedroom and grabbed Lucy's unyielding face with my good arm. 'OK, I know you're in there, Lucy. You can't bloody well die, be absorbed or whatever else it is that you AIs do when you're taken over. You have to wake up now because I need you – we all need you. Somehow when I wasn't looking you became one of my best friends on Earth.'

A loud crash came from the outside door of the flat as the demon crashed into it. I glanced round to see Cristina piling even more things into the barricade as the whole door shook in its frame, splinters beginning to appear in it.

I turned back to Lucy. 'Look, you, I will be so absolutely pissed off if you don't try to fight for your life.'

The blue light around her glimmered more strongly. My heart surged. At last, a damned sign!

'That's it! Come back to us, Lucy – come back to me. Please!'

For the first time her lids started to flutter, her eyes now moving beneath them like someone experiencing REM sleep.

'You can do it,' I said as the splintering sound from the door grew louder.

With small jerks, Lucy started to move her head from left to right and back again.

I grabbed her shoulders, which gave slightly at my touch. 'That's it – fight it!'

With a moan, she began to thrash around on the bed as if she was having some sort of fit. I heard the chilling sound of the furniture we'd piled against the door being scraped backwards across the floor by the thing pushing hard from the other side. The air had grown even icier around me.

'Show me what to do to help you!' I shouted, shaking Lucy's gradually softening body.

I glanced up to see the swirling shadows now pressing into the windows, seeping in through the cracks. It wouldn't be much longer until this was all over, one way or another.

A huge crash came from the next room and Cristina screamed. I was instantly on my feet and running towards the bedroom door. I entered the study just in time to see the demon smash Cristina aside with a powerful strike of its smoke-wreathed arm. She slammed into the wall, shattering the plaster, and she slumped down to the floor.

And then there was only one.

I stood in the doorway to the bedroom, blocking the creature's path as it stalked towards me, each footstep sending shudders through the entire flat. It stopped a couple of metres away, fixing me with its eyes, looking me up and down as though it were measuring me up...probably for the coffin I'd soon be in.

'You're going to have to fucking come through me if you want Lucy!' I shouted.

The monster's eyes grew brighter, like two burning red dwarf stars, as it pulled its arm back ready to obliterate me with a single blow. I braced myself to fight this thing, even though I knew I had absolutely no chance of winning. But then I felt gentle hands taking hold of me from behind, moving me out of the way as if I were a young, stubborn child being manoeuvred by a parent.

My heart soared as I turned to see Lucy smiling at me.

'I think the phrase you humans use is "hold my beer".' She stepped past me, her whole body blazing with blue light as the demon rushed towards her.

I backed away. A sound like a clap of thunder rattled the entire college as the two AIs crashed into each other. Lucy locked her hands round the creature's chest, swung the beast around her and hurled it towards the window. It crashed out through the glass and the black fog swallowed it like a lake of dark water pulling down a drowning man. Without even pausing, Lucy leapt after it, not even considering the five-storey drop to the ground below, and she disappeared from view into the fog.

I rushed to Cristina. She was groaning, blood pouring from a gash in her head.

'Are you OK?' I asked, grabbing an old cushion from an overturned chair and pressing it into her wound.

'Every single muscle in my body feels as if it's been run over by a lorry, but I'll live.'

'Thank god for that. Here, hold that cushion in place. I want to see what's happening out there.'

Cristina nodded and then winced as she adjusted the temporary bandage on her head.

I headed over to the shattered window and peered out. The fog was beginning to thin as the demon that was Red grabbed hold of Lucy in the courtyard below. He spun her like a crazed discus thrower before letting go.

My heart crowded my mouth as Lucy crashed into the far wall, cracking the stonework and sending slates tumbling down from the roof above. The college groaned around us as large lumps of plaster smashed from the ceiling onto the floor.

'Come on – we've got to get out of here before we get crushed to death,' I said.

Cristina nodded, grimacing as she tried to stand.

Looping my good arm beneath her shoulders, I pulled her to her feet. Together we headed for the stairs.

The floor had begun to buck beneath us by the time we reached the steps and started to stagger down. The battle outside sounded as if it was tearing the entire college apart, brickwork cracking with explosions of mortar, the air thick with dust.

We'd barely reached the bottom of the staircase when an avalanche of masonry crashed down into the stairwell behind us. It billowed out in a cloud of shrapnel, forcing us to exit in exactly the place I'd been hoping to avoid: the AI battlefield that the quad had become.

The shadow birds spiralled round the combatants as they traded earth-shattering blows. The impacts sent shockwaves of air like sonic booms through our bodies, making me cry out in pain as the wound in my arm opened up.

Lucy spun round, her eyes briefly locking on to mine.

It was a momentary distraction, but it was all that Red needed. He wrapped his smoke-encircled arms round her from behind and slammed her head hard onto the floor, sending fissures spidering through the icy cobbles.

Lucy lay motionless as the demon rolled her onto her back. Fear gripped my heart as he leant down close to her. Then, with a crackle, red tendrils of light burst from his eyes and lanced down over her. The flickering ribbons of energy played over Lucy's body, sucking away her blue aura.

'It's killing her!' Cristina shouted.

Whatever the consequences, I couldn't just stand by and let this happen. Wincing, I picked up a heavy lump of fallen masonry and rushed towards Red. He was pushing home his attack on Lucy, sucking her dry of energy like an AI vampire.

I raised the lump of stone and brought it crashing down on the shadowy figure's back. But my improvised weapon struck something like hardened steel at the core of the dark phantom and the masonry splintered on impact. My right arm screamed with pain as the vibration of the impact shot through my body.

I grit my teeth as the thing turned its red eyes towards me. I felt the energy flow out of my body, like ice was creeping first through my blood and then my mind. I could only stand frozen to the spot, unable to resist. Cristina rushed forward to help me, but then she staggered to a stop, struggling against the invisible force that was now holding her too. I knew then without a shadow of a doubt that we were all going to die in this.

Still, I shouted, 'You'll never win!' grounding out the words between my teeth.

But then, despite Red still pressing her head into the ground, Lucy turned her head towards me. Her gaze widened as she witnessed what was happening. In an instant the look of defeat faded from her eyes, replaced by one of pure rage. With a scream, she twisted free and a pulse of blue light surged through her body, throwing the demon backwards with a howl of fury.

'No one touches my niece, you utter bastard!' she shouted. Lucy strode towards Red and leapt at him.

Just like that, Cristina and I were released from Red's supernatural grip. We staggered backwards together towards the edges of the quad as the shadow birds spiralled in closer to the two battling figures.

The AIs danced and spun round each other, attacking with blows and kicks of impossible power that sent pummelling shockwaves rippling out into our bodies with a series of ear-shattering sonic booms. Red rushed forward, grabbing hold of Lucy's head and raising his knee to crack it into her face. She staggered backwards as he battered her, blow after blow.

'Lucy, you can beat that bastard!' I shouted out, tears streaming down my cheeks. There was absolutely nothing I could do to help as Red pulled his fist back to punch through her skull.

But maybe my words did reach Lucy's ears, because she raised her head, eyes blazing with light and fresh determination. She grabbed Red's fist as it hurtled towards her, spun round and, using his momentum, flipped him over her shoulder, smashing him into the ground. An earthquake rippled out through the floor as if its surface had turned to water, throwing us to the ground.

Cristina's hand sought out mine as unearthly bellows came from the demon. Lucy rained blow after blow down on him, her fists nothing but a blur in the air. The demon's eyes began to dim as a curtain of shadow birds closed in tight around both combatants. Then a pulse of red light burst between the cracks in the birds' wingtips before fading again, followed by a blue blaze of sustained light that kept building until it was a phosphorus brilliance. Heat radiated from it, burning away the shadow birds that evaporated into wisps of smoke.

We had to turn our heads away as the light increased to starlike intensity, melting the snow and starting to burn my exposed skin. But then it faded away, the heat too.

I blinked hard, battling the afterimage burned into my retinas as a blurred figure began coming into focus, walking towards us.

'Will you look at what that bloody AI has done to our home, Lauren?' Lucy's voice said.

My vision cleared enough to see Lucy reach out and wrap both Cristina and me in her arms.

We hung onto each other, no one saying anything as the sky cleared and golden light fell across the quad. I turned my face up towards the sun that had appeared directly overhead.

Then that ruined version of Oxford faded away around us until suddenly we were back in the lab and people were rushing towards us, led by Jack.

CHAPTER TWENTY-FOUR

PEOPLE WERE CRAMMED into the lab, mostly clearing the shattered remains of the downed WASPs that seemed to be scattered everywhere. A small team was dampening down a number of fires caused by some of the drones' lithium power packs exploding. Jodie and Ruby had already left to help with the injured from the main assault, whilst the rest dealt with the immediate aftermath of the battle in the lab.

Much to my relief, the first things I'd seen on my return to the lab were the merged micro minds that now glowed a healthy blue within the shattered remains of the Cage. Lucy was very much in charge again. So far she hadn't reached out to make contact back in the real world, but I wasn't worried as she probably had plenty of housekeeping to do over in E8.

I'd been telling Jack what had happened over in E8 while he'd been sorting me out with a temporary sling for my broken arm from a bandage he'd grabbed from a first aid box. Jack had shaken his head in wonder as I'd described the alternative version of Oxford I'd found myself dropped into and the incredible supernatural battle that I'd witnessed between Lucy and Red.

'That's quite the story, Lauren' he said as I finished.

'Isn't it just? I still can't get my head round half of what I witnessed.'

'I bet,' he said as he tied off the sling. 'OK, that will see you through until I get you down to the sick bay.'

'There's no rush; you've pumped me with enough painkillers to hit the snooze button on a charging rhino.'

'All part of the service, ma'am,' Jack said with a smile.

Mike headed over to us, walking very fluidly on his prosthetic leg, the MP7 still clutched in his hands.

He gave me a very gentle hug, careful not to jar my arm. 'Thank god you're all right.'

I nodded, pulling back from him. 'It was a bit touch and go over there in E8 for a while.'

'So what happened exactly?'

'I'll tell you everything once I've had a chance to catch my breath.'

Jack gestured towards Cristina, who was standing at one side of the lab with Alice. 'I can't believe you finally persuaded that woman to see sense about us being the good guys.'

'She took some convincing, but we got there in the end.'

I noticed that Cristina had tears in her eyes. Alice reached out and took her hand in hers, nodding. It was obvious that this was a heart-to-heart. It was probably only now that it was starting to sink in for Cristina that her family were really alive – not to mention the fact she'd been fighting for the wrong side all this time. I had a strong hunch that it was going take Cristina a long while to forgive herself for having been manipulated by Alvarez.

Tom appeared through the doorway that we'd blown with our C4 charges, his eyes taking in the destruction everywhere. 'Looks as if you had quite the firefight in here.'

'Like you wouldn't believe,' Jack replied as he closed the medical box.

'And you, Tom? How about you and the rest of the assault team?' I asked.

'A few wounded, some seriously, but miraculously everyone's alive – thanks to you and Jack not following orders and letting Poseidon into the hangar. If you hadn't, by the time we would have got there, many more lives would have been lost.'

'Yes, for a Lauren seat-of-pants plan it played out rather well,' Jack said.

'I am so not taking the credit for this – it was very much a team effort,' I said. 'And Jodie's hack was pivotal in winning the battle.'

Mike nodded. 'I couldn't be prouder of her, but we also need to thank Ruby. Luckily for us she returned to the vent in the cavern air duct to see how we were doing and did enough sniper shooting to hold back the Mircats and WASPs so that Jodie could install her patch. Then cool-as-a-cucumber Ruby abseiled down into the lake directly beneath the vent, took over the control of the WASPs we'd accessed and flew the nads off those things. I think that's what probably turned the tide seriously in our favour.'

'Without a doubt, but despite everything we all did that tide would have quickly turned back if Lauren hadn't seized the initiative and headed over to E8 to help Lucy,' Jack said. 'Talking of which, next time you're taking me with you, Lauren. I was worried sick about what was happening to you over there.'

'I didn't know what I was getting myself into. Besides, you had your hands pretty full here,' I replied. 'In my defence, like usual, I was making it up as I went along. I didn't have much time to think it through.'

Tom shook his head. 'Same old Lauren, in other words.' He turned to Mike. 'And what's this I hear about you going all Rambo and helping to defend the lab against the WASP swarm?'

'Yes, I sort of surprised myself there, including with how well

I can manage with my prosthetic leg. All the physio in the infirmary obviously paid dividends.' Then Mike's face grew serious as his gaze settled on Jack and me. 'And about that accident, guys. I've not really been myself since then.'

'We noticed,' I said. 'But anyone wouldn't be after something like that.'

'I'm sure some would have handled it better than me. Anyway, when I watched you head out without me on a mission, I immediately realised I'd made a huge mistake in staying behind. Yes, I could help Jodie, but she has more than enough people to assist her now that she has her own Forge team. And since I was forced into wearing my prosthetic by the battle, I realised I could actually deal with it. So, I was wondering if...' His gaze dropped to the floor.

Relief surged through me. I knew exactly where this conversation was going.

Jack obviously did too, because he smiled. 'You want to rejoin us on future missions, right?'

Mike met our gazes. 'If you can put up with me. Besides, apart from anything else, I think Jodie's patience is starting to run thin with me poking my nose into all her work.'

'In that case, we'd better save you from yourself and from ruining your relationship,' I said. 'And for the record, we so missed having your perky disposition on the mission.'

'That's the god's honest truth, buddy,' Jack added.

Mike gave us a relieved smile. 'That's great news – the band is back together.'

'I would say we should celebrate, but maybe right now is not the time." I smiled wearily. 'All I want to do is crawl into bed.'

'After we set your arm up with a proper cast in the medical bay,' Jack said.

I huffed at him. 'You're such a nag.'

'But you love me anyway.'

'Such a sweet couple,' Mike said, raising his eyebrows at Tom.

'Aren't they just,' Tom replied, shaking his head. He turned his attention to the shattered remains of the Cage. 'It looks as if that's going to be offline for a while.'

'It may be a few days before we have it up and running again,' Mike said.

'Good,' Tom said. 'I'm sure we all want to talk to Lucy about what happened, as well as what we can do in the future to make sure that something like this never happens again.'

He had a point. We'd come dangerously close to losing everything. I also knew that he and many others in Eden would insist that we had to put measures and procedures into place to protect this base from anything like this happening in the future. I had a pretty good idea what the implications of that would be. We couldn't afford to have Lucy accompany us on a mission again. She was far too valuable to risk, as had just been proved. She wouldn't like it, but she'd eventually come to accept it, because it really was the right decision.

'Right, time to get you down to the sick bay, Lauren,' Jack said, unaware of my thoughts running on overtime.

I gave him a vague nod as my gaze lingered on the glowing micro minds. I was desperate to talk to Lucy about what had happened in Oxford. The experience of that dystopian version of the city had rattled me. Had it just been an AI version of a nightmare we'd fallen into, or something more? It was something I was desperate to find out the answer to.

CHAPTER TWENTY-FIVE

THREE DAYS after we'd successfully retaken Eden, I sat in Alice's lab with Jack, Niki and Cristina waiting to begin our first chance to debrief with the others. Cartons of takeaway Thai from the Asian food hall was a testimony in itself to the fact that slowly but surely Eden was returning to normal. Alice, Mike and Jodie were due to join us any minute. But Tom, Ruby and Troy had been called away on some secret mission using *Ariel*. Whatever their mission was we hadn't been briefed about it yet.

My right arm nestled in a sling as I ate with my left. Lucy, who had finally reached out and made contact, had offered to let me recuperate over in E8 with her. But that wasn't an option as I would have spent every moment worrying about what was happening in Eden. So I'd stayed, helping in any way that I could to deal with the aftermath of the battle.

The spring roll that I'd been trying to eat with chopsticks, dropped between them back into the carton for the umpteenth time.

Jack leant across to me. 'You do know they don't use chopsticks in Thailand, right?'

'I know and I'm normally up to the challenge, but on this occasion...' I stuck my chopsticks into my pile of noodles, took hold of the spring roll and popped it into my mouth.'

Jack snorted. 'Don't you ever change.'

'I have no intention of doing so.'

The door to Alice's office, which had been boarded with sheets of ply until the walls could be properly replaced, opened and she entered the lab in her wheelchair with Jodie, Mike just behind her and walking even more naturally on his prosthetic leg. It turned out that since the battle he'd taken to it like a proverbial duck to water. I'd even found him running around the Olympic-sized track in the gym complex earlier in the day. Yes, the guy was definitely starting to not only come to terms with his life-changing injury, but in a way embrace it too.

'Hi everyone, sorry we're late to the party, but the guys here wanted to step me through the changes to the server room for Eden,' Alice said.

'How has the Delphi's code patch been going? Will it protect her systems from any future hacks?' Niki asked.

'Maybe I can answer that,' Lucy's voice said from the speakers in the lab. A moment later her synaesthesia hologram appeared within the Cage.

'Be my guest; I'm famished,' Alice said as she headed over to the lab bench with Jodie and Mike to help themselves to our feast.

Lucy peered out at us with something approaching uncertainty in her face as she chewed her lip. 'It's good to see you all again, guys.'

Jack gave her a straight look. 'Yes, about that, why have you been hiding yourself away all this time?'

'Is that really a surprise after what happened around here?' she replied.

I sought out her gaze with mine. 'Are you trying to say you feel responsible for what happened here, Lucy?'

'Of course I am. Fourteen members of your security team lost their lives because of my failures during Red's initial takeover of the base.'

'Nobody thinks that was because of you,' Niki said. 'Everyone understands that was because you'd been badly damaged and that was what allowed Red to take over your systems.'

'You try telling that to the families of those whose names are about to be added to the memorial wall in the landing bay next door. Their blood is on my hands and I'm not sure that I can ever get over that.'

Before I had to chance to weigh in and argue with Lucy, of all the people in the room to spring to her defence it was actually Jodie.

'No - you're as responsible as any computer program, albeit a conscious one that's been infected by a virus, can be,' Jodie said. 'For example, would you hold responsible a system that's been taken over by a virus that then threatens to wipe all of the user's files unless they hand over a ransom? Or the person who wrote that virus in the first place?'

Lucy just shrugged. 'I'm not sure that's a valid comparison for my monumental screw up.'

I shook my head. 'Look, I can tell you from personal experience that it's hard not to feel that every death on a mission is down to a bad decision that I've made. And I'm sure that we could all lecture you not to beat yourself up about this until there was no oxygen in the room, but you'll still do it anyway. So let's take that as a given.'

Cristina, who'd been silent to that point and just listening to the conversation, put down her green curry and crossed to the Cage. She looked directly at Lucy on the other side of the glass.

Of course, unlike the others who were gazing at the monitor to see her, like me she could clearly see Lucy without any electronic assistance thanks to her own synaesthesia ability.

'Look, I know we haven't had much time to get to know each other but I'm telling you that this isn't on you,' Cristina said. 'If it's on anyone it's on me. When Red first imprinted on me I was filled with grief and raw anger because I believed my family had been murdered. And I'm certain that had everything to do with what happened here consequently in Eden. And for that I'll always be sorry for that to the bottom of my soul.'

This time it was Alice who shook her head. 'Actually, if the responsibility lies anywhere, once again it is with the Overseers. They were the ones experimenting on that micro mind like it was a lab rat.'

Lucy slowly nodded. 'Maybe you have a point there. They put thousands of volts through him to see what would happen, as well as drilling into his crystal matrix. It's little wonder that his core defence mode was activated.' She headed up to the glass wall in front of Cristina and pressed her hand against it. 'The only part that you unwittingly played was to give a focus for Red's anger towards myself and my family here at Eden.'

The use of the word *family* by my friend in that glass room almost brought a lump to my throat. Yes, at some point we'd become so much more than just a bunch of humans that an AI had come to know.

'Lucy's absolutely right,' Jack said. 'And don't forget you were just as much a victim as anyone else in all of this, Cristina.'

She gave a small nod, but her expression was still drawn.

Alice looked at her with kindness in her eyes. 'Everything we've just discussed is why I had that memorial wall built in the first place. These latest deaths will join all the others that have directly or indirectly lost their lives at the hands of the Overseers. And that wall's not just to remember those who have fallen but also exactly what we're fighting for. So yes, we should all feel the pain inside of us, own it, but use it to fight harder for what's right in the future.'

Everyone fell silent for a moment, tears in many of our eyes, including Lucy's. It was finally Mike who broke the silence.

'And right there is why you're paid the big bucks to be in charge.'

Everyone laughed, even Christina, who smeared away her tears with the back of her hand.

'Okay, I think that's enough self-recrimination for one day, so let's get this debrief going,' Alice said. 'First thing we need to discuss are the steps that Lucy herself has taken to make sure that nothing like this ever happens again. Jodie, maybe you'd like to brief everyone about this as you've been working closely with her regarding Delphi's systems.'

Jodie nodded. 'Yes, with a considerable amount of help from Lucy, I have installed a permanent firewall program specifically designed to stop her, or any other micro mind for that matter, taking over Delphi's systems again.'

'And just how robust is it?' Niki asked.

'As bullet proof as I can make it, even from myself,' Lucy replied. 'I threw everything I could at the firewall, but couldn't open up so much as a single crack in the code. There should be no chance of any rogue micro mind ever being able to seize control ever again. The downside of this is that I won't be able to snoop on you all anywhere in the base like I used to.'

'Oh thank god for small mercies,' Alice said, which made everyone laugh.

Lucy's gaze fell upon me. 'But as an extra precaution, I've also taken it a step further and have introduced a kill code worm virus into my own matrix. Lauren, I've installed what is effectively a self-destruct control into the Empyrean Key. As a measure of last resort, you will be able to destroy me and any micro mind linked to me.'

'Bloody hell, that's an extreme step and one that I have no intention of ever using.'

'Which is the right answer, but it's there just in case and to also hopefully restore any confidence that you may have all lost in me.'

'I can't talk for anyone else, but I never did,' I replied.

Every person in the room, even Niki - who I thought might take a dim view of our AI after what had happened - nodded.

Lucy flapped her hands towards us. 'Can we please change the subject because otherwise you beautiful people are going to make me seriously blub in a minute.'

Alice smiled and turned to Niki. 'I believe in Tom's absence that you've got an update to give us from the repair crews?'

He nodded. 'Yes, progress is good and power has now been restored to the transformer room, although it was a considerable amount of work removing all that rubble from the roof collapse.' His gaze zeroed in on Jack and me.

'Hey, don't look at us, you're the one who set the charges.'

He scratched his neck. 'Yeah, yes I did, didn't I?' Then he gestured to the lab around us. 'As you can see, repairs are well in hand here and across the rest of Eden. At the rate we're going we should be fully operational and back on track by the end of the week.'

'That's excellent news,' Alice replied.

'Oh it gets better,' he replied. 'It turns out that there are some major upsides to this whole episode. Not only have we got an army of WASP drones that we can put into the field but we have also inherited a sizeable workforce of Mircats too.'

'Which sounds great, but I have a question for Lucy,' Mike said. 'How come Red managed to speed up production so dramatically and create so many units in such a relatively short space of time?'

'When I successfully integrated his system, that gave me access to information I had lost since I was attacked by the Kimprak virus. It turns out that each micro mind has a different skill set and they all combined in our linked AI matrix. Red's speciality was production processes, hence the notable increase in the factory output.'

'And what is your speciality, Lucy?' Mike asked.

'To think more like you, using empathy and compassion to augment logic, a key component of what makes an AI capable of reaching its full potential.'

'And what about Poseidon?' Jack asked, sitting up a fraction.

'I think it's better if I let him answer that himself.'

The air shimmered next to Lucy and then Poseidon was standing there, no longer wearing a toga, but now in a T-shirt and jeans.

'Liking the new look, Poseidon,' I said.

'You can thank me for that,' Lucy said. 'His wardrobe was so out of date.'

Poseidon make a 'humphing' sound. 'Well, it has suited me perfectly well for nearly ten thousand years.'

'Precisely.' Lucy shook her head at her fellow AI.

He ignored her and turned his attention to Jack. 'To answer your question, I am basically a historian. I took on the role of curator among my siblings, focusing on human anthropology and preserving it.'

'You mean we're not just talking Atlantis here?'

'That is correct. I can give you a major insight into every ancient human civilisation there has ever been.'

Jack's eyes grew wide. 'Holy crap, I mean think of the possibilities for research.'

'It sounds to me like you just hit the archaeological jackpot,

Jack,' I said.

He scraped his fingers through his hair with a look of wonder in his eyes. 'Too right it does and I'm going to have a ball exploring everything you know, Poseidon. I can still come over and visit Atlantis with you in E8?'

'Anytime, my friend,' Poseidon replied. 'And not just there either. Although there are some significant gaps in the database thanks to the Kimprak virus, I still have a significant number on file. And if I have it, that means I'll be able to recreate it, if that is something you'd be interested in?'

'Do bears crap in the woods? Damned right it is.'

'Well before you two get into a full-blown bro love fest, I'd like to know about the micro mind from Peru, what was its speciality?' Jodie asked.

'Communications, and it was that knowledge that enabled me so effectively to hack all those systems since I merged with him,' Lucy said.

Alice sat forward in her chair and her gaze focused in on Lucy. 'So if you've inherited Red's expertise, is there any way we can use that knowledge to generally accelerate production around here?'

Lucy gestured towards Mike with a smile. 'Do you want to tell her about our secret project?'

All eyes turned to Mike, who put down the large box of noodles he'd been about to start on.

'Oh right. Yeah, I've been crossing over to E8 to work directly with Lucy on updating our Mircats using Red's knowledge of automated systems. Do you want to show what we've been up to, Lucy?'

'Of course.'

She and Poseidon stepped into the corner of the Cage and air shimmered next to her as an eight-foot-high Mircat appeared.

'Learning from what Red did to the Mircats, we've now

programmed them to run under a Delphi AI system so we can accelerate production of X103 and X104 craft. And based on our projections, once we build more units like this, we should be able to increase our existing fleet tenfold within a year. As a test, we had three of the Mark II Mircats working on the *Pangolin* prototype and if everything goes to plan we should be able to complete it in the next three weeks.'

'And you're just telling me this incredible news now?' Jodie asked, staring at her boyfriend.

'Hey, you were rather tied up getting the lab up and running again, not to mention your Forge group's projects, so I thought it would be a nice surprise.'

'Oh my goodness, I can't wait to see Troy's face when he hears this,' Alice said. 'This is going to bring the whole proposed mission to that asteroid way forward.'

'Talking of Troy, what's this secret mission that he and the others are on?' Jack asked.

'Don't worry, they'll be joining us shortly and then you'll find out.' Alice cast a smile towards Niki, who returned it like they had a secret they weren't about to share with the rest of the class.

As I gazed at the Mircat a thought struck me. 'Hang on, Lucy, you've been able to help directly in producing a robot with Mike that's several decades beyond what we're capable of producing by ourselves. I thought that prime directive coding of yours prohibited you from giving us tech we hadn't produced ourselves?'

'No flies on you, my little sunflower,' Lucy said.

Cristina looked between us.

'Just don't ask,' I said as I cast Lucy a frown.

Lucy did her best to suppress a smile. 'Anyway, yes, the restriction triggers built into my knowledge base would normally have prevented me from aiding you in this way. That is, if it hadn't of been for Red running through my subsystems like a bull in a china shop. One of the unexpected positive consequences was that it loosened some of the restrictions built into me when Red hacked through my firewall layers in his attempt to take me over. It means that now I too can circumvent some of the coding protocols that previously stopped me from sharing at least the mid-tier tech knowledge. That includes major improvements to your REV drive, which will switch the drive ring from mercury plasma over to Element 115 - also known as ununpentium. It's far more efficient for full anti-grav drive design – like those used on craft like the Tic Tac type UFOs. This will greatly enhance possible speeds with craft like *Ariel* to Mach 10.'

Alice eyes widened. 'That's quite the performance boost, Lucy.'

'It certainly is and that's just the start. It now also means that I can supply you with a small fusion plant to power your new helical drive on a *Pangolin* too.'

Now Mike was gawping at her. 'Do you know how long our species has been trying to get a fusion reactor up and running? And you're just going to hand over a working version?'

She beamed at him. 'Hey, I'm just all heart. And I've already designed the alterations to the *Pangolin* prototype to accommodate it. With so much more power to drive it you'll be able to hit sixty-five percent of the speed of light. A significant increase of your current record of forty percent with the probe, and that will significantly reduce mission times out to the asteroid belt.'

'You're not trying to tell us you're going to have this ready in three weeks too?' I asked.

'With our new Mark II Mircats on the case, I most certainly do. I just wish I could share even more advanced technology with you, but for the foreseeable future I'm afraid that's going to remain on the top shelf, well out of the reach of your species.'

Alice shook her head. 'Considering the way that this conversation started off, I think that isn't an issue when you consider everything else that we've gained. This is going to greatly accelerate all our efforts to prepare for the Kimprak's arrival. Apart from anything else, it means that it will cut down transit time to the asteroid from months to weeks.'

Lucy grinned at her. 'Exactly. You'll have a whole battle fleet of *Pangolins* and *Ariel* class craft ready by the time that the Kimprak get here.'

But Jodie was pulling a face that I noticed.

'What is it, Jodie?' I asked.

'There's one major fly in the ointment. Isn't Element 115 meant to be extremely rare?'

Now it was Mike's turn to beam at his partner. 'It is, but Lucy and I have already been working on the advanced production system that she found in Red's databanks. It's a very advanced linear particle accelerator and without boring you all to death, we fire calcium ions into Americium atoms and the result is Element 115.'

'Americium, now you're just making things up,' Jack said.

'Honest to god that's actually a real synthetic radioactive element named after the Americas and a nod to the Europium element that is located just below it in the periodic table.'

'And that was named after Europe?' Jack said, with a look that said he still wasn't sure that the piss wasn't being taken out of him.

'You see, you're an utter genius when you want to be,' Mike said grinning.

That was rewarded with a crooked mouth scowl from Jack.

But apart from that, everyone in the room was now smiling and nodding, apart from Cristina who had noticeably grown quieter. It was pretty obvious to me that even surrounded by so many people - who if she realised it or not were now friends - that Cristina was thinking about her family. And who could blame her?

It was at that exact moment that a bleep came from an electronic panel built into the arm of Alice's chair. She took an earpiece out of her pocket and slipped it in.

'Tom, good to hear from you. Was your mission successful?' A wide smile filled her face as she listened to the answer, then responded. 'Excellent. And what's your ETA?' There was a pause. 'Wonderful. See you very soon, my friend.'

She slipped the earpiece out and gazed at us all. 'Okay everyone, the time has come for me to reveal the secret mission I sent the others off on this morning.' There was something unreadable in her expression as she turned towards Cristina. 'Earlier today, Tom followed through on some intelligence that Lucy supplied us with. He set out with Troy and Ruby for a farm high in the Andes mountains in Peru, where two people very special to you were hiding out.'

I stared at her as my heart literally skipped several beats.

Cristina's eyes had become saucer-wide. 'My family?'

Alice smiled. 'Yes.' She glanced at her watch. 'And *Ariel* will be landing with Gabriel and your baby boy onboard in about five minutes, so I thought you might like to go out to the hangar to meet them. What do you say?'

A squeal burst out of Cristina's mouth and then she was on her feet, rushing over to Alice to hug her. 'Thank you, thank you so much!'

'If anyone around here, it's Lucy that you should be thanking,' Alice said. 'The sleuthing she did to track your family down was absolutely incredible. Anyway, we are going to resettle you all to someplace where the Overseers will never be able to find you and you'll all be safe.'

Cristina nodded, kissing Alice on both cheeks before heading over towards the Cage and pressing her hand against the glass wall. Lucy did the same on the other side. Genuine smiles filled both their faces.

'I will never be able to thank you enough, Lucy,' Cristina

said.

'Hey, it's just good to help someone get a happy ending around here,' said Lucy.

Cristina put her hand on her heart and then pressed her palms together in act of prayer. Then she turned and headed straight towards me, arms out. I stood and we hugged each other hard. No words because there was absolutely no need. By the time we broke apart there were tears on our faces.

Jack tapped on his watch. 'We better get a move on if you want to get this welcome party organised.' He held out his arm for her.

Cristina laughed and hooked his. A moment later she headed off with him and the others towards the hanger. But I hung back and headed over towards the Cage.

'You look as though you still have a question to ask me?' Lucy said as I approached.

'I do.'

Poseidon looked between us. 'I'll give you two a moment alone.'

Before I could say anything his body became transparent and he disappeared.

Lucy gave me an expectant look. 'What did you want to ask me, Lauren?'

'We still haven't had a chance to discuss that twisted version of Oxford where we found you. What was that all about? Presumably something to do with Red?'

A troubled look filled her face. 'Actually it wasn't him, but something I can only describe as like a waking dream. You see, I was dropped into the equivalent of a human sleep cycle after I was damaged in that crash.'

'So we were living in one of your nightmares then?'

'No, it wasn't that either, but came from somewhere deep within my matrix, a part of which even I can't pretend to understand. The best explanation that I can give you is that it's the equivalent of an AI's subconscious, where dreams happen, but in this case I'm actually worried it was something more.'

'What sort of worried?'

Lucy looked at the floor. 'There is an element of Angelus AI's that links us all together via quantum entanglement. And sometimes those connections can even breach the barrier of time.'

I stared at her. 'What, you're saying you had a premonition of the future from one of your kind about something dreadful that's going to happen to Oxford?'

'I can't be sure, but maybe. Of course, it could also have just been a nightmare, just like you said.'

'Let's hope so for all our sakes,' I replied.

Lucy peered at me. 'Hey, enough of the long face. You should be celebrating the big reunion with the others out in the hangar, right now.'

I met her gaze and nodded. 'Maybe I should be.'

'Good, but there's one last thing I'd like to ask you whilst it's just the two of us. In that service Alice intends to hold for everyone who died during the siege, I'd be grateful if you act as my proxy and lay some flowers at the memorial wall for them.'

I gazed deep into Lucy's eyes as a lump filled my throat. 'Of course I will.'

'Thank you, my dearest friend.'

Lucy placed her hand to the glass like she had with Cristina, and I did the same.

We stood gazing at each other and maybe understanding each other far better than we ever had in that moment. Then I took a deep breath, turned and headed towards the hangar door, knowing that Lucy was watching me every step of the way. And part of me just wished she could be physically here to share in the joy about to happen in the hangar, because goodness we all deserved to share in a bit of that right now.

LINKS

Do please leave that all important review for **Earth Howl** here:
https://geni.us/EarthHowl

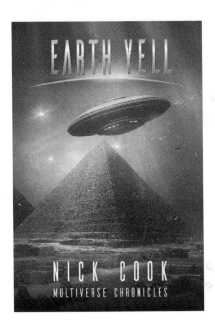

BOOK 5 - EARTH YELL: Something is happening in the ocean off the shores of Cuba an why are Russian Spy ships and subs congregating in the area? When a local diver goes missing, Lauren and the team head off on a mission that is going to stretch them all to their limits as they journey to the bottom of the sea to discover an extraordinary secret that will change everything. Pre-order here: https://geni.us/EarthYell

Whilst you are waiting for the next book, how about reading the Fractured Light trilogy, part of the Multiverse Chronicles? This continues the story of the AI called Sentinel, six years after the events covered in *The Signal*. A secret hidden in human DNA is about to be unlocked, but can college student Jake and his underground hacker friend Chloe solve the mystery before reality itself starts to break down? The **Fractured Light** trilogy can be found here: https://geni. us/FracturedLightTrilogy

OTHER BOOKS BY NICK COOK

Prequel to the Multiverse Chronicles

The Earth Song Series (The Multiverse Chronicles)

The Fractured Light Trilogy (The Multiverse Chronicles)

AUTHOR NOTES

So here we are at the end of *Earth Howl*. To say I geeked out whilst writing this book would be a serious understatement. There are various bits of tech that stuck their heads above the parapet in this book, especially towards the end... the helical drive in the *Pangolin* in particular. This will have a much bigger role as the series unfolds towards its conclusion in the seventh book. As for the helical drive design, the proposal for a high-performance drive that can almost reach the speed of light really exists. The problem comes in supplying it with sufficient power to perform at such a level, hence the inclusion of the mini fusion power plant! And for those of you who have read my *Fractured Light* trilogy, you will recognise it from the technology that Sentinel supplies our race with to try to protect our planet from another threat beyond our reality.

If you are interested in learning more about helical drives, check out this video: https://www.youtube.com/watch?v=CK-T5zlnw-MM&t=78s

Anyway, back to *Earth Howl*...

I greatly enjoyed researching possible locations for Atlantis, and everything related to it that I've written about in this book really does exist. The Richat Structure is an extraordinary site in the Sahara that still hasn't had a major archaeological dig. The big controversy about whether it really could be the site of Atlantis revolves mainly around its current altitude above sea level. Significant seismic activity is one possible cause of the discrepancy, but there's also evidence of a huge inland lake having once been there. One proposed explanation is that the Earth swaps its magnetic poles on a regular basis. It's long been theorised that this would create major problems, but one proposal is that it may also coincide with a shift in the Earth's axis that has led to rapid climate change in the past as it's changed the angle of the planet to the sun. The theory is that it was this pole-swap that turned the once-green Sahara into the desert that we know today. If you're interested in this subject, I can't recommend the Bright Insight channel on YouTube highly enough. Jimmy, the channel's host, is like a modern-day Sherlock Holmes, and has pieced together various clues that have been found at the Richat Structure. Listening to the evidence, it's certainly hard not to conclude that it's a serious contender for the location of the mythical city of Atlantis. Here's the link to that video:

https://www.youtube.com/watch?v=U5kEzxOb-3c

You can probably tell that I really enjoyed writing *Earth Howl*. It contains one idea that absolutely took on a life of its own – Poseidon recreating Atlantis in the higher dimension of E8. This was a genuine bolt of creative lightning that struck during the writing of those chapters. In many ways I wish I'd thought of the idea before now, as I would have made more of it in previous books, but now it's here I'm going to make the most of it in the future – not necessarily in the *Earth Song* series, but...pauses for dramatic effect...in the series that comes after it that I've been dying to write for years. I won't say any more about it for now, but

I hope that piques your interest.

We met a new character in *Earth Howl* – Troy Armstrong. His surname was inspired by Neil Armstrong and suggested by one of my readers, Chris Green. As for his first name, those on my Facebook page (where you really should be following me) will know that it's a nod to Troy Tempest from *Stingray*. (I did say I was a bit of a geek.) And if I could get away with a character called Marina, I so would! Troy's characterisation is partly inspired by Chuck Yeager, a real-life United States Air Force officer made famous by *The Right Stuff*, written by Tom Wolfe and brought to life on the screen by Sam Shepard. Chuck was an extraordinary test pilot who was always, to quote the book and test pilots everywhere, 'pushing the envelope' and breaking records. Troy is my own small homage to this great man, and will be a major character in the next series too.

Word of mouth seems to be spreading about *Earth Song*, and the series has been steadily climbing up the charts. I'm eternally grateful to you for being part of that success – you buying this book enables me to keep doing the thing I'm most passionate about: writing. I've also been truly humbled by some of the emails I've received and that sort of feedback really does help to make it all worthwhile. And thank you to everyone who has left a review, as that is the single most effective way of raising the profile of a book and getting the word out there.

As is customary, I need to thank my fantastic editor Catherine Coe for making sure I really do deliver my best work. A huge thanks also to my proofreader Beverly Sanford (I was very tempted to deliberately misspell her name to see if she spotted it) for doing such a great job scooping up all those pesky typos. She also went above and beyond and helped to add that final bit of polish and sparkle to the book. But there is one person above all that I have to thank – my ever-wonderful wife, Karen. She has been my rock, especially during the pandemic, which has made life so difficult for everyone. I'll sign off here and get on with writing the next book in the *Earth Song* series, *Earth Yell*. If you like lots of cool underwater sequences in your novels, get ready for exactly that!

Nick Cook, November 2020

Made in the USA
Middletown, DE
18 May 2023

30856647R00165